Rescue My Love

by

Lynn Story

Lynn Story
Newport News, VA

---

1.   http://www.bookdesigntemplates.com/

To Larry, with love.

Acknowledgements

Thank you to my wonderful husband, Larry for his willingness to discuss endless ideas and plot twists. My editor, Heather August without whom none of this would be possible. And William Heavey at Bold Fox Designs for his wonderful artwork.

Also, by Lynn Story
The Gates Point Series
Ginny's Christmas Wish
The Primrose Heart
Love at Bay
Her Private Chef

Chapter One
Ethan

We had just wrapped up a fugitive warrant case, it had been one of those inter-agency cooperation things that always gave me a headache. Now, I just wanted to relax, listen to some good music, and maybe have a bourbon or two before going home to an empty house. The Ironclad promised me the comfort I was searching for tonight. The Ironclad sat close to the banks of the southernmost point of the James River where it met the Chesapeake Bay. The area was recently revived attracting of lot of micro-breweries, trendy restaurants and shops. The Ironclad was a bar and grill known for its bourbon and featuring local and nationally known blues artist. And while I avoided the trendier establishments in the area, I enjoyed the atmosphere of the Ironclad, lately it was becoming my home away from home.

My wife, Diane, had called earlier to say she would be out late with friends at a book club meeting or something, honestly it didn't matter we hadn't been spending much time together lately. It seemed that after sixteen years of marriage we had drifted too far apart to drift back together again. The end was inevitable.

The sign in front of the Ironclad announced Charlie Pickens was playing tonight at nine o'clock. Charlie had gotten his music career started here in Gates Point before he was discovered and found national fame with his unique style of blues. I found a seat at the bar, ordered a drink and scanned the room, an occupational hazard; my eyes stopped at a table in the far corner. It was so deep in the shadows that most people probably wouldn't even know it was there. I wouldn't have paid any attention to it myself if it weren't the woman sitting there alone. She looked oddly familiar; I couldn't place her. Over the years I have traveled to one conference or other, been part of too many task forces to count, and even taught a few classes at Quantico.

Hell, maybe I had just seen her in here before. As, the warm-up band ended their set the music was replaced by the din of the bar. There were snippets of conversation, glassware clinking together, cheers, and laughter all blending together as the setup on stage was rearranged.

As soon Charlie Pickens took the stage, he crowd cheered and I cheered right along with them. I remembered the woman in the corner and glanced in her direction. She sat motionless focused on the stage; she wasn't cheering. Something about her tugged at my brain, I pushed it away. I had come here to relax, and I didn't need to be creating more headaches than I already had.

The music made me forget about the woman in the corner hidden in the shadows, and instead I thought about my failing marriage. The woman I had loved with all my heart was someone I didn't know anymore. Charlie's songs had a way of making you think about such things and tonight it was hitting too close to home. We didn't fight like so many couples do these days, we were more like roommates than soulmates. The kicker was my daughter. I didn't want to turn her life inside out. I still loved my wife, just not the same way I used to, still, I harbored no ill feelings. I had very few feelings at all. I felt sad for the loss of the relationship it felt like a tragedy in one of Charlie's songs.

Charlie played for an hour and a half before calling it quits. I turned my attention back to the woman in the corner. She was still there quietly sipping her drink. A local band was taking the stage now and would carry the crowd until closing time. I decided I had to know who she was, it was really annoying that I couldn't place her.

Before I could get off my barstool a young man approached her table. I had no idea what was being said, one minute the man was standing there with his back to me blocking my view of my mystery woman and the next minute his back was on the floor. The woman was settling herself back into her chair, her attention was no longer on her drink. Sensing there might be trouble I rushed over.

"Anything I can do to help?" I asked the woman.

"Not unless you're in charge of waste disposal." She never took her eyes off the man who was now getting to his feet.

He looked like he wanted to say something to her as she cocked an eyebrow at him, and he stood there as if he was trying to make a decision. I had to admit I was pretty impressed. Even more curious now than I had been before.

"It might be best just to walk away." I said in a low tone to the young man. He nodded and walked away. Then turning my attention back to her I asked, "How do you like that self-service?" She almost smiled. "May I?" I asked cautiously I didn't want to end up on the floor.

She nodded silently.

"My name is Ethan." I held out my hand.

"Kennedy, my friends call me, Kay." She took my hand.

There was a surge of electricity up my arm and straight to my heart when we touched. By the way she pulled her hand back she felt it too. At that moment I realized that it wasn't that I recognized her from somewhere, we had never met before, it was that somehow, I had known her all my life without having met her. We were somehow linked. The moment I touched her I knew it. Some might call it love at first sight, but it was so much more.

"What's your poison?" I indicated her empty glass.

"Bourbon."

I turned to get the attention of a waitress who nodded and appeared at the table with fresh drinks. "Have you always been a fan?"

She glanced up at the stage and nodded. "Yeah."

The corner was dark, and it was keeping most of her features in the hidden what I could see, I could tell she was beautiful in that smoky, dark sort of way you normally only see in those trendy ads for perfume or expensive cars.

"Are you a local or just visiting?"

"Both."

Okay, I could see she wasn't a talker, this was going to take a little work on my part. That was okay getting people to talk was sort of my thing, so I was up for the challenge.

"Home for a visit then."

She made eye contact with me and gave me a small, appreciative smile.

"Exactly."

"Well, then I can see why you love the blues if you're from here. It gets in your blood at an early age."

"Yes, it does." She looked at some point off in the distance and I wondered if it was the music taking her away from me or the bourbon.

"And what about you Ethan? Are you a local or just visiting?"

"Local."

She nodded and sipped the fresh drink.

I watched closely and I had so many questions. I had this urge to know everything about her even though I felt like I already knew the answers.

She frowned up at the band on stage, they weren't bad, but it was hard to follow someone like Charlie Pickens.

"Wanna take a walk?" I asked, thinking I would risk the rejection.

To my surprise she nodded. I looked around for the waitress. The same one that had brought us refills appeared.

"Thanks, Emily." Kay said the waitress. "I'm going to call it a night."

"Okay well let me bring you your change."

"No, keep it."

"But..."

"Keep it."

"At least let me pay for mine." I offered.

"No, I prepared, when I came in tonight, so you're covered."

I didn't pretend not to be confused, but the waitress looked happy so I went along with it. Kay let me hold her elbow and guide her through the crowd out on to the sidewalk.

I took a deep breath of the fresh night air. It was humid and promised rain.

Under the glow of the streetlights I could see she wasn't just beautiful she was exquisite. The full lips and the high cheek bones. I could tell her hair was dark and thick despite being pulled back at the base of her neck in a clasp. Her eyes were dark too, although I couldn't see the exact color. It didn't matter because it was the way the light danced in her eyes that held my attention.

"Where to?" she asked.

"This way." I thought a walk along the water in the moonlight might be nice and I would be able to learn more about her without having to shout. It took a minute for my hearing to adjust.

"So, what brings you home for a visit?"

"Oh, just had to take care of some family business. It can be difficult to try and do things long distance at times." Although her tone was casual, I could tell it was forced. Whatever had brought her come was anything but a casual visit.

"I understand. I've tried that myself a few times it never really seems to work."

She nodded in agreement and we walked on. I wondered about the family business.

"Where do you live when you are not here in Gates Point?"

"Pretty much everywhere and nowhere."

Again, she was trying to sound casual and not give too many specifics. I didn't blame her; we had only just met, and it is never a good idea to give too much personal information to a stranger.

"You're pretty good and not answering questions, aren't you?"

"I'm sorry. I didn't mean to be evasive." She looked over at me. I could tell she was sincere in that.

"It's okay. We just met and I don't blame you for not wanting to tell a stranger your life story. It's just that most people will talk without thinking twice."

"Meaning?"

"Meaning either you have had some training in evasive tactics or you're an extremely private person."

She laughed out loud. It was an honest laugh and one that sounded like crystal windchimes. It was light and the warm breeze carried it away.

"I guess I'm just a private person. I'm a photojournalist so I'm more about telling other people's stories, not mine."

"Now that makes sense." I smiled; I was relieved to know she wasn't in some sort of law enforcement. It was refreshing to talk to someone that didn't involve an investigation.

"And what about you Ethan, what agency does that badge on your belt represent?"

I was surprised that she noticed it. I wasn't trying to hide it but, I wasn't flashing it either.

"FBI,"

"Really? I had you pegged as an NCIS man."

"I know a few of them and they are good guys."

"Yeah, they are." She agreed.

"Has your family always lives in Gates Point?" I asked changing the subject back to her. She smiled. It was a loaded question and she knew it. Gates Point prided itself on first families and old money.

"As far as I know they have. And what about you?"

"Oh, at least a few generations."

We reached the Chesapeake Bay. It is an impressive site I don't care how many times you see it. Tonight, the moon was full and reflecting on the water.

"So, you're a photojournalist and home for family business, where are you working right now?"

"The Middle East,"

"That must be tough,"

"It's the job." She shrugged.

"Wanna sit?" I pointed to a bench.

"What's your favorite thing about the city?" I looked back over my shoulder I was determined to get her to open up to me. I had to know more about her. She smiled a little and I congratulated myself.

"I love the music."

I nodded. "Do you play?" I asked.

"I play a little guitar now and then."

I had a feeling she was being modest.

"What do you play, Ethan?"

"I play the piano from time to time and sometimes the harmonica."

"I bet you're good. I'd like to hear you play sometime."

I wanted to take her back to my place and play something for her, it might be hard to explain to Diane. It was weird though, I should feel more guilty about going for a walk in the moonlight with a beautiful woman, I didn't.

"I'd like that." We both smiled. I felt like we had a bit of a breakthrough.

"Tell me a little more about you." I leaned in a little. "Do you have siblings?"

"No, and that's okay. I don't mind it. Big families seem to be too complicated. I like things simple."

I smiled. "How's that working out for you?"

She laughed a little. "Not so well, the rest of the world seems to like things complicated."

"You are not wrong, there." I agreed.

I watched her eyes crinkle into a genuine smile. I wondered what she looked like with her hair down instead of pulled back. I had the urge to reach out and loosen the clip that was holding hair and watch it cascade over her shoulders. We talked about music some more, debating the best live performances and the best albums.

"It's getting late." She said looking sad.

"Can I walk you home?"

"It's an awfully long walk. I'll catch a cab."

"Are you sure. I'd like to know you made it home safely."

She smiled a soft warm smile. "How about I text you when I get in."

"Deal." I smiled and gave her my phone number.

"I'll text you and then you will have mine."

"Okay." I nodded.

We walked back to the street and she whistled for a cab and waved to me as it pulled away from the curb. I felt deflated and walked to my car and drove home. About thirty minute later my phone buzzed.

"Home safe. Thank you."

"Glad you're safe."

I wanted to say more but didn't know how to say it or if I should, so I left it at that.

***

The next day, I felt more alive than I had felt in a long time. Even Diane noticed.

"You look like you finally got some sleep," she said as she poured coffee.

"Yeah, I did. I'm sorry I didn't wait up."

I actually hadn't thought about what time Diane had gotten in. It had to have been past midnight. I wondered if she had the same kind of evening I did. I smiled to myself because I genuinely hoped that she had.

"That's okay. We sort of got sidetracked from the book and drank more wine than we read." She laughed.

My daughter bounced into the kitchen. Madelyn was a morning person. I have no idea where she got that from, it certainly wasn't from me or her mother.

"Morning, don't forget Mom, you said I could spend the day with Angie."

"I didn't forget, just check in with me or your dad once in a while so we know you're okay."

"Wait," I interrupted, don't you have school today?"

"No, it's a teacher workday so, Angie and I were going to hang out." Madelyn smiled and popped bread into the toaster.

"Hang out where?"

"Oh dad!" She sighed.

"I'm serious."

"At her house, mostly her mom doesn't work so we'll probably get a ride to the mall or something."

Diane touched my shoulder sensing I was about to ask more questions.

"That's fine, I've already talked to Ms. Harper, you still keep in touch today, okay?" Diane instructed as she moved about the kitchen putting necessities into her briefcase.

"Okay." Madelyn smiled plucking the toast out of the toaster and plopping it onto a plate."

"Careful, don't burn yourself," I said.

Madelyn just rolled her eyes at me and started to add jelly to the toast.

"Okay, okay." I said putting my hands up in the air. I concentrated on my coffee and the headlines in the paper.

Just as Madelyn was finishing her toast the doorbell rang.

"Oh, that's Angie."

"Wait." I said putting my hand up. "Finish your toast and put the plate in the sink. I'll get the door."

Diane nodded to her and she took the last bite of her breakfast.

"Good Morning Mr. Craddock." Angie was standing on the porch beaming at me.

"Morning, Angie." I said stepping aside to let her in. I waved to her mother sitting out in the car.

"Okay, see you later!" Madelyn said as she and Angie headed back out the door.

I bent down and Madelyn kissed my cheek. It made me smile.

"Have a good time and behave yourself."

"I always do." She said and ran to catch up to Angie.

I shut the door behind her and walked back into the kitchen. Diane had her keys in her hand.

"Where are you off to?"

"Work." She looked at me with concern. "Aren't you working today?"

"Yes." I was actually looking forward to it. I'd even considered walking to work and enjoying the fresh air.

"Okay, have a good day."

I watched as the women in my life left the house each with their own independent lives to lead. I turned off the coffee pot and headed to work. I knew Charlie Pickens was playing a second night at the Ironclad and I thought about going after work just to see if Kay would be there.

It was another long day and nearly midnight when I was done at the office. I needed to go home and get some sleep, the thought of Kay haunted me. I went to the Ironclad instead. It took a minute for my eyes to adjust to the dimness. And Charlie Pickens was almost done with his set, Kay was sitting in the same spot as the night before. She smiled when I approached the table.

"I hoped I might see you again." She said.

My heart did about three flips and I sat down. "I hoped you'd be here." I smiled.

The same waitress from the night before brought two bourbons to the table and left without a word.

"You've almost missed the set."

"I've heard it before." I shrugged. Tonight, I really didn't care about Charlie Pickens. I wasn't really listening to the music anyway; I was too busy admiring the color of her eyes. I felt her touch my hand. I looked down in surprise.

"You were pretty far away there; you didn't hear a word I was saying." She smiled playfully.

"I'm sorry."

"Come on." She said standing up.

I had no choice but to follow.

The waitress rushed over.

"Your change."

"Keep it." Kay said.

"I can't really."

"Yes, you can." Kay gave the waitress a sweet smile. "It's okay. Keep it."

It was the same scenario as the night before.

"What's the deal? Why doesn't the waitress want the tip?"

"I have no idea, but she better learn to accept them is she is going to make any money in this job." Kay shrugged.

I turned back and saw the waitress look down at a one-hundred-dollar bill. That was a big tip for a journalist, or at least I thought it was. I honestly, had no idea if being a photojournalist was a lucrative career or not. I guess I always thought of journalist in general as being the stereotypical starving artist type. You know the one you always see in the movies, who always looking for that one big story that will win them a prize or something.

"Where are we going?" I asked catching up to her.

"I don't know. Someplace quiet I think."

"Okay."

I fell in step next to her and we walked for a while talking. We passed the veteran's cemetery and I realized we were heading into the Garden District. I wondered if she somehow knew where I lived. We turned in the opposite direction of my house and I breathed a sigh of relief.

We walked through an iron gate. I realized the property contained a beautiful garden, a large house with a small one to the rear. I was familiar with the property in passing. It stood out because it took up an entire block. I followed her to the smaller of the two houses.

"Is this where you live?"

"It's where I'm staying while I'm home."

She opened the door with a key, and I followed her in. I scanned the room, there was nothing of a personal nature, it was a definitely guest house.

"Have a seat," She motioned to the cluster of chairs and a sofa. I chose the sofa. "Do you want something to drink?"

"Maybe just a club soda, I have to be up early. I'm working on a new case." To her credit she didn't ask what the case was about, and I was grateful. I didn't want to talk about it. I wanted to talk about her. She handed me my drink and joined me on the sofa, kicking off her shoes and tucking her legs under herself.

"This is a nice place."

"It's comfortable and quiet." She sipped her own club soda.

I nodded. I suddenly felt very awkward.

"What about you?" She asked.

I looked at her confused for a moment.

"Do you have siblings?" She asked picking up the conversation from the night before.

I smiled. "No."

She nodded and looked at my hand.

"You have a wife; do you have children?"

"A daughter." I answered feeling awkward at the mention of Diane. I hadn't brought it up before because I wanted to learn about her and because I frankly hadn't given it much thought.

"Just the one?"

"Yeah. She is so beautiful." I smiled a little.

"She must take after her father."

I looked up at her. It was the first personal thing she had said, and I felt all the blood rushing to all the wrong parts of my body.

"How old is she?" she continued.

"She ten going on thirty." I sighed.

She nodded.

"No one special for you?" I asked.

"No, long distance is tough, and the dessert isn't really the best place to meet your soul mate." Her eyes looked like she was looking into my soul.

I thought of her with a boyfriend and a new feeling I hadn't felt in a long time rose up in my gut.

She noticed my glass was empty and she got up to get me another. She leaned over to take my glass from me, and her face was so close to mine. Too close. She smelled like vanilla.

"Let me get you another."

"You don't have to do that." My voice was hoarse.

"Sure, I do." She whispered back.

In that moment I have never wanted another woman more. Not even Diane and that bothered me. I am not the man that looks at other women, I don't cheat on my wife no matter what kind of problems we are having. I'm just not that guy. But there was something about Kay, that I had no control over. I couldn't control my feelings and I already felt like I had known her my whole life. She must have sensed how uncomfortable I was because she quickly stood up and walked to the kitchen.

"Maybe I should call it a night." I said not trusting myself to be alone with her. The look of disappointment on her face pierced me through the heart. I didn't want to leave. I was afraid if I didn't, I might lose control. I couldn't stay and risk doing something I might regret, because I knew I wouldn't regret it and that was the problem.

She put both glasses on the counter and walked back over to me. She sunk down on the sofa closer than she had been sitting before.

"I wish you didn't have to go. I've really enjoyed spending time with you."

"I am enjoying it too."

"So why leave?"

"Because,"

She looked at me. I was hoping she wasn't going to make me say it. What if she didn't feel the same way and then I would sound like a total idiot. But I believed with every fiber of my being she felt the same way.

"Because I might do something that I shouldn't."

She raised her eyebrows at me. "Are you sure?"

"Am I sure about what?" I asked my thoughts were getting cloudy.

"That you shouldn't?"

Oh god, here we go. She was tempting me. She knew how I felt. She leaned back into the sofa and drew circles on the back of the sofa with her finger.

"Yeah, I'm pretty sure."

"Because of your wife."

"Yes."

"I understand. I do not want to be party to any stress or unhappiness in someone else relationship."

She looked up at me. Her eyes were on fire. "I have to leave tomorrow. I'm going back to my assignment. If we are meant to be together, we will meet again. And if not, I'll treasure these past two nights with you."

It took all my power to stand up and prepare to walk out the door. She stood up and followed me.

"Kay, I..." I couldn't bring myself to say the words.

"I'm going to miss you, Ethan." She stood on her toes and kissed me gently. Her tongue touch my lips for the briefest of moments. I wanted to pull her close to me. I wanted to explore her mouth with my tongue. I wanted to carry her to the bedroom and spend a week exploring her body. I felt the blood pulsing through my veins, and I needed to leave now, or I would never be able to go.

"Kay." I whispered again. Then I turned and walked away. I didn't look back instead I waited to hear the door close behind me. It didn't, not as long as I was in earshot.

Chapter Two

Kay

I had only been stationed in the Middle East for six months when my mother died. The cancer had been in remission, but it came back with a vengeance. My mother had called to tell me the prognosis and I started making arrangements to return home immediately, unfortunately, she passed while I was in route, Eddie, my mother's personal driver provided by the family business met me at the airport and gave me the news. Fortunately, when my father died two years previously, he had seen to it that things were put in place, so that at the time of my mother's eventual demise, the legal aspects of the family business and the private property would be a matter of me signing a few documents. I was an only child so the will was pretty straight forward. I received the real property, some money and the family business. There were sizable donations made to various charitable organizations in Gates Point.

My first order of business upon arriving home was to meet with the family attorneys; one for the estate and one for the company, Port City Industries. The family attorney for the real property was a very brief meeting. We went over the will I signed a few papers accepting the house and the monetary funds so they could be transferred into my personal account. Then I met with the corporate attorneys to sign the necessary documents that granted Elliott Goode limited power of attorney. Elliott was the corporate attorney for Port City Industries, he had been with the company for more than twenty years. But my father had taught me well and I only allowed him to exercise control over what might be considered minor items for the day to day operation. Anything major short of a vote by the shareholders would still have to be forwarded to me no matter where I was in the world. And even the items that went to the shareholders came to me, as I owned the majority of the stock in the company.

As we sat in the conference room on the twentieth floor of the Port Cities Industries building, I was starting to get a headache from the whining of the corporate attorney.

"Ms. Dandridge, are you sure you want it set up this way?" Elliott protested.

"Yes, I'm sure."

"You are living in a war zone at the moment what if something urgent arises?" Elliott continued.

"You have my cell number, call me. As you pointed out, I'm in a war zone, not another planet." There was no way I was going to budge on this matter, and I would fire him if I needed to, I was not signing away control of the family business. "And I want to meet with the employees while I'm home."

"That's impossible." Elliott blurted out allowing his frustration to show.

"Not for the ones here in the corporate headquarters." I leaned back in the leather chair that my father had occupied for so long. I don't think my mother ever came up there even though she was the head of the company after father's death. "Listen, I realize that mother pretty much handed over control to you and the staff here during her tenure, but she never understood the business side of things. I do and I intend to be just as involved as my father was."

"From the other side of the world?" Elliott was incredulous.

"I will make it work."

"Hmmpf." Elliott was clearly annoyed.

"It's like this Elliott, I will make it work with or without you. The choice is yours and there will be no hard feelings." Elliott turned red in the face and looked around the room. It was only himself; a junior attorney, Michael; the administrative assistance, Sherry, and me.

"I wasn't implying that I would not be supportive, I am merely trying not to over burden you at this time." Elliott was a little thin-lipped weasel of a man and I wasn't sure if I could trust him. I sure as hell wasn't taking any chances while I was halfway around the world.

I held up my hand to stop him. "I appreciate that Elliott and I wasn't implying anything different." He let out a sigh and relaxed a bit.

His junior attorney spoke up. "I think we can all agree that this is a stressful time, maybe we should just focus on the paperwork today and then

Sherry can organize the meeting you've requested." He looked at Elliott and then me.

I liked him; he wasn't afraid to speak up. "That's an excellent idea. I need to get to the funeral home."

"Of course, I apologize." Elliott offered.

"Thank you, Michael for keeping us on track." I smiled. He nodded and avoided eye contact with Elliott.

"Sherry how soon can you have business cards made up for me?"

"I can have them here tomorrow," she responded.

"Perfect. Do that and set up the employee meeting for after mom's funeral."

"Yes, ma'am."

I shook each one of their hands before leaving. I had the company car and driver at my disposal now. It felt silly. But Eddie had insisted. He said it was no time for me to worry about things like traffic and getting to meetings on time. We drove away from the corporate offices, then to the funeral home to sign the final papers that would allow my mother's funeral to move forward as she had planned.

She had pre-paid and picked out her own casket the day she found out the cancer was back. It seemed morbid to me at the time, but today I was grateful for her forethought. She'd be placed next to my father in the family crypt. I had a space there as well, although I had not made any pre-arrangements. However, today I was thinking it might not be a bad idea considering I'd be going back to the Middle East when all of this was over.

With the corporate lawyer confrontation over I had just one more hurdle this week. My grandfather. His car was in front of the house when I returned.

"Grandpa!" I smiled as I walked into the house.

"Kay, there you are!" He advanced on me for a hug. "Where have you been?" he asked holding me at arms-length.

"At the office to get things straight with the lawyers."

"And did you give them hell?"

"Yes, sir."

"That's my girl." He laughed and squeezed my shoulders. Richard Beauchamp was my maternal grandfather and he was the Secretary of the Navy. We kept the family connection very quiet for the sake of my career. I didn't want any special treatment and I didn't need the hassle of everyone assuming I was getting special treatment.

"Are you staying here?" He asked leading me over to the sofa.

"Out in the guest house. I just couldn't..."

He patted my arm. "It's okay."

"Besides, you and your security detail will need the privacy of the house anyway." I tried to smile.

"That is very thoughtful, but not necessary," he soothed.

"I like the guest house."

He nodded. "Now tell me how things are going in the Corp?" He hadn't been a fan of me being imbedded with a military unit, particularly a Marine unit. But I had wanted to go where the action was and I learned as a child, the Marines saw a lot of action.

"Squared away, sir."

"I know you are. Are they giving you a hard time?"

I shrugged one shoulder. "Some do, some are coming around."

"Hang in there." He smiled.

"I will."

"You've got a lot on your shoulders right now anything I can do to help?" he offered.

"No, I have everything under control."

"You always do. You are your father's child." It was a family joke that my grandfather was happier than anyone when my father proposed to mother. At the time my father was a marine and the son my grandfather never had.

I gave him a small smile. "Want to have dinner together tonight?"

"That sounds good." He agreed.

"I'll see what we have in the kitchen." I got up and left grandpa with his security detail I was certain he had work to do.

I found everything I needed for seafood casserole and cornbread. I made sure there was enough for the security detail, as well. It seemed security details were a way of life in our family. My father as CEO of Port City Industries didn't have a detail but he had Eddie. Eddie's title was company driver. When he was with my father outside of the office, he never let my father out of his sight. I never got the full story of their relationship. I knew they had served together when my father was a young man. My grandfather, being Secretary of the Navy, couldn't go anywhere without his detail and pre-checks and sweeps. For every one of my grandfather's security team that I saw I was sure there was another I couldn't see.

The rest of the week was a blur, the funeral was well attended, and my mother would have been happy to see so many of her friends. My grandfather had to leave the day after the funeral, and frankly I was surprised he stayed as long as he did. The meetings at the company headquarters to review new contracts and address the employees went along without further problems from Elliott. I gave each employee my personal cell phone and told them to call me if they had any concerns about their jobs or the company itself. A personal touch is what my father believed. It didn't matter how big the company got or how many cities were located. He made sure each employee knew he was approachable and would take the time to listen to them no matter the concern.

I remembered accompanying my father to visit employees or employee's family member in the hospital. He'd set up a scholarship fund for employee's children to attend the college or trade school of their choice. He was always looking after the employees as if he was still a small company of only ten people and I believe that was the secret to his success.

Finally, it was all over. The meetings, the funeral. I returned my family's home, now my home. The Garden District was a historic area and most of the families had lived there for generations. It was a quiet neighborhood with a lot of pride. No matter how big or how small the house, it was well kept, lawns attended to, flowers and garden flags proudly displayed, some with fences, many these days with children. It was a wonderful picturesque place and I was grateful for it today.

I walked up the wide front steps and entered the house. It was quiet without my grandfather and his men. Amidst the emptiness everything to hit me at once, my mother was gone. My father had died two years earlier. Now the house felt so completely empty. I couldn't bring myself to sleep in my old room, so I returned to the guest house. It was close enough but without the constant reminders of what I had lost. It didn't take long, and I was tired of staring at four walls I needed a distraction. Something to cheer me up a bit. I decided I needed fresh air and a fresh perspective. I could hear my mother telling me to hold my chin up and get on with it. I decided to walk downtown for a little entertainment. As luck would have it, Charlie Pickens was playing at the Ironclad. The Ironclad was home to two of my favorite things, bourbon and blues.

I went in and selected a seat in the corner. A lady never sits at the bar alone and I wasn't looking for company of any kind. I just wanted to try and forget that I felt like an orphan at twenty-eight years old. I paid the waitress one hundred dollars to bring me bourbon until the money ran out or until I passed out. Not that I had plans to get blind drunk. But, just as a precaution I gave her Eddie's number and told her if it looked like I couldn't make home on my own to call that number and someone would come and get me. I promised her a huge tip if it became necessary for her to call that number. Her eyes had widened at the sight of the one-hundred-dollar bill. She looked too young to have been waitressing long and I hoped that worked in my favor. I didn't want to give her one hundred bucks and end up in the alley out back or worse.

Things were going as planned until some guy made his way to my table and asked if he could buy me a drink.

"No thank you, I prefer to drink alone."

"You're too pretty to drink alone, let me keep you company."

He was insistent. "No thanks, I'm not looking for free drinks or company."

"Why not?" He pressed harder.

I was getting annoyed. "Does it matter? Go hassle someone else."

"You don't have to be such a bitch about it." That was the moment I lost what little patience I had. I stood up and sucker punched him. You don't get imbedded with a Marine unit without learning a thing or two. He guy landed on his back. He looked pretty angry and I thought for sure my evening was over.

"Anything I can do to help?" I looked up to see a second man standing at my table. My first reaction was of annoyance until he smiled.

I made some comment about solid waste management and he smiled even more. I felt my heart flip and then start beating again. The guy on the floor got to his feet and the second man whispered something to him. I couldn't hear what exactly, but Mr. Romance didn't look twice at me and scurried off. I noticed a glint of gold from a badge hanging from the second man's belt. So, whatever he said to Mr. Romance, apparently, he could back it up.

"May I join you?" the man with the badge asked.

I shrugged then nodded. He sat down cautiously and introduced himself. His name was Ethan. That name seemed to fit him perfectly. He seemed to sense I wasn't looking for company and new drinks arrived. There was something about him. I couldn't explain it, but it was everything. His crooked smile. The warmth of his touch. It was like an electric spark and pulsed through my body and gave my heart a jump start.

The remaining two days in Gates Point was spent with Ethan. We sat and talked for hours. In the end I learned that he was married. I told him I wouldn't be the cause of any break of a marriage even one on the rocks. And told him if we were meant to be together, we would meet again. I wasn't sure if I believed that at the time. What else could I do? He wasn't looking to have a romantic relationship and cheat on his wife. He was lonely and in need of a friend.

As I sat on the plane headed back to the Middle East and my assignment for Beatty Images, I wondered how life seemed to be going on around me without a care. Didn't the airline crew and other passengers realize, my life had just been turned completely upside down? Both of my parents were gone, I was the new CEO of a manufacturing company, and I had just met the man of my dreams only to find out he was married? My life is nothing if not complicated.

As I arrived back in Kabul I longed for the clean breezes off the bay while I was pelted by sand of the dessert.

"Hey Kay, I'm was sorry to hear about your mom."

"Let us know if you need anything." Chris, Dev, Micah, and Oliver stood staring at me all nodding.

"Thank you. I've got everything under control." I smiled.

These four men were my team, at least my core team anyway. I was the only female here and these four guys were the only ones that didn't give me shit on a daily basis. Most of the men here didn't think I could hack it. I guess I don't blame them. I got all sorts of comments about sleeping my way in and other crass jibes, and notes left on my bunk. I had thick skin and I let the comments slide. All these guys were high strung type A personality types and you needed that in this job. I wasn't about to do anything to disrupt the status quo other than being a female.

I followed these guys around night and day trying to get the images that told the real story of this war. The costs on all sides. Most people didn't appreciate my being here and considered me a liability. I was told under no uncertain terms that if I stepped out of bounds and got myself kidnapped; I was on my own. The commander wasn't going to risk his men or their mission just because some photojournalist wanted to take a picture. It was fair enough. I knew the risks when I volunteered for this assignment. Actually, getting into this unit was nothing short of a miracle. These guys did what no one ever got to see. The real stories were here, these men all of them what they sacrificed, what they endured and what they did without thinking twice as incredible. The civilians we encountered their stories were both heartwarming and heart wrenching.

But my team, my guys as I thought of them, we all looked out for each other and they took care of me. I tried not to be in the way or complicate their missions. I wouldn't do anything that would jeopardize their safety.

Chapter Three

Ethan

"Morning, boss."

"Morning." I mumbled in return. I came to work carrying my second cup of coffee for the day and it wasn't even eight o'clock yet. I hadn't slept well and spent most of the night on the couch so that I wouldn't wake Diane. The relationship was becoming more distant and I knew the inevitable was coming. She had made an appointment with a divorce attorney. It was only a matter of time.

"You see the notice from DC?" Jared checked in.

My phone had started buzzing the moment I took it off the charger this morning. "Yeah, we need to get started on that, what do we know locally?"

I set the coffee down on my desk and looked around the room. Agents Logan Watson, Jared Walker and Stephanie Fisher were already hard at work.

"Rough night?" Stephanie asked.

"No rougher than usual." I sat down at my desk and logged into my email. "What do we know so far?" I pressed.

"DC has picked up on chatter that something is being planned locally, they don't know who yet. We don't know the target or the players." Jared reported.

I looked to the three agents. "Where's the chatter coming from?"

"Other groups advising their people to stay out of the area this week." Logan replied.

"We have nothing," I sighed, "Well, let's get to work." The office was a concert of keyboards.

An hour later Logan spoke up. "I might have something."

"Let's hear it." I said, hoping for something useful.

"There was a warehouse theft two nights ago of demolition equipment and supplies." Logan continued.

"From where?" I stood up eager or details.

"A construction company warehouse." Logan's eyes scanned the screen as he read out the details.

"The report say what was taken?" I pressed.

"Some tools, small equipment," Logan looked up from the screen, "and the interesting part, explosives."

"Logan, you and Stephanie go interview the owner of that warehouse." I instructed.

"On it." Logan pounced.

"Jared, see if you can get a copy of the police report on the break-in."

"You got it, boss."

I continued searching our database of known terrorist groups that might be operating in the area. We needed to find a way to determine the target. The question was, what to search for first? The potential target or the potential bad guy, one could lead to the other. It was a catch twenty-two. But we had to look at every angle until we came up with something. It wasn't glamorous, it wasn't like all the excitement you see on television. It was hours of digging through files, listening to chatter, interviewing people, searching more files.

"Boss, there is a report of some weapons reported missing at Camp Allen." Jared had found something.

"How many weapons?" I asked.

"About ten automatic rifles and a case of grenades."

"Better give NCIS a call. Maybe they will be willing to share intel." I instructed. I blew out a sigh. This was going to be one of those long drawn out cases and I was feeling antsy. I needed something more to occupy my mind. It was a product of too little sleep and too much caffeine.

"You look tired." Jared added.

"Comes with the job."

He nodded and went back to work.

I didn't want to talk about it. Besides it really wasn't anything I could put into words even if I wanted to. Jared wouldn't understand regardless. Life hadn't kicked him in the teeth enough yet. Maybe in about ten years, he might get it. I got up and walked to kitchen. I really didn't want any more coffee. I went to the fridge for a bottle of water instead. I imagined my body protesting at something that wasn't coffee or alcohol.

Back at my desk and tried a different approach. I found where a tip had been called in that someone bought a lot of farm grade fertilizer recently from a feed and seed store.

"Jared I'm going to go talk to Saunders Feed and Seed, I'll be back later."

Jared nodded and I left him alone to handle the research. I couldn't sit at a desk today, I need to be outside in the fresh air and moving otherwise my mind was going to dwell on my personal problems when I needed to be focused on this case.

I got back around six and we sat comparing our notes from the day.

"Something doesn't sound right." Stephanie said

"What do you mean?" I asked, appreciating her ability to see the larger picture.

"Well grenades, from a military base, explosives from a construction warehouse and fertilizer from a feed store?" She was thinking out loud. "That feels like two completely different MO's. Grenades are more personal, suicide bomber style."

"Okay." I was interested to see where she was going with this line of thinking.

"Fertilizer is a broader more widespread impact. Less personal."

"Unless you pack the grenades together, create a big boom that way." I offered. "So, you're thinking the two aren't connected?"

"Not sure I'm willing to go that far yet, it isn't very straight forward."

"Is it ever?"

"Guess you have a point." She nodded.

It was getting late and so far, we had a bunch of different pieces of a puzzle and nothing was fitting yet. It felt like we were chasing our tails. "People we really need to figure out the target."

"It would help if we knew who was doing it. No luck on the credit card from the feed and seed?" Stephanie asked.

"Stolen card. The card holder is a college student whose wallet was stolen." Jared said.

"Great." My eyes were tired. "Why don't you guys call it a day, we can look at this fresh tomorrow."

"You sure?" Logan asked.

"Yeah, it's late, you guys get out of here." I waved my in the direction of the door.

"What about you?" Stephanie asked.

"I'm going to call it a night too." At least I was thinking about it.

They all gathered up their things and went home.

I made sure the office was secure then I went and made a fresh pot of coffee. I wasn't fooling myself. I wasn't going to be able to sleep tonight anyway. So, I might as well try looking at this from a different angle. The office was so quiet you could hear a pin drop. The silence was ringing in my ears. It was almost worse than too much noise. I paced back and forth trying to get a handle on this case.

Stephanie was right; grenades and fertilizer implied two different styles of attack. I could almost take the fertilizer as a coincidence if a stolen credit card hadn't been used. Jared had left his computer running the facial recognition program on the images we got from the video camera above the register at the feed and seed.

My cell phone rang.

"Craddock."

"Ethan, it's John, I hope I haven't caught you at a bad time."

"No, I'm still at the office, What's up?"

"I am hearing rumors of a possible attack on the city." John's voice conveyed his concern.

"I imagine it was part of your security brief this week, yes." Frankly, I was surprised I hadn't gotten a call before now.

"I know the FBI is working very hard to uncover if the threat is real or not so please know if there is any resources the city can offer you, let me know."

"You know, I'll keep you in the loop once I have anything to share."

"I know you will Ethan."

"Good night, John."

I clicked off. John St. Clair and I had known each other a long time. Our kids went to the same school, our wives were in the same clubs. He never used his position or our friendship to curry professional favor, so this phone call was interesting. There had to be more to it and if John didn't tell me over the phone, I trusted that it was because he couldn't.

I got up and check Jared's computer. Still nothing. I had a bad feeling about this case. I felt like we were missing a big piece. I scanned the headlines, for any stories of anyone important visiting the city this week that could be a potential target or any recent court cases that might have caught the interest of any local radical groups. Other than local dinners and functions I didn't see anything that would garner the attention of someone with enough juice to steal from the Camp Allen armory and a feed and seed brazenly as they had. Maybe they just got lucky.

I sat down at my desk and stared up at the ceiling. I was starting to get past the idea of a divorce as Diane had filed the paperwork with the court and had moved to North Carolina as part of our one-year separation. I kept the house since it seemed like I wasn't the only thing she was tired of around here.

It was an amicable split and I could see Madelyn whenever I wanted. There were no restrictions and Madelyn was too wrapped up in her own teenage life to care too much about what me and her mother were doing or not doing. Things really could be a lot worse. Diane had her own career and she wasn't looking for support from me. I, of course, provided support to Madelyn and that was more from a requirement than anything Diane pushed for. She made more money than I did as a corporate tax attorney working down in Charlotte. So why was I so miserable? I have an ex-wife that wasn't demanding. I could see my daughter whenever I wanted, I had a good career going with the FBI and I drank too much and slept too little. I could try and blame in on the cases, that wasn't it. Sure, I lost a bit of sleep due to the more stressful ongoing cases, but I rarely let them bother me after it was over. There was always a new one to take its place so there was no point in getting hung up on one case or another.

If I was honest with myself what had been keeping me up at night was the thought of Kay. I don't know why. I had thought of her over the years and wondered if I would ever see her again. I hoped I would. I had filed that weekend under the category of two ships passing in the night. It was a great memory, but realistically I doubted I'd ever see her again. But, lately my thoughts of Kay were different. I felt like it was less a memory and more of a sense that she was in danger or something. I scanned the newspapers for anything that might mention her. I had no idea if she was still in the Middle East. I thought about doing an internet search or even a database search. I sat staring at the computer for several long minutes. Then I shook it off and decided the most important thing right now was to focus on the case but that wasn't going to happen tonight. I admitted defeat and went home.

The next morning, I came to the office with a renewed sense of purpose. I floated my idea to the team about any large local events happening that would be an easy target for someone.

"Maybe it isn't anything as high profile as all of that." Jared offered.

"That doesn't help." I was frustrated that we were getting nowhere. "Anything more on the chatter?

"Nothing yet." Stephanie shook her head.

"Okay, so who are our main players around here for mayhem?" I started pacing. "Who do we know that has access to the base and the port and who is behind most of the big problems around here?"

"I like where you're going, boss." Logan said. "So, we have the gangs, the drug runners and the Dixie Mafia."

"So, let's start with a drug angle. Focus in on our typical players involved in moving a lot of weight."

"So, you think they need explosives to do what?" Jared asked.

"I know, but maybe it's a turf thing. Maybe someone is planning on taking out a rival in a big away."

"Okay, I'll check with the local PD for recent conflicts and see if there is anything to indicate a big move by the rivals. Maybe, somebody smoked another gang member or something." Stephanie frowned at her screen in concentration.

"Okay, that or someone is stepping on someone else's drug turf." I offered.

"On it." Jared said as he ducked his head behind his computer monitor.

"And think of any of our informants that might know what is going on. Maybe, someone who is part of the chatter telling people to stay away? See if there is anything we can get from that angle." I suggested. With everyone tapping away on their computers. I decided my time would be better spent elsewhere. "I'm going to go over and talk to Chief Corey." I grabbed my keys and headed out the door. It only took me about ten minutes this time of day to drive over the police headquarters. I had called his office once I was in the car to let them know I was on my way.

"Ethan what a pleasant surprise." Chief Corey extended his hand when his assistant let me into his office.

"Jim, thank you for seeing me on such short notice." I shook his hand.

"Anytime at all. Come on in."

His was a simple office with a few pictures adorning the plain walls. The chief had been on the Gates Point PD his entire career and he had moved up through the ranks and therefore had the respect of the people who served under him. He also knew everyone and where all the bodies were buried in this town. He was a valuable friend and a terrifying enemy. Not that he would do anything outside the law, but he knew the dirt on everyone and everyone in Gates Point had dirt.

"How can I help you today?"

"Well, this chatter we've all heard about and the thefts at the warehouse and over at Camp Allen."

"Yeah, we have to stop this before it turns into a shit storm for all of us." He took a seat behind his desk and I sat across from him in a leather guest chair.

"Exactly, I have to admit I'm not getting much of anywhere yet, which is disturbing. So, I am trying a different angle. Maybe it isn't an outside terrorist but something closer to home?"

"Certainly, possible but what did you have in mind?"

"Well, I was thinking is there anything that might be a local gang retaliating on another or a big drug shipment coming in that you might have heard about on the local chatter that I haven't heard?"

"Well that is definitely an angle we should be looking at so hang on and let me call Lt. Taylor and find out what he knows."

"I'd appreciate that."

The chief spoke briefly into the phone.

"He'll be right in."

"Okay, thanks." I leaned back in the chair.

"I'm sorry to hear about you and Diane. I know it's been a while, but I haven't really had a chance to talk to you in private since then, I don't think."

"Thanks, just one of those things." I shrugged.

"Yeah, I know what you mean. You stay in touch?"

"Yeah, we do. She's just down in Charlotte so I see Madelyn once in a while when I'm not working."

The chief nodded. Divorce was a common thing in police work at every level. It was tough, dangerous, long hours and unpredictable schedules. It was hard on the families.

The door opened and Lt. Dale Taylor stepped inside. I had met him once before.

"Agent Craddock, good to see you again."

"Yeah, you too."

We shook hands and the lieutenant sat down.

"Ethan and I were just talking about the recent thefts. We were wondering if it could be drug and gang related. Ethan isn't getting much traction on the international front of things."

"It is possible, I mean there is always some rift or other going on."

"Why don't I pull up some data and we can go over it maybe see if we can find a new pattern or something going on, we've missed." Taylor offered.

"Okay, what can I do to help?" I asked.

"Maybe your database might be able to pull some information from other states and we can compare notes."

"That sounds good, I can send one of my techs over if that helps?" I offered.

"That would be great."

We all stood up and shook hands. "I really appreciate the help gentlemen."

"Anytime." The Chief said.

I drove back to the office and sent Greg our tech guru over to police headquarters to work with their drug and gang's units.

I tried to do some more research on the case, but my mind was wandering today, and I kept picturing Kay. I wondered if she was in some sort of trouble or if something about her was connected to this case. Gates Point had a long tradition with alternative theories on one's destiny. I think it started back in the seventeen or late eighteenth century. I wasn't one to believe it one hundred percent and I wasn't one to discount it out of hand either. Things happen for a reason and you should trust your gut, hunches, intuition or whatever you wanted to call it. Mine were usually right and there had to be a reason Kay had jumped to the forefront of my thoughts recently. Still, I need to get some work done.

"Boss, I think we might have our first real lead." Jared's head popped up from behind his monitor.

"What have you got?" We all walked over to look at his screen.

"I got a hit on facial recognition from one of the security cameras at Camp Allen."

"Who is it?" I asked.

"A former Army sergeant turned private security named Joseph Branigan. You know one of those big firms that work over in the Middle East?"

"Yeah, which one?" I said feeling a little impatient.

"Russo Security."

"Good work! I clapped Jared on the shoulder, "Logan, check with Russo Security and see what the status of his employment is with them."

"I'm on it." Logan returned to his desk.

I turned back to Jared. "What else you got?"

"He was dishonorably discharged for fighting. Apparently, he has quite a temper."

"Wonder if he holds a grudge?" I mused.

"He might." Jared agreed.

"Who filed charges against him for the fighting?" I asked.

Jared typed away. "Whoa, looks like he was charged with manslaughter and got off with a dishonorable, because the witnesses changed their testimony. They said Branigan didn't start the fight and acted in self-defense when they previously stated he was drunk and started the fight inside the NCO club. The man he was fighting with died of head injuries sustained in the fight."

"Okay, we are going to need more on Joseph Branigan, I'm going to call GPPD and let them know what we found." I said reaching for the desk phone.

"On it, boss." Jared got back to work.

"What can I do to help?" Stephanie called out.

"Look into his known associates while he was on active duty and the witnesses to the fight to see if maybe they can tell us more." Jared instructed.

I was pumped, it finally felt like we might have a solid lead. At least we had something to focus on at the moment. I reached Greg, our resident technology whiz kid, so that he and the GPPD would look for local connections and see what Branigan was into these days. It didn't seem likely he would steal weapons here if he wasn't planning on using them here. Unless he was going to try and smuggle them out through the port.

I called over to the port authority and put them on alert as well. Jared emailed all the other local departments Branigan's picture from his Army file and what we pulled off the surveillance camera. He looked scruffy now, so I had a feeling he wasn't working for Russo Security anymore. From what I knew all the Russo employees were clean cut and very military in style and dress. Unless, they had something going undercover.

Logan hung up his phone.

"Branigan is no longer employed by Russo and they didn't want to talk in detail over the phone. They're sending someone out to talk with us."

"All the way to Virginia?" I was surprised.

"Apparently, so." Logan confirmed.

"That's interesting." I said trying to think of a reason why they would go to the trouble.

Stephanie and Jared looked up.

"Either they know he is into some heavy stuff or they are seriously paranoid." Stephanie offered.

"Yeah, so why not talk on the phone if there isn't anything to tell?" Jared added.

"You have a good point. Logan, did they say when they would be here?" I asked.

"Tomorrow."

"I think it might be a good idea to let our friend the chief know as well. This might be worse than we thought." I reached for the phone again.

Chapter Four
Ethan

It was a rainy Tuesday afternoon as I sat in Chief Corey's Office with Mike Russo from Russo Security.

"We appreciate you coming all the way up here to talk to us, but I have to admit I'm a little curious as to why we couldn't do this over a secure phone or video chat."

"I understand your confusion. I'm afraid the area of concern is at my end rather than at yours."

"You think you have a leak in your organization?" I asked.

"It might be worse than a simple leak. I have suspended all our activities at the moment because I believe our files have been severely compromised. I think the only way that could happen is from the inside." It was clear, Russo was trying to get ahead of the situation.

"And you think Joseph Branigan might be involved?"

"I think it is not out of the realm of possibility, especially since you called asking about him." Russo postulated.

"Why don't you start at the beginning Mr. Russo." Jim sat down behind his desk and waited.

"As I'm sure you already know," Russo began, "Branigan was dishonorably discharged from the Army for fighting."

"Yes, I am aware, and it makes me wonder why you would hire a man with such a record."

"Listen, I'll admit not everyone I hire is a boy scout and sometimes you need someone who is willing to get their hands dirty to get a job done." He paused and held up his hands. "I'm not talking about breaking the law and certainly not in the U.S. As you know the laws are somewhat different in a war zone and we are not held to the same standard as the U.S. military. We often can get things done the military cannot."

Jim and I both nodded.

"I was aware of Branigan's service record and I was also aware he had a lot of friends and contacts in a lot of places that might be helpful to our overall mission."

"So, you were willing to overlook a few indiscretions in order to get to bigger fish?" I asked.

"Exactly."

"Go on." Jim encouraged.

I knew Jim understood Russo's reasoning; it wasn't an uncommon practice in law enforcement anywhere to offer some leniency to a small fish if it helped you take a bigger one off the streets.

"I fear I may have underestimated Branigan. He is full on pyscho. Whether that is by circumstance or if he has always been that way and no one bothered to make note of it, I'm not sure. And it doesn't matter at this point." Russo waived his hand dismissively.

"So, you think that Branigan has contacts still inside your organization willing to help him?" I asked.

"It's the only explanation I can come up with. The problem is, I don't know what they might have bugged or might be tracking so I haven't been able to get very far with an internal investigation. I didn't have enough to take to the police until now."

"I see." Jim leaned back in his chair and tented his fingers. A clear sign he was thinking deeply about something.

"Are you sure you have been bugged?" I asked thinking that his taking a meeting with the FBI and the GPPD he might be a target, if he wasn't already. "Your phone, laptop? Maybe a button on your clothing?"

Russo looked down at his shirt.

"Do you have your clothes dry cleaned?" I asked.

"Yes."

"You might want to buy some new clothes while you're here and maybe a burner phone for the time being." I advised.

"You may have a point." Russo seemed to understand that he may have been compromised.

"If you like I can have our tech guys look at your laptop and phone to see if they have been tampered with in anyway." I offered.

"Yes, thank you."

He handed me his laptop and phone. I would drop them off with our IT guru Greg on my way out. "Do you have a place to stay yet?" I asked Russo.

"No, I came straight here."

"Okay that's good if they were tracking you, they wouldn't have tracked you to a hotel yet. I would suggest leaving here, buying some new clothes and checking into a hotel, preferably one with security cameras."

"I can put some plain clothes officers in place to help keep an eye on you Mr. Russo." Jim offered.

"Thank you." Russo nodded to Jim," I have to admit I'm a little out of my element. I'm used to having my own team around me if needed. I don't know who I can trust anymore."

"It's best in these situations to let someone from the outside handle things." I reassured him.

Jim called for two plain clothes officers to shadow Russo as soon as he left his office and to stick with him, discreetly. I headed back to my office with a promise from Greg to let me know the minute he found anything on either the phone or the laptop.

"How'd the meeting go?" Jared asked as soon as I walked back into the office.

"Promising. This may be bigger than we thought. Greg from IT is going over Russo's phone and laptop for anything that we can trace back to Branigan. And he gave me a list of employees known to be close to Branigan when he worked for Russo Security so that might give us a few more leads." I split the list between Stephanie, Jared and Logan.

***

It had been a long day. My head was pounding as I walked to my car music drifting on the night air caught my attention. It sounded like Charlie Pickens and reminded me of Kay. I wandered down the street in the direction of the music. I hoped I would find her sitting at a table alone listening to the music and waiting for me. I stepped inside a small night club, but it wasn't Charlie playing. I looked around and didn't see any signs of Kay. I thought my mind was just playing tricks on me I shook my head stepped back out onto the sidewalk.

An old blind woman sitting on a bench just outside the door reached out and grabbed my hand. "The one you seek is not here; she looks for you as well." She released my hand went back to swaying to the music. I stared down at my hand and walked back out into the street. The words haunted me all the way home. It had been a long time since I had encountered a seer. I remembered my grandmother talk about and old woman that lived back in the woods, that would see the future and tell fortunes.

Images of Kay filled my thoughts as I laid in bed. What it would be like to be with her again? Now that I was divorced, we could have a real relationship. I imagined her in various stages of undress. At some point I drifted off to sleep, I woke with a start and sweating. I sat up and listened. Had there been a noise? I thought about the Branigan case and wondered if what had woken me was related? Not hearing anything I laid back down panting. I had been dreaming of Kay but instead of her beautiful smile and the way I imagined she would look with her hair down I dreamt she was hurt and alone somewhere dark. She needed help and was calling my name; I had no idea where she was or how to get to her.

The clock read three in the morning. I knew I wouldn't be able to sleep tonight. The old woman's words came back to my mind. Had they been prophetic? Had they incited the dream? There wasn't much point in staring at the ceiling. I dressed, went downstairs, made coffee and went to the office.

I picked up the list of associates and suspects off Jared's desk and started working them. I typed the name Joseph Price, into the system and the screen lit up. Joseph Branigan scared back at me; I had more information than I could have hoped for. Joey Price, a.k.a Joseph Branigan, was into a lot of bad shit. I double checked Branigan/Price's personal history it seemed Price was his mother's maiden name. Bingo! I also had a more recent picture to go along with the new name and I began sending it out to every law enforcement agency in Virginia. Price was a member of the Southern Gentleman's Club which was nothing more than a home-grown terrorist group. They professed to be patriotic, yet they burned churches, temples and mosques. They were anti-government and anti-establishment. They pretty much didn't like anyone that didn't belong to their little club.

At six am Jared came into the office. "Hey boss, you're here early."

"Yeah, I found our boy, too." I said smiling at him.

"No way!" Jared exclaimed.

"He is using his mother's name, Price, these days. I pulled up the picture on the screen. I've sent it out to all the LEO's."

"Why didn't I think of that?" he chided himself.

"You would have eventually." I smiled enjoying the moment.

"Maybe, but it might have been too late." Jared shook his head.

"Well, we still don't know what he is up to and when. But now we can at least draw some better lines between him and known associates and maybe get a better handle on this thing." I tried to reassure him. There was certainly plenty of work to be done on this case yet.

Jared sat down and got to work. About half an hour later Logan and Stephanie joined us. By noon, we had a much better picture of Joey Price's network.

Greg's face appeared on my computer. "Hey boss, you there?"

"Yeah, I'm here Greg what have you got?"

"A lot! So, you were right about Russo's phone. Someone had a remote tracker on it so it could not only track his movements through the GPS, and it was capturing keystrokes."

"So, all of Russo Security files are exposed?" I needed to know.

"Yes, not just company files but his personal files too." Greg elaborated.

"Okay, well we know Mike Russo is a target. But, is he the only target?"

"I'll keep digging." Greg said.

"Greg, do you know what hotel Mike Russo check into last night?"

"No."

"Okay, I'll call the chief." I hung up and then dialed Jim's number.

"Corey, here."

"Jim, it's Ethan. Look we got a good line on Branigan using the name Price. And Russo is definitely a target. What hotel did he check into last night?" I asked.

"Damn! He is staying at the Renaissance. I'll call the two officers watching him and tell them to stay close." He answered.

"Thanks Jim, I'm on my way over there. We can put him in a safe house." I said, thinking that would be a better situation.

"Alright, then." Jim clicked off.

"Logan you're with me." I turned to Jared and Stephanie, "keep connecting the dots."

We were almost to the hotel when my phone chirped.

"Craddock."

"Ethan, it's Jim. I just spoke to my two officers and they say that Russo is gone, looks like he was taken by force."

"Damn!"

"Sorry, Ethan."

"Thanks for the heads up, Jim. I'll call you later." I clicked off.

"What's happened?" Logan asked.

"Looks like Russo is gone, maybe kidnapped." I sighed in frustration.

We were met in the lobby by two plain clothes and two uniformed officers.

"Gentlemen, I understand from Chief Corey, that Mike Russo is gone, what can you tell me?" I asked showing them my credentials.

"There looks like there was a struggle up there and his personal belongings are still in the room. We think he was taken by force." One of the plain clothes officers answered.

I looked at Logan and he was already pulling out his cell phone and dialing our forensic team to get over here right away. "Show me!" I demanded.

The two plain clothes officers took me upstairs. The door to the room was still open and there was yellow tape across it.

"You touch anything in there?"

"No, we came up here when we got the call from the Chief that you were on the way and once we realized he was gone, we stepped out and called the station as soon as we saw this mess." The officer looked around at the overturned furniture and blood stain on the bed."

"Great." I ran my hand through my hair. "FBI has jurisdiction over this scene now."

"Yes, sir." They replied and walked away.

Logan came up and looked around. He let out a small whistle. "What a mess."

"In more ways than one." I added.

"You think Price did this?" Logan asked looking around the room.

"I'd bet my Redskin's tickets on it."

Logan whistled again. "Forensics will be here soon."

"Okay, well let's wait out here." I stepped back out into the hallway to make sure no one disturbed the scene until our team could get there. "Call the office and tell Jared and Steph what's going on."

Logan nodded and stepped away to use the phone.

I called Greg. "Greg can you and the team there check the traffic cameras in the area. I'm going to go talk to hotel security as soon as the forensic team gets here. "

"On it."

"Okay, thanks." Just when I thought we were getting ahead of this thing; I shook my head.

"You okay boss?" Logan asked as he slipped his cell phone back in his pocket.

"Just frustrated."

"Yeah, I know how you feel," he agreed. "You seem worse for wear lately, anything going on?"

"No, no. I'm good." I lied.

Logan wasn't one to press. We'd worked together a long time and he knew me as well as anyone. He wasn't going to push the issue and I was grateful for that. How do you explain dreaming about a woman you only ever spent two nights with, and it wasn't even intimate? I sounded like a crazy person even to myself.

I shook my head. I needed to focus on Joey Price and our missing security executive.

"We're here Agent Craddock!" Andria Chapman called from the elevator.

"Good, it's a mess in there so you'll have your work cut out for you."

"We got this." She replied.

"I know you do."

I left Andria and her assistant to get to work. I had work of my own to do. I went down to the lobby in search of the security office. I flashed my badge and finally got access to the security feed. Three men wearing trench coats entered the lobby at eleven thirty-five. Due to the bad weather no one questioned their attire.

All three went up to the twelfth floor. When they exited the elevators, they were wearing ski masks and used spray paint to block out the cameras in the hallway.

Then they exited through a side entrance on the street level with Russo in tow. A camera near the pool was aimed only at the door so there was no way to know which way they went after they were outside or what kind of vehicle, they were in. I text the information to Greg in hopes the traffic cameras would give us more information. I knew it would take time and it was time we didn't have. Our investigation had been elevated to a kidnapping case. Logan and I drove back to the FBI office.

"We need to find out if Russo has any next of kin and if there has been a ransom demand yet." I said as we walked through the door into the office.

"I'll coordinate with the office in Georgia where Russo's security firm is based." Logan offered.

"Okay, try to find out where he lives you might need to call the Atlanta field office." I stood looking around the office for a moment thinking of what to do next. "We also need to find out if anyone in their organization is in jail at the moment." I was trying to wrap my head around all the possibilities as to who may be after Mike Russo.

"On it." Stephanie added.

"You think they are looking for a trade rather than straight revenge, boss?" Jared asked.

"I think there is still a lot we don't know about this case. We know some of the players, but we still don't know the motive." I said, going back to basics.

"True enough." Jared agreed.

"We have got to figure this thing out people." I was stating the obvious to a room of professionals, but I wanted everyone to keep focused on this case. This certainly wasn't their first kidnapping or terrorist threat. I just had to get it off my chest. I had to put it out there in the ether, to the universe for whatever help it may have to offer. Things were escalating quickly. They had already kidnapped a high-profile target right out from under our nose and we didn't have the first idea of where they may have taken him. At this point we could only hope they made some sort of demand so that we might buy a little time and track them down before things got worse.

The day was just as cloudy and rainy as the night before and it didn't do anything to help my mood. I was still operating on more caffeine than sleep. I couldn't shake the feeling of the nightmare I had about Kay or the woman's words in the bar. I had a missing CEO and only an educated guess as to who took him. A wild guess as to why and no idea as to where or what they might want in return if anything. It could be that Joey Price just wanted to exact revenge on his former employer. If it was that simple, I didn't hold out a lot of hope that would be able to find Mike Russo in time if at all. I was feeling edgy and short tempered.

It was close to eight o'clock in the evening and we weren't much closer on finding Mike Russo. No phone calls and no demands. Our Atlanta office was with the wife, waiting for contact from Price for a ransom and protecting her as well.

"Why don't you all call it a night." I told my team. "No sense in staying here if you're exhausted. Better to get a fresh start in the morning."

"What about you?" Logan asked as he stood up to leave.

"I'll close up the office and go home." I reassured him.

Logan was a good friend and I knew he meant well.

I locked the door behind them and started to try and organize my desk a little when the phone rang. The caller ID indicated it was from our forensics office.

"Andria, what are you doing working so late?"

"Same as you, I suppose."

I nodded, touché.

"I just wanted you to know that Williamsburg Police fished a body out of the Chickahominy River."

"Was it Russo?" I held my breath waiting for the answer.

"No, it was a man named Joseph Price."

"Price?" That was a surprise.

"Yeah."

"Any cause of death?"

"Not at the moment but they are going to send him over to me in the morning. So, I'll know more around noon tomorrow. I just thought you should know in case it has anything to do with the business at the hotel."

"Okay thanks." I hung up. My frustration level had reached its breaking point for the day and I angrily shoved a stack of files onto the floor as I headed for the door. It wasn't going to do me any good to stay here tonight so I drove home. I needed to run a few miles on the treadmill and work out this tension. I needed to try and get some sleep. I hoped my dreams of Kay were more peaceful.

Chapter Five
Ethan

"Boss, I think we may be onto something." Logan called from his desk.

"Whatcha got?" I looked up hopeful.

"Traffic cameras picked up a van that parked behind the hotel the night Russo was kidnapped. And fifteen minutes later it has seen leaving the area."

"Can you track it?"

"I did. It stopped near warehouse over near the port."

"You have an address?"

"Yep."

"Send it to GPPD and have them meet us there."

We all grabbed our gear and headed out to the parking lot. I drove one SUV and Jared drove the other.

We pulled over half a mile from the warehouse to wait for GPPD.

"Remember team. We know they have explosives, grenades, high-powered rifles and a hostage. Let's end this safely."

We all acknowledged and descended on the warehouse. As FBI we took the lead and went to the front of the building. We sought cover behind some metal shipping containers. Gates Point Police Department took up positions surrounding the building. They also had snipers on nearby roofs.

Agent Brian Newsome, the FBI hostage negotiator arrived just as we were taking up positions.

"Have you made contact yet?" He asked.

"No." I answered.

Brian and I had worked together enough that there was no need for pleasantries in these situations.

"Okay, good. Do we know if there is a landline in there?"

"You need to check with Greg in the GPPD tech van over there." I pointed to where the van was parked further back from the rest of us.

Brian ran over and disappeared inside. A moment later his voice came over our earpieces.

"My name is Brian Newsome; who am I speaking with?"

"Well Brian, my name is not of your damn business."

"Okay fair enough but can you tell me how Mike Russo is doing?"

"He's just fine and will stay that way if you and whatever ever pathetic force you rolled up in here with leave and let us do what we came here to do."

"And what is that?"

"Make our voices heard."

"Okay, I'm listening."

"You don't matter, Brian. You're a nobody. We want the whole country to hear us."

"And how is Mike Russo going to help you with that?"

"Well, he has access to files that could be quite useful to our cause. He also had contacts in Washington that need to hear what we have to say."

"Okay, and what is that you have to say? I know a few people in Washington, myself."

"I bet you do."

Silence.

We all listened straining to hear anything. I thought perhaps they had hung up until a gunshot thundered in our ears.

"Ah!" I pulled the earpiece out instinctively.

"Hello? Are you still there?" Brian was frantic on the phone.

"Well, if you're the man Brian I guess we didn't need Mr. Russo anymore."

Logan and I looked at each other. Had they just killed Mike Russo?

Logan whispered to me. "That voice sounds different."

"You think it is a different person?" I whispered back.

Logan nodded. If there was no hostage there was nothing stopping us from storming the building, except possibly the explosives. Brian hung up the phone.

"We need eyes inside that building, now!" He ordered over the comm system.

Two GPPD officers crept up the side of the building looking for a place to insert the micro camera. Another officer set up the infrared equipment so we could try and determine how many people were in the building.

"What I want to know if Price/Branigan is in the morgue and Russo is in there dead, who the hell else is in there?" I said into the mic.

"I'm working on it, Boss." Greg answered. "Okay, the camera is live inside the building. Looks like we have about ten individuals, but we can't see Russo. They are loading barrels into the back of two vans."

"That's got to be the explosives." Logan said.

"I'm not sure we are going to be able to wait much longer. We can't let those vans leave here." I ordered.

"I think we are going to have to move fast because it looks like they are almost finished loading the vans." Logan said to me in a low tone.

"We go on your orders Craddock." A voice shouted.

"Okay. Everyone get ready." I paused and checked my gun and ammo. I looked to make sure everyone was wearing their tactical vest. "Now!"

We rushed the building from all sides. There was an entry door next to the bay and Logan pulled it open and I went in low.

"FBI, don't move!" Of course, they all moved, they always do. I went to my right down the wall with Logan behind me. Jared and Stephanie down the wall to the left. GPPD was filing in behind us. Two guys ran for the vans.

"Stop the vans!" I yelled into the mic.

Two uniformed officers stormed each van and pulled the drivers out.

The rest of the people fled to the back of the building.

"Their headed for the back!" Logan yelled.

We pursued them knowing uniformed officers would be there to meet them if they got to the rear doors of the building. Seeing that they were trapped a few them turned and began firing. I pushed Logan behind a crate, not that the wooden crates would offer much protection, but it was better than nothing right now. I felt a bullet hit my vest. It knocked me back onto the floor.

Logan stood up and returned fire. The wind was knocked from my chest. I couldn't breath and it hurt like hell.

"We have an agent down, repeat agent down!" I could hear Logan yelling but I couldn't speak to tell him I was going to be alright. The next thing

I know he had me by the shoulder and was dragging me across the floor. Everything seemed to be in chaos at the moment.

Logan suddenly appeared in my field of vision. "You're going to be alright, boss. Hang in there."

I tried to tell him I knew that already and to go get the bad guys, but it hurt to try and talk.

"Stay with me boss," he encouraged.

I just needed to close my eyes for a minute and catch my breath. Damn this hurt. After a few moments I realized the shooting had stopped so I opened my eyes. Logan and Jared were staring at me.

"Did we get them?" I whispered with what little air I could manage.

"Yep. We got'em. Jared smiled.

I nodded and closed my eyes again.

"Boss? Stay with me the EMTs are here."

"I don't need EMT's." I said trying to sit up.

"Yes, you do." One of the EMTs answered and gently pushed my shoulders back to the warehouse floor.

"Fine." I gave in. I was getting my breath back. They removed my vest and cut open my shirt.

"The vest stopped the bullet from penetrating, but I think you might have a couple of broken ribs. We will get you to the hospital and get you x-rayed."

"I'm fine." I tried to sit up again.

"Boss, you're going to the hospital even if I have to sit on you to get you there." Logan threatened.

I had no doubt he would make good on that threat too. I cooperated as they put me on a gurney and loaded me in the ambulance.

"Stay here, work the scene." I said to Jared and Logan.

"Okay, I'll come by and pick you up later." Logan smiled.

"Don't wait too long." The ambulance doors shut, and I couldn't hear what else Logan said. I thought it sounded like he said, 'stubborn bastard'.

***

I hate the way hospitals smell. I think it is the mixture of disinfectant and alcohol.

The EMT was right as I had two broken ribs. They bandaged me up, gave me something for the pain and told me to stay home for a few days. My shirt was useless, so I tossed it in the garbage. I had my jacket. I don't know what happened to my vest. I was at the counter signing paperwork so I could get out of there when Logan finally showed up.

"So, you're gonna live?" he joked.

"Looks that way."

"I'm glad to hear it." He clapped me on the back. "I was worried for a minute."

"Just a couple of broken ribs, nothing serious." I told him.

"Here I brought you this." Logan handed me a t-shirt.

"Thanks." I slipped it on as we walked out the door.

"So where are we with case?" I needed to know where we stood now.

"Well we arrested everyone in the warehouse except one."

"Oh?"

"Yeah, the guy who shot you didn't make it." Logan said.

I paused and looked at Logan. "You take him out?"

"Well, yeah. He had just shot a federal agent so what was I supposed to do?" He just stared at me.

"You did good." I smiled. "Did we get all the explosives?"

"Yeah, we did. We still don't know the extent of the plan yet; do you want to hear the kicker?"

"There's a kicker?"

"Oh yeah. I big one." He smirked.

"Well, then you better tell me." I wasn't sure I was ready for it. It had been one hell of a day already.

"Mike Russo is alive and well and asking for his lawyer."

I stopped and looked at Logan.

"Yep, I'm not kidding. He faked his own kidnapping to cover up his involvement in all of this. I suspect Branigan was going to be a scapegoat all along."

"So, who got shot when the negotiator was talking to them?" I asked.

"Apparently, Russo shot the guy on the phone because he thought he was talking too much."

I shook my head. Well at least we had round them all up. "So, you're sure we got everything?"

"Yes. We have someone from Camp Allen coming over to confirm the inventory of items."

I nodded. I felt tired. It must have been the meds they had given me. My knees were a little weak.

"You okay?" Logan paused.

"Yeah, just tired."

"Why don't I take you home."

"No, office."

Logan shook his head. I knew he disapproved. He had no room to talk as he was a former Marine and a tough son-of-bitch and he would have done the same thing. Besides, we were going to have a ton of paperwork to do and putting it off wasn't really an option.

"Boss, should you be here?" Stephanie looked up when Logan and I came through the door.

"No." Logan answered again showing his disapproval.

"Getting shot only adds to the paperwork; it doesn't make it go away." I went to my desk and started sorting through the files.

Chapter Six

Kay

I woke up in a hospital. I remembered a blast of light. Everything was silent as a bright white light blinded me. Then as quickly as it had appeared it was gone and all that was left was chaos. Screaming, shouting, and gunfire. Someone was yelling at me. Everything was grey and black, like all the color had been sucked out of the world. I could barely see anything. It took me a minute to realize what had happened. We had been hit with an RPG. I couldn't fine the new kid that had been standing next me,. He was a young Marine that had joined the team recently and Chris had taken him under his wing. The rest of the team was to my left and they were on the ground. I needed to move and fast. I tried to run. It felt like something was attached to my leg and it was making it hard to move. I didn't have time to investigate. I looked down and saw my camera on the ground. I grabbed it and then crawled over to Oliver as he was the closest to me. I needed to get to the rest of the team. Oliver was unconscious so I went to check on each of the others. Chris was semi-conscious and in a lot of pain.

"Get my pack." He looked to the right. "First aid kit." He managed to say.

I crawled over and grabbed it.

"There is a morphine injection in there you are going to need that for Oliver."

"Why?"

"Look at him; he has a huge hunk of wood sticking out of him you need to remove it."

"What are you talking about? I can't do that!" I exclaimed.

"Well, normally I would but I can't right now, so you have to be my hands." He replied.

I wanted to argue further but I knew he had a point. I could see his right arm was mangled. "Why don't we fix you first and then you can help the others."

"He is dying while you are arguing." Chris grabbed me with his good hand. He was right, I could see the blood pouring out of Oliver. He would certainly bleed to death if I didn't do something.

I took a deep breath and did what Chris told me to do. I had never been squeamish about blood before, but I hadn't seen it from the inside out either, not like this. With Chris's help I started to get Oliver stabilized while whoever had launched the RPG was approaching. I could hear the whine of a vehicle engine and shouting. I turned to look at Chris.

"What do we do now?" Just give me direction, I thought.

"Grab Oliver's gun!" He didn't leave me any room to argue. "Point and squeeze." He showed me as best he could with his functioning hand.

I was near panic. This was all too much, the blood, the mangled bodies, the smoke and that awful smell .

"Devon!" Chris shouted. "Grab your weapon Marine!"

I wasn't sure what injuries Devon had but I knew he hadn't moved since the blast. He moved now. Micah began to move too. I thought it must be auto-reflexes because they all were pretty seriously injured as far as I had been able to determine. The ones that could move did so to take what cover was available. I got behind an overturned table. I wasn't a pacifist, but I never learned to fire a gun my mother had thought it undignified.

"Stay calm, Kay. Wait until they are close." Chris whispered.

I had hoped they assumed we were dead and would just leave. Apparently, that wasn't going to happened.

The door opened. Four men with rifles entered. Their faces were covered with ski masks. Not definitely here to rescue us. My heart sank and I felt sick. There was no time to think about any of that as I concentrated on the four men. They walked around kicking debris out of the way. I knew if they found us alive, they would kill us. I couldn't let that happen.

I heard Chris whisper. "Now."

I braced the butt of the rifle on my shoulder the way I had seen them do before. I aimed and squeezed. My arm jumped. I wasn't expecting the gun to be so powerful. I refocused and tried again. I could see the intruders aiming at us and firing but I couldn't hear anything. I looked to my right and saw Chris and then to my left and saw Devon and Micah firing their weapons. Oliver was still unmoving on the ground. I aimed and fired. I don't know how many times.

Finally, all the intruders were on the ground. Chris laid back down and closed his eyes. I had been imbedded with these guys for months. I had watched them work. I knew what to do. I got up and carefully checked to see if the intruders were dead. They were. Then I collected their guns and I looked outside. I didn't see anyone else around. I crawled back over to Chris.

"Can you hear me? We got them all."

Chris opened his eyes. I could see he was in pain.

"Tell me what to do." He shook his head and closed his eyes. "Dammit!" I crawled over to the others and checked on them. They were in the same condition as Chris or worse.

I needed to be able to stand. I looked down at my leg. I wasn't in any better shape than they were. I was bleeding and my leg below the knee wasn't anything recognizable. I was pretty sure there was debris in there from the explosion. I knew we had to get out of here. I went back to the first aid kit and found what I thought I needed to wrap up my leg. Then I found two table legs and made a splint. I limped outside there was a beat-up pick-up truck, I assumed it belong to the four dead guys. The keys were in it. I limped back inside.

"Chris, we have a truck and we need to get out of here. Get up!" I commanded as he groaned. "Get up, Marine!" I tried lifting him by the shoulders which was useless as he was too big and heavy. "Come on, get up, we have to go!" I begged to each one of them.

I could see they weren't going to be much help. I rolled Oliver onto a blanket. I then took the tabletop and made a ramp for the truck. I was able to drag him outside and up the ramp. My leg screamed in protest the entire time and when I was done, I was sweating, and it wasn't from the heat. I had three more marines to go. It took me some time to recover from Oliver and I found half a bottle of water. I wet my lips and then I took it to the others. I talked them through what I was doing even if they didn't respond. I had to load them in the back because I couldn't get them to cooperate enough to put them up front in the cab. I was the only one with any chance of driving and that was going to be iffy at best.

Chris revived a little after the water and was able to help me get him into the truck. He chose to ride in the back and look after Oliver.

I got my cell phone out and kept redialing phone numbers to the base. I just wanted to make sure they didn't shoot us when we approached. I had all the guns I had collected plus our own in the front with me. I had given Chris the first aid kit. I was finally able to reach the camp. "This is Kennedy Dandridge; I am in a stolen truck with four injured marines and I'm driving to the camp. Don't shoot!!!"

"Ma'am, can you repeat?"

"This is Kay, don't shoot, I'm in a white pick-up truck!" I could see the camp coming into view as I got closer and I could see the MP's standing at the ready. "It's me, I see the MP's. Please don't shoot, I have injured marines in the back!"

"Slow down and approach slowly." The voice on the other end advised.

I did as I was told when I got close enough, I stopped and held my hands out the window. The MP's approached on high alert They looked at me and, in the back, and waived to the gate. One of them called on the radio for medics.

I leaned my head back on the seat and closed my eyes.

"Kay, Kay can you hear me?" I heard a voice trying to revive me.

"Yes."

"Can you open your eyes?" the voice continued.

I tried to open them, but they felt incredibly heavy. I managed one than the other. It was the Unit Commander.

"What happened? He asked.

"RPG, I think and then four men with guns." I replied a bit in a trance.

"Where are they?" he pressed.

"Dead." I told him. He nodded to me and then to someone else and I closed my eyes again.

***

When I opened my eyes there was a stench of rubbing alcohol in my nose. I had tubes in my arms and hands. I had something on my face. I could hear beeping and clicking. I tried to move; my whole body screamed. Everything hurt like hell.

"Hey there, glad you're awake." A nurse leaned into my field of vision.

"Where?" I whispered.

"You're in the hospital at Ramstein Air Force base." She informed me.

"Team?" I continued.

"You need to rest." She was in nurse mode.

"Team!" I said with all the strength I could muster. My throat was dry, but I was determined to make her understand me one way or the other.

"They are all here, too." She said, understanding I was not going to give up.

"Alive?"

"Yes." She smiled. I relaxed back into the pillow.

When I woke up again there was a doctor leaning over me.

"Good to see you awake." He smiled.

"How long?" I asked. I no longer had an oxygen mask covering my mouth, so it made it easier to speak.

"Have you been here?" He asked. "They brought you in four days ago."

"Team?" I asked.

"All still here." The doctor was checking my vitals while he was answering my questions.

I nodded.

"Want to see them." I felt weak like breathing was too much effort. But I needed to know the guys were okay.

"I'm afraid that is going to have to wait." The doctor pulled his eyes away from this tablet to look at me. "Ms. Dandridge you are severely injured. You need to rest."

"Need to know how the others are doing." I insisted.

"You need to stop talking." The doctor insisted.

"Water!" I demanded my throat was on fire.

He frowned.

"Nurse, bring Ms. Dandridge some ice chips on the condition she stays in this bed and rests." He smiled down at me. I frowned up at him.

"We need to talk about you." He continued as if my steely gaze had no effect on him. Which apparently it didn't. He pulled up a chair and sat down next to the bed. I fumbled with the buttons on the bed so I could see him better. He reached over and helped me.

"Better?" he asked. I nodded. "Okay, so here's the deal. I'm not going to sugar coat anything."

I nodded again.

"Your left leg is pretty bad. I've saved it although, I'm not sure how long that will last. I am making sure there is no secondary infection. I won't lie to you. There is still a chance you could lose it."

I thought I had fallen asleep again and was having a nightmare. I was thinking I needed to try and wake up. The doctor reached over and touched my arm and I knew I wasn't dreaming.

"Ms. Dandridge?" He looked concerned.

"Save my leg." My voice sounded calmer then it should have. I wanted to shout at him to demand that he do everything he could, but my body and my mind didn't seem to be syncing at the moment.

"I am certainly going to do everything I can." He patted my hand reassuringly. He started to get up.

"Wait!" I said reaching for him.

He sat back down.

"Details." I demanded.

"What kind of details." He asked.

"About my leg." I said. He looked at me curiously and then nodded.

"Okay, tell you what. I have to go check on a few other patients. Then I'll come back, and you and I will have a long talk, okay?" he said clearly trying to placate me.

I nodded. "Promise?"

He smiled. "Promise." He left and a nurse appeared with ice chips.

I was done sleeping now. I had a new mission now. I had to figure out how to save my leg. "Can you bring me a phone?" The nurse gave me a sympathetic smile.

"Sure." A moment later she was back. "Can I call someone for you?" She indicated all the tubes in my hands.

"No, thank you." I needed to handle this myself.

She nodded and left. At the moment Eddie's number was the only one I could remember. I took a deep breath and punched in the numbers.

"Hello?" Eddie's voice sounded like home. I wanted to cry. I wanted to ask him to come get me and take me home. But I knew that wasn't possible. Not yet.

"Eddie, it's Kay."

"Kay, where are you? You sound like you're in a barrel." Eddie's voice already conveying his concern.

"I'm in a hospital Germany." I heard a sharp intake of breath.

"Are you hurt?" He wanted to know.

"Yeah." Was all I could manage to say.

"Is it bad?" His voice was hoarse.

"Yeah." I squeaked.

"Oh god." He said more to himself than to me I'm sure.

"Listen Eddie, I need you to do something for me, can you do that?"

"Of course, you know I would do anything for you."

"I need Michael to come over here and I need either you or him to find the very best reconstructive orthopedic surgeon. I don't care about the cost just get him and bring him here."

"Kay tell me how bad you were hurt." Eddie's voice trembled.

"I was in an RPG attack and my leg is pretty bad, Eddie." My voice cracked a little. I refused to cry, not yet.

"Oh god." He said again.

"Can you get Michael and the doctor for me." I got back to business; it was the only way I was going to keep sane in this situation.

"Of course, I will. Eddie promised.

I lost my cell phone, so you'll have to call me back here at this number to reach me."

"Kay, are you going to be okay?" He was beginning to panic.

"I'll be fine Eddie. I'll be home soon." I tried to soothe him. I thought I heard him crying when I hung up the phone. I laid back on the pillows. There wasn't anything more I could do at this point. I closed my eyes and thought about Ethan and walks in the moon light; the smell of the salt water, the warm breeze on my face. I imagined he was here to hold my hand the way he did that night at the Ironclad. Thinking of him made me smile.

The next day there was a knock at my door and Dr. Gordon poked his head in.

"Ms. Dandridge you have a guest." He announced.

He stepped aside and a man who looked to be about forty, with blonde hair and horn-rimmed glasses stepped inside.

"Hello, I am Dr. Klaus." He smiled. I had been expecting someone older. His youth took me by surprise, as did his Bavarian accent.

"I'm glad to meet you Dr. Klaus." I greeted him.

He walked over to the bed and shook my hand. "I understand you have an interesting proposal regarding your leg."

"Yes. I do." I smiled up at him.

"Do you mind?" He pointed to the blanket.

"Go ahead." I nodded.

Dr. Klaus turned to Dr. Gordon. "Of course." Dr. Gordon insisted.

Dr. Klaus started to remove my bandages. I watched intently; I had a long incision from my ankle to my knee. "Do you know what sort of shrapnel did this?"

Dr. Klaus looked from me to Dr. Gordon.

"Um, well." Dr. Gordon looked uncomfortable. "There were some metal fragments from but mostly it was bone."

I cringed as I knew that the only thing left of the new kid was what they dug out of my leg and left side.

"Bone?" Dr. Klaus asked.

"Yes," I filled in the blanks. "There was a Marine standing next to me when we were attacked. He took a direct hit." It broke my heart, a young vibrant life reduced to less than a pound of bone, placed in a six-foot coffin and draped in a flag. That made me want to cry more than anything.

Dr. Klaus looked horrified. "It doesn't matter how many times I see or hear about war injuries I never get used to it." He shook his head and looked at me. "I am very sorry."

"Thank you." I nodded reassuringly.

"I must also say you are very lucky to be so close and to not have suffered more life-threatening injuries."

I nodded. I had to admit I wasn't feeling so lucky at the moment although he did have a point. Things could be worse.

"I've looked at your x-rays and the video from your surgery. I don't see why we shouldn't be able to save your leg if you're up for another surgery."

"If it will save my leg. I'm up for anything." He nodded gravely. "I do have one small request though." I looked to Dr. Gordon.

"Oh?" Dr. Gordon raised his eyebrows in my direction.

"I want to see them first." I said definitely. "I want to see all of them, my team."

I had one IV still in my hand which they hooked to the back of a wheelchair and insisted that a nurse escort me. I didn't mind, my chest and shoulder still hurt and manuring the wheelchair on my own would have been a little too much.

"Oliver?" I said quietly as the nurse parked me next to the bed and waited. He opened his eyes slowly. "Oliver? It's Kay."

He looked over in my direction and tried to smile. "Hey Kay!"

I noticed that he was missing his left arm from the elbow down. I tried not to let my anger show.

"Hey how are you feeling?" I asked. "Oh, I don't know they keep me pretty doped up." He looked down at his arm. "What am I going to do? I can't be a marine with only one arm!"

I could see the panic in his eyes, and it broke my heart. "I'm so sorry, Oliver." I felt the tears building. "I wish I could have done more to help you."

"It's not your fault. You saved us. Because of you we didn't end up in some torture chamber or worse." Oliver smiled a weak smile.

"I'll fix this." I promised.

"What about you?" He wanted to know.

"Oh, I'll be fine, don't you worry about me." I assured him. It was tempting to tell him I was hurt too but he needed to be strong and didn't need another sob story.

"Is your arm the only thing they took?" I was afraid I already knew the answer.

"No, they took part of my leg too."

I looked down the bed. I felt the anger rising in my chest. Why hadn't Dr. Gordon told me? Why had they taken his leg and not mine? Dr. Klaus might have been able to help Oliver too.

"Have you talked to your family?" I changed the subject before the tears escaped.

"Yeah, mom and dad are flying over and they should be here tomorrow. They say I'll be in rehab for a while though."

"Yeah, we all will. That is okay we will get through it together." I patted his shoulder.

"Will they let us go to the same hospital?" He asked.

"I'll do what I can to try and make that happen." I promised him.

He nodded and his head fell back on his pillow.

"You get some rest okay? I'll come back and see you again." I whispered.

"Promise?" His eyes refocused on me.

"Promise." I smiled and then nodded to the nurse.

The nurse wheeled me down the hall. I visited Devon, Chris and Micah before returning to my room. Chris, Micah and Devon weren't hurt as bad in that they hadn't lost limbs, but they were still not going anywhere soon.

"Please tell Dr. Gordon I really need to see him as soon as he can spare me a minute." I told the nurse once I was settled back in my bed. She nodded and left.

I was more exhausted than I thought I would be. Without the fog of the morphine my mind was free to wonder. I had two choices; I could lay here and get angry about what had happened to our unit or I could try to think of something else. I needed to think about anything else and the only thing my mind would settle on was Ethan Craddock. I fell asleep thinking about his smile and the way he looked in the moonlight along the waters of the Chesapeake Bay.

Chapter Seven
Kay

When I woke up I again, Michael was sitting next to my bed typing furiously on his laptop.

"Hey." I said my voice hoarse.

He immediately put his laptop down and came over to the bed. "Ms. Dandridge, how are you? What can I get you?"

I smiled and looked over at the table next to the bed.

"What? What do you need?"

"Ice chips." I pointed. He smiled and handed me a cup.

"Thanks." I croaked. For a moment when I first woke up, I thought it was Ethan sitting there. That he had come to rescue me. I took a few ice chips and Michael put the cup back on the table.

"This okay?" He indicated the location.

I nodded.

"I brought you a laptop as well." He gave me a small smile.

"Thank you." My voice was still hoarse.

"If you don't mind my asking," He looked uncomfortable. "Why did you want me to come here?"

I smiled. "In case I die, we have to make sure the business is taken care of."

"Oh." He looked surprised then shook his head. "I never met your father; from what I hear you are a lot like him."

"You never met him?" I was confused. Maybe it was the medication.

"No, your mother hired me. She didn't like Elliott." Michael laughed a little.

I nodded. "He has his own way of looking at things." I wondered why my mother kept Elliott if she didn't like him.

Michael nodded. I thought for the first time that things may not be easy for him at the company. I had no idea if he and Elliott got along but if I had to guess based on this new information I'd say not.

"Does he give you a hard time?" I wondered out loud.

"No, not really. I can and have learned a lot from him I still have my own way of doing things."

"Listen, thank you so much for coming all the way over here. I know it must be a burden on your schedule and your family. Honestly, I didn't know who else to call."

He smiled.

"I don't trust many people." I admitted.

"I gathered that. And I am honored that you called me and asked for my help." He sat down and picked up the laptop. "What should we work on first?"

Ethan

I went home dog-tired from the day; I was too tired to sleep. I poured a bourbon and glanced at the mail. A heavy cream envelope slipped out of the stack and onto the kitchen counter.

I set the rest aside to examine the envelop. It was a good quality stationary. And it was addressed to me in an elegant font. I was both suspicious and intrigued. I opened it carefully.

Inside was a matching folded invitation with the same elegant font.

You are cordially invited to the Mayor's Dinner
to honor this year's Chamber of Commerce Outstanding Businesses of the Year
A kind reply would be appreciated by April 15th.

I must have been on some list from when Diane and I were still together. I checked the address again. No, it was addressed to only me. I had the urge to toss the thing in the garbage but instead I removed the RSVP card, checked the box that I would attend and slid it into the return envelope. I had a feeling my friend Vice Mayor John St. Clair had something to do with this. But, why not see where this was leading. It was three weeks away that gave me a little time to investigate it further.

***

"I'm out of here tonight, see you all in the morning." I announced to the team as I left the office.

Every one of them looked up surprised. "Leaving early?" Stephanie asked.

"Yeah." I left them hanging.

"Everything alright?" Jared asked.

"Sure. Why wouldn't it be, Jared?"

"I don't know you're always the last to leave."

"Leave the man alone, maybe he has a hot date." Logan joked.

"Maybe I do." They all stopped laughing and stared at me. I smiled and left.

I went home and showered, shaved and changed. The Mayors dinner was a formal so I had to dust off my tuxedo. It has been at least six years since I had worn it and I was pleased with myself that it still fit. I drove to the Boxwood and let the valet park my car. He was young and looked at my Dodge Hellcat with envy.

"Son, you see this badge?"

"Yes, sir." He replied.

"You know what it means?"

"It means if I scratch your car you can kill me?" He stammered.

"Exactly." I leveled a stare at him.

"Yes, sir."

I let my stare burn into his brain as he slid behind the wheel and slowly drove away. I stepped into the lobby where a young lady sat with a list.

"Good Evening." She smiled.

"Evening, Ethan Craddock."

The young lady checked her guest list.

"Yes, sir. Right through there."

I followed her gaze to a crowd of people. I was having serious second thoughts. Maybe I should just ditch this thing and head downtown for a soft-shell crab and some music.

"Ethan! So glad you came!" The vice mayor called to me with an outstretched hand.

"John, good to see you." I shook his hand.

"I'm pleasantly surprised to see you. I wasn't sure you would come. Are you alone?" He looked around for my plus one.

"I'm a little surprised myself. Uptown isn't normally my thing and no; I didn't bring a date."

"Good for you!" He slapped me on the back and guided me to the bar. "What'll ya have?" John asked.

"Bourbon." I told him.

John was pleased once I had a drink in my hand. He started steering me back towards the crowd. "Come on over and let me introduce you to some people."

Great. Just what I had hoped to avoid, a lot of hand shaking and smiling at people I didn't know. I followed John counting the minutes that I could duck out. This was really not my thing. I shook hands with various members of the business community and I even knew a few having been a customer at some point. There was going to be dinner, a presentation and then a reception to follow.

They called for everyone to take their seats and John had managed to seat me at his table.

The Mayor leaned over and whispered in my ear. "Good job on that terrorist case."

I smiled and nodded. It had been a couple of months since we had taken down a terrorist cell. Which was less a terrorist cell and more of one-man wanting revenge for the loss of a large government contract at the shipyard. I hoped Mike Russo rotted in jail for the rest of his life. The Mayor slapped me on the back and went back to the other guests at the table.

I surveyed the room; it was large, and it was so packed it was hard to see all the faces. I got a brief glimpse of a face that caught my attention. But, it was gone in an instant. There was something about it, something familiar. Before I could think about it, the food began to be served and I was distracted by the dinner conversation.

Finally, the dinner and dessert had been served, speeches had been made and people recognized. It was time for the reception. We all got up and moved to another room. I thought about ducking out, having made my appearance and shaken enough hands to run for office. John was having none of it.

"Come on, this is the best part. There's music. He knew my weaknesses. I cursed and followed him. He pushed a fresh bourbon in my hand and offered me a cigar. I refused the stogie but took the drink. John immediately saw a friend and was off, leaving me to drift to the edge of the crowd.

I was scanning the room. There was certainly enough security here that my services were not needed. Still it was a hard habit to break.

Something to my left caught my attention. I turned to see the back of a gorgeous woman. I couldn't see her face; her dress was open all the way to her lower back. It was an emerald green with pearls along the edges. She had short dark hair slicked back. If only I could see her face. What I could see was exceptional. I tried to pull my eyes away. I began circling around trying to find a better position to observe her.

It was odd as I had no interest in another woman. Kay had done it for me six years ago. I hadn't looked or thought about another woman since then. The divorce hadn't helped either. This woman had me drawn in and I hadn't even seen her face, this was crazy. Why was I even doing this? I needed to call it a night. We had a missing persons case to work and I needed to be in the office early. I started to turn away as the woman tossed her head back and laughed. I knew that laugh. It was like a crystal wind chime. It was light and floated on air. I spun back around in her direction. It had to be her.

She had broken away from the trio she had been talking to and was walking away from me. I wanted to call out her name and run to her. I didn't imagine pushing people to the ground at a black-tie event with the mayor was going to do much for my social standing, not that I cared. But I hadn't found out why I had been invited to this shindig yet, so I didn't want to blow it before I solved that mystery.

"Ethan!" John appeared in front of me and cut me off. He'd had a few more drinks since dinner.

"John."

"You enjoying the party?" His speech was slightly slurred.

"Yeah, I am but I think I might need to call it a night soon. I need to be in the office early. You know how it is." I was looking over his shoulder trying to track the green dress. She was gone.

"Sure, I understand. Got to keep Gates Point safe, right?"

"Right." I didn't think it was the time to split hairs and remind him of the chief of police had that honor.

"We'll get together again soon." John slapped me on the back and moved on.

I looked around the room and the woman in the green dress was gone. I went in the direction I had last seen her which led out into the lobby of the hotel. She could have gone anywhere from there. I stood staring the ceiling.

I needed to go home and get some sleep. I had too much bourbon and too little sleep and was probably chasing ghosts of my past. I knew I shouldn't drive, and I wasn't sure where my car was parked. I walked out to the valet stand and gave the attendant my ticket. He brought the car around. The office was closer than my house, so I drove very slowly and parked the car in the parking lot. I would walk home from here. The fresh air would do me good anyway.

I had a place on Third Street. I walked past the cemetery and thought about the night Kay and I went to the guest house she was staying in that weekend. It as part of one of the statelier homes and out of my price range. I hadn't thought about why she was staying there at the time. Did she know the people who owned the larger house? She said she was home visiting for family business so was it the family home? I was surprised I never thought of that before. The night air had cleared my head a little. I started walking in the direction she and I had gone that night six years ago. Was I crazy? Had the bourbon made me see things that weren't there? I still had to know. I continued walking questioning my sanity with every step.

I found the house and stood across the street. There were lights on inside. Was it occupied by the same people six years ago? I couldn't see the guest house from the street. It was obscured by hedges. I stood there long enough that I started to feel like a stalker. I turned and walked home. I had the feeling that I had lost her all over again.

Chapter Eight
Ethan

"Morning...., damn boss that must have been some party last night you look like death warmed over." Jared greeted me as I walked into the office.

"Thanks." I headed for the coffee pot. "You find anything more on our missing schoolteacher?" We had a local schoolteacher and her child that had gone missing and we hadn't heard from the kidnappers, which had me worried.

"Not really. What I have found is nothing so that is something." Jared smiled.

"Jared, man I can't do riddles this morning." I sat down on the edge of my desk ready to taste the coffee.

"Sorry." He tapped on his keyboard.

"Angela Posten hasn't touched her bank account since the day before she went missing."

"Okay"

"So, if she left on her own, she would probably have withdrawn a large amount of cash or used an ATM card in the past week or something." Jared explained.

I turned to Logan and began questioning him as well. "Has her cell phone been equally as quiet?"

"Yes, at least in the city. It must be turned off or destroyed because I can't get a location off the GPS in the phone."

"Okay, we'll keep on that." I instructed Logan and turned back to Jared. "So, if her bank account hasn't been touched the motive isn't likely money."

"No, she isn't rich, but she isn't poor either. She has about twenty thousand and change in the bank."

"She have any other sources of income?" A theory was staring to form at the end of my mind.

Jared began checking. "Not that I can see. Nothing coming into this account."

"Check and see if she had any other accounts."

"On it." He continued searching.

I sat down and started combing through the tips we had received on her sighting. The family was wanting to put out a reward and I knew that would bring in more tips and some of them would be people just seeking the money. I wanted to get through as many of the tips we had already before the onslaught of new ones came with the promise of a reward. We were going to have to route some of them to other offices as we weren't going to have the ability to go through them all.

Stephanie came in all smiles. Stephanie was cursed with the morning person gene.

"You look extra happy this morning." Logan teased.

"Have you seen the paper this morning?"

"No, why?" Jared looked up.

"There a very dashing man on the society page."

Logan frowned. "So, what else is new?"

"What is new is that this dashing man is one we know!" Stephanie pulled a copy of the paper from her bag.

"Really? Who?" Jared asked.

I suddenly had a feeling I didn't want to know. I concentrated on the computer screen.

"Whoa! Is that you with the Vice Mayor?" Jared looked up from Stephanie's paper.

"Probably." I still stared at my screen. I was struck with a thought, what if the picture caught the woman, I was chasing last night.

"Can I see that?" I asked.

Jared and Stephanie exchanged looks.

"Sure." Stephanie handed me the paper.

I looked at it carefully. "Is this the only picture?"

"No, there are a few more on the next page." Stephanie looked at me curiously.

I flipped the pages quickly. I scanned the pictures. I saw nothing. No beauty in the green dress.

Jared came over and leaned on my desk.

"You were working a case, weren't you? Looking for someone?" He turned to Stephanie and Logan. "I knew you wouldn't just go to some fancy party for the heck of it. You were working."

"Something like that." I nodded at Jared.

"I knew it!" Jared pleased with himself punched the air.

"Does it have something to do with our current case?" Stephanie asked.

"No, it's a cold case from a long time ago." I lied. I didn't want to explain Kay to them.

"Oh." She looked slightly disappointed.

The room went quiet and I handed Stephanie her paper.

Maybe I had imagined it all. Maybe that bourbon was stronger than I thought but I didn't think I was that drunk. I was just over worked. I'd hadn't taken in vacation in over ten years. Maybe I should take some time off.

"You okay?" Jared asked.

"Yeah." I went back to combing through tips on the computer. I couldn't get the woman in the green dress out of my mind. Could it have been Kay? I really couldn't tell, the hair was shorter, of course, but that didn't mean anything. She could have had it cut. There was nothing else to make me think it was her other than the way I felt. Kay was the only woman who had ever made me feel the way I did right now, and I couldn't imagine there could be two women like that in the world. And what if it was her? Why hadn't she come find me? She knew where I worked. In fairness she had no way of knowing I was divorced; I just needed to find her and tell her myself.

I had been staring at the same screen for fifteen minutes. I got up and walked around.

"Everything alright?" Jared asked.

"Yeah, I just need some air." I walked outside and stood taking in the morning air. It was warm and the promise of summer's heat was coming off the bay riding the breeze.

"Ethan?" Logan stepped out the door to stand next to me.

"I don't need a babysitter."

"Did I say you did?"

"No," I shook my head." Sorry, no you didn't."

"Just the same, you seem like something is really bothering you and I know it isn't this case."

"Yeah, no. hell I don't know." I shuffled my feet and look off in the distance.

"Only one thing can get a man tied up in knots like this."

I knew where he was going with this, so I let him say it.

"What's her name?" Logan asked.

"Why do you think it is a woman?" I glanced over at him.

"If it's not a woman then I am going to have to assume you're terminally ill or something and you better start talking."

I chuckled. Leave it to Logan to take to the next level.

"Yeah, alright fine. I'm not talking about this at work."

"Fair enough." He turned and walked back inside.

I didn't want to talk about it. I knew it would sound crazy and I didn't need that right now. I also didn't need pity stares from my agents.

We worked until about nine o'clock and then we called it quits. Logan hung back.

"Wanna go grab some roasted oysters and beer?"

I thought about saying no but what good was it going to do to go home and stare at the wall. "Sure, why not?"

"I'll drive."

I climbed into Logan's truck and didn't ask where we were going. I just let my mind wonder for a while. We stopped at a little house near the water back off the road. I hadn't been paying attention to where we were, and I was surprised when we stopped.

"What's this place? I asked getting out of the truck.

"My place."

"I've been to your place and it is bigger than this."

"This is my weekend place."

I surveyed the area. It was well screened by trees. There were lights on all corners of the house that I could see and very discreet cameras. I suspected for every security measure I would see there were five more I couldn't. Logan was very cautious.

I followed Logan inside. It was surprisingly light and airy. I expected something darker from his man cave.

It was masculine and took advantage of the southern exposure and allowed the windows to pick up the breeze off the water.

"This is a nice place."

"Thanks." He said with his head in the fridge.

"You come here every weekend?"

"Most weekends if we're not working." He handed me a beer.

"Thanks." I said accepting the icy beer. I held it up and gave him a salute and took a swig.

He took two pulls from his bottle. "Okay, oysters." He announced pulling a jar from the fridge.

"Looks good. Anything I can do to help?" I offered.

"Stay out of the way."

"Copy that."

We walked outside. Logan had an impressive outdoor kitchen setup. I stared off across the water at the lights on the far shore while he did his thing.

"Ready?"

"Yeah." I sat down at a wooden table. Logan put a shallow pan of roasted oysters between us. There was a large bottle of hot sauce and a fresh beer.

"You're a good host." I said. Logan shrugged.

We ate and drank way too much. It was getting late and the bottles were filling up the trash can on his deck.

"So, what's her name?" Logan finally asked.

"Kay."

"Kay, what?"

"I don't know her last name."

"What?" Logan laughed. "I didn't have you pegged for the love 'em and leave type, Ethan."

"It wasn't like that."

"Tell me about it."

"I went to the Ironclad one night. I was still married then and I gone to listen to Charlie Pickens."

Logan nodded. He was a music lover as well.

"And I saw her sitting there alone. So, I went over and started talking to her. We sat listening to Charlie and drinking. Then we went for a walk along the river and talked for hours."

"Just talked?"

"Yeah we just talked."

"Okay." Logan raised an eyebrow in my direction. I wasn't sure if Logan believed me, but it didn't matter, though.

"I went back to the Ironclad the next night and she was there again. So, we sat and listened to music and drank bourbon. This time we walked to the place she was staying in the Garden District. We were talking and I told her I was married. She said she wouldn't be the cause of a marriage breakup or anything and that if we were meant to be together, we would meet again." I shrugged. "And I left."

"That's it?" Logan looked disappointed.

"Yeah."

"How long ago was this?" He asked holding a beer to his lips.

"Almost six years."

Logan almost spit out his beer.

"You've been holding onto this for six years and you never tried to find her?"

"No."

"You care about her?"

"More than any other living creature on this planet," I paused, "it's hard to explain as I was leaving that night she reached up and kissed me. As soon as her lips touched mine. I knew in that moment why I had been put on this planet."

"That's pretty serious. I'm confused why you didn't try to find her."

"Well, okay, I did try after Diane and I split up. I didn't have much to go on, but I did have her cell number. When I called it was no longer in service. She said she was from here but didn't live here at the time. She was just home visiting, and she was staying in a guest house. And I never got her last name."

"Well Kay isn't that common of a name so how hard could it be to find her?"

I shrugged. "Harder than you think."

"Okay, that was six years ago, and databases have improved so what else do you know about her?"

"She was working with the military, a journalist, I believe she said and was just home to take care of some family business."

"Now we're getting somewhere. We can look through the DOD database for anyone named Kay. How many could there be?"

"I don't know, I keep thinking about what she said that if it was meant to be, we would meet again."

"So, you just going to sit back and wait for her to walk through the door?"

"I don't know." I wasn't a superstitious kind of person, but there were those locally that belong to the older generation and they believed in such things as fate, karma and other powers. My grandmother had taught me about such things. I was pretty good with a divining rod too, so I knew there was some truth to what the older generation believed. And I thought about the old woman's words outside of the night club a few weeks prior.

"Dude, this woman has you this messed up and you are willing to sit around just waiting for her to fall in your lap?" Logan shook his head.

"I don't know man. I don't know what to do."

"So why has she come up all of a sudden. You haven't thought too hard about her until lately."

"I thought I saw someone that looked like her at the Mayor's dinner. I never got a good look at her face. So, I don't know if maybe I just imagined it. I'd had a couple of drinks that night."

"Okay, well we can work with that too. If we can get the guest list maybe, we can find her on it that which is a much smaller list than the DOD database."

"Yeah, I can ask John for the list."

"The vice mayor?" Logan raised his eyebrows, "You know him for real?"

"Oh yeah, we go way back."

"Well there you go. Now all you have to do is sober up."

I laughed and then passed out. I woke up on Logan's deck in a chair with my feet propped up in another chair. The smell of something bitter and strong had interrupted my dreams.

"Wake up sleeping beauty!" Logan kicked the chair out from under my feet.

"Ah!" I rubbed my stiff neck.

"Coffee." He pointed to the mug on the table and then disappeared.

"Shit." My neck hurt. I tried to rub the muscles into a more relaxed state. I drank some of the coffee. I coughed and sputtered.

"Holy shit, what is that?" I yelled towards the house.

Logan stuck his head out the back door. "Coffee."

"Bullshit."

"Chicory coffee with a little hair of the dog."

"Good god! That is terrible." I said walking into the kitchen.

"Yeah, it will cure what ails you."

"I don't know." I eyed the mug suspiciously.

"Stop your whining and drink it. We've got to go to work."

"I need a shower."

"Yeah, you do." Logan laughed "I'll drop you by your place."

"Okay."

"Drink your coffee."

It was nearly nine o'clock when I got to the office.

Stephanie and Jared refrained from making any comments about Logan and I coming in late. Our case load was stacking up. We had the missing schoolteacher which was a priority. We also had a fraud case and a possible misconduct case of a police officer. I put Jared and Stephanie on the missing teacher while Logan and I focused on the rest of the workload.

After Stephanie and Jared left for the night, I got up to stretch. Logan had barely moved from his computer all day.

"Logan, you've been at it all day. Go home."

"Yeah, I am. I've just been tracking down this lead."

"It can wait."

"If you saw a picture of that woman Kay, you'd recognize her right?"

"Sure, I'll never forget her. Why?" My heart leapt into my throat.

"Well, I think I may have found something. I'm not sure it's the right person, says her name is Kennedy Dandridge."

"Okay, well let's see it." I remembered something about her telling me her name was Kennedy and her friends called her Kay.

Logan tapped a few keys and then swiveled his monitor around.

Kay was staring back at me. Her hair was indeed shorter. She was just as beautiful as I remembered. I wanted to reach out and touch her cheek. The photo was professional.

"Where did you find this?"

"It took some deep digging on the web, I found it on a business news page."

"Business page? What kind of business page?" I was curious.

"It would appear that your mysterious woman is in fact the owner and CEO of Port City Industries." Logan raised his eyebrows at me.

"What?" I laughed.

"Kay Dandridge, Port City Industries." Logan smiled. "You always were one lucky bastard."

"That's ridiculous. I mean not that it matters as she never said anything about the family business. She said she was working in the Middle East or something."

"She wasn't lying. She was a photojournalist and it looks like she mostly worked with the military, in the Middle East, Africa and a few other places. Logan looked distant for a moment and while I thought there was something more he was thinking on that front, I was more focused on Port City Industries. They had a huge building on the other side of town, and you could see it from our office. I started thinking that all this time she could have been that close, and I wouldn't have even known it. And again, I felt a pang in my chest that she hadn't looked me up.

"You said she told you she was home on family business six years ago?"

"Yes."

"Well, apparently six years ago her mother passed away which left the company to Kay."

"So that was the family business she was home to take care of, then." I moved to stand behind Logan looking at the obituary over his shoulder. "She was home that weekend to bury her mother." I felt sad and a bit ashamed that I had flirted with a woman who was grieving in her own way. I felt like a total jerk.

"She seems to be a complicated woman." Logan said reading my thoughts.

I went back to my desk and sat down. "I don't want to know any more about her from a computer. I want her to tell me. I want to learn about her over a cup of coffee or a walk along the river. I don't want to read about her in a file like a suspect or a victim."

Logan nodded. "Fair enough. What are you going to do?"

"I don't know." And I didn't know. I had so many thoughts running through my head that I couldn't answer a simple question.

"Okay. See ya tomorrow." He turned off his desk lamp for the night.

"Okay." I said not looking up. I heard the door close behind Logan and I just sat staring at the ceiling. I knew what I wanted to do. I knew what I had to do. The question now was how to do it.

Chapter Nine
Ethan

I drove home, allowing the thoughts of Kay fill my head. Before I had tried to push them aside but tonight, I couldn't do that anymore. I had to think about her. I had to remember her, and I wanted to find her. I tried to remember our conversations all those years ago, but I couldn't. I couldn't remember the words; I just remembered her eyes. I remembered how they looked when she was angry at the guy that had hit on her. How she looked in the moonlight along the river. How close her face had been to mine when we were sitting on the sofa in the guest house.

I drove without thinking about where I was going. When I looked up, I realized I was at the address where Kay had been staying. The same house I had walked to after the Mayor's dinner. I wondered if the larger house had been her mother's house and she had stayed in the guest quarters. It made sense. The larger house was fitting for the CEO of a large company based here. The Garden District was home to several such people. I sat staring the dark house. I wondered if she had sold it. Maybe the house wasn't her style. I leaned my head back for a moment. I needed to find her. I wanted to tell her that I was divorced, and I wanted to ask her to dinner.

I woke up with the sun shining in my face. I sat up with a start. I was still parked in front of the house I believed to belong to Kay. I looked around. I was surprised no one had called the police. I rubbed my hand through my hair. I looked towards the house one more time. Nothing seemed to have changed. No movement. I started the car and drove home for a shower and a change of clothes.

Kay

I left the office late. I wasn't sleeping at night and figured I might as well be productive. The traffic getting home was better at that time of night anyway. The house took up the block and had a driveway on the back, which made it was easy to drive straight into the garage and go straight to the house.

Eddie, my company driver and self-appointed bodyguard, didn't like that I drove myself to and from work. He said it was undignified. My father had always had Eddie drive him. Lately I had been keeping such odd hours it didn't seem fair to Eddie or his family. I had hardly been able to shake Eddie since I had gotten home from the hospital. He had taken on the role of my personal bodyguard. He was at least sixty, and not the type to work out, so I'm not sure what he had in mind should I actually be attacked. We had fallen into a comfortable routine, he would drive me if I was going somewhere on company business but to and from work was out of the question.

The house was dark, and I left it that way. I knew my way around I didn't need the lights. I looked in the fridge. There wasn't much there to speak of and I didn't feel like cooking this late. I opted for a yogurt. I was restless. I thought about walking across the street to the cemetery and hanging out with the souls that didn't sleep at this hour.

When I looked out the front window there was a car parked out front with someone inside. I instinctively pulled away from view. Was someone watching the house? Or were they watching the graveyard? I stood to the side and watched to see if there was something illegal about to happen. If someone thought, they were going to deal drugs on the street in front of my house they were going to get more than they bargained for, but nothing happened. I stood there so long my legs started to go numb. Finally, I decided I was being paranoid. The car could have belonged to a guest of one of my neighbors, or someone else who liked visiting cemeteries at night or any number of legitimate reasons. I left my window and went to bed.

I woke up early and showered. I checked out the front window and the car was gone. I decided that my imagination was running away with me caused by too much work and too little sleep.

"Morning!" Sherry, my all too happy secretary greeted me as I came into the office.

I'll be the first to admit I am not a morning person. And bless Sherry for never letting that thwart her in her efforts to start my day off in a cheerful manner. Today it was less inspirational.

"Morning." I regretted the look on her face when I didn't pause at her desk and continued into my office. I tapped my computer back to life and settled my cell phone in its cradle.

Sherry came in quietly and set a cup of coffee on my desk. I had told her repeatedly she didn't need to make me coffee every I didn't want her to feel like she was 'serving' me. She insisted. Today, I didn't protest.

"Thank you, Sherry."

"You're welcome. You have a pretty full day today. Do you need me to cancel anything?"

Her persistent caring made me smile despite myself.

"No, I'll be okay thanks. Just a bad night. I'm sure I'll be fine after a cup of your coffee."

She brightened and proceeded to sit down so that we could continue with our daily routine of going over my schedule.

Sherry was the model of efficiency. She was in her thirties and a single mom. She had never remarried, and I could only assume that was a personal choice. She was attractive and held back mid-life curves with daily yoga after work. She had a business degree and a good head for numbers. I had offered her opportunities in budget and finance a number of times, but she refused. She said she enjoyed her job with me. I couldn't argue with that I don't know what I would have done without her.

After half an hour we were finally done, and Michael appeared in the doorway. He helped himself to coffee.

"Whoa, you look like roadkill." He said when he sat down across me. Sherry gave him a sour look as she got up to leave.

"Thanks." I concentrated on my email. Michael had become part of my morning routine just like Sherry.

"Are you feeling okay?"

"I'm fine." I responded in a tone that possibly suggested otherwise and asking about it further would be futile.

Michael waited for Sherry to close the door behind her. "Are you having nightmares?" He pressed.

Despite the fact that it was Ethan I had wanted to be there for me when I was in the hospital, I wouldn't have made it without Michael. "Only the one I'm having right now." I deleted a few messages and flagged a few more to read later.

"Funny," he responded, undaunted.

"I thought so." I quipped.

"Listen, I thought we'd review our contract before out meeting later today with Chemlab." He was back to business.

"Why?" I wondered aloud.

"We'll need to make sure we are asking for everything we need. We want to be covered from a liability standpoint if any one of our devices fails based on some faulty plastic, they provide us."

I guess this is why we have lawyers. "God, this stuff makes my head hurt." I leaned back in my chair. When I took over the company, I created a new branch to produce high tech prosthetics for veterans. Chemlab Corp was providing some of the materials used in construction.

"I know, but you need to be aware of this and we also need to protect you personally as well as the company. You know how people are, they will sue whoever they think can afford to pay them."

"I know I know. What if what Chemlab provides us is a good quality product but how it is applied creates a faulty part, are we covered for that?"

"Yes, we have those bases covered with assembly quality control and testing. And also, the manufacturing aspect, which is all Port City Industries, I have the main core of the company shielded in case this arm, no pun intended, fails."

"Your turn to be funny." I rolled my eyes.

Michael scooted close to the desk. "Look, it just makes good business sense."

"I know it does and you make sure this is all on the up and up as I don't want anything to even have a whiff of impropriety."

"Listen if you go down, I go down and I like my lifestyle. I'm not going to risk it on some half-assed scheme. No offense."

"None taken."

Michael checked his watch. "Well, it's almost time for your first meeting of the day, I'll see you later." He stood and straightened his Tom Ford suit and strolled out of the office.

Sherry frowned at him again as she came in to remind me of my meeting. She handed me a file. "They are already seated at the table."

"Good. Thank you."

I walked down the hall to the large oval conference room. It had an impressive view of the city.

"Good Morning, sorry to keep you waiting." I said as I walked in.

Eight faces turned to greet me.

Chapter Ten
Ethan

I drove to the office and parked the car and then walked down the street to a coffee shop. I needed something different than the normal office coffee. I stood watching people come and go as I waited for my order. I wondered how many times Kay and I had unknowingly passed one another in the city, maybe even in a coffee shop like this one? It didn't seem possible. I would have known her on sight.

I got my coffee and walked back to work lost in my own thoughts. I really needed to snap out of this rut I was in. Maybe Logan was right, maybe I needed to forget all this business about fate bringing us back together and go find Kay.

Logan was already at work when I arrived.

"Morning." I said as I came in.

Logan looked up didn't immediately say anything. I let it go.

"Where's Jared and Steph?" I asked.

"Out in the field." Logan stood up. "Ethan, we are friends so I feel like I can say this."

"What?" I looked up, bracing myself for what seemed to be coming.

"I didn't think it was possible for you to look worse than you did but you look like you've been on an all-night bender."

"Shut up, Logan."

"I'm serious, you are not okay, man." He was sincere.

"I wasn't on an all-night bender and I didn't even have anything to drink last night."

"Really?"

"Yeah, really. I just." I hated to admit it even to Logan. "I fell asleep in my car last night."

"What? Where? In your driveway?"

"No on the way home."

"At the wheel?" Logan looked alarmed.

"I had pulled over. I was parked."

"Ethan, this is getting dangerous; man, you need to do something." It's not often Logan gets this concerned.

"I was doing something." I skirted the issue.

"What?" He was relentless.

"I was sitting outside her house. I think it was her house anyway." I confessed.

"Dude, this is off the rails sort of behavior. I feel like you need an intervention or something and I don't know how to do one."

I laughed. "It isn't as bad as it sounds."

"I sure as hell hope not because it sounds pretty bad." He countered.

"Why can't you just look at the positive side?" I tried to reason with you and set his mind at ease.

"What would that be?" He asked frowning at me.

"I got some sleep last night."

Logan laughed and returned to his desk shaking his head. "You like to live on the edge, man."

"I've got it under control." I was justifying my behavior, even to myself.

"Yeah, okay."

My phone rang. "Craddock."

"Boss, it's Jared. I think we found the teacher and the kid. We need some back up." I jumped up getting Logan's attention. I repeated the address out loud so Logan could map it. "Okay Jared. Stay out of sight and let me know if anything changes; we are on our way." I looked to Logan "Grab your gear call the local PD. Jared and Steph have a location on the teacher."

Logan was up and racing for the door. "I'll drive." Logan said, speaking volumes about more than just the case.

I didn't argue. I punched buttons for the local police to provide some tactical backup. We pulled up behind Jared and Steph. I slipped out the passenger side door and crept up to the window. Stephanie was waiting for me.

"What's the status?" I asked.

"A Woman and child matching the description of our missing teacher was rushed into the house about an hour ago," Jared reported.

"We sure it is her?"

"A neighbor called it in said she recognized the teacher from the news reports." Steph glanced back at the house.

"What about the person with her." I asked.

"Tall male wearing a hoodie. She couldn't see his face and is not sure if it was the man who lives there or not." Steph replied.

"Do we know anything about the owner of the property?" Logan asked.

"It's a rental and the neighbor says no one seems to stay very long. She isn't familiar the current occupant," said Jared.

"Okay, hang tight." I crept down the block to where the local police were waiting.

"Agent Craddock?" I nodded and held out my hand.

"Lt. Bradford," He shook my hand "What do we have?"

"We believe the teacher and her son are inside with one suspect. It was called in by a neighbor, said the woman was rushed inside by a man wearing a hoodie. Any way we can try to get eyes inside?"

"Let me see what we can do." Bradford offered.

"Thanks."

The lieutenant walked down the line to a van and spoke with a couple of people. He returned after a few short minutes.

"Agent Craddock, we are going to send a few men around with scopes to try and see in any of the windows. We are also setting up a heat seeking detector to find out how many people are inside and where they are."

"Thank you we really appreciate the help."

Bradford nodded and walked away again. I went back up to let Jared and Stephanie know what was going on. For the moment we would have to wait. I was getting antsy. Logan was better at waiting that I was. He could sit there all day with his eyes closed and not even flinch. I think I had been living on caffeine for too many months, maybe years to be able to do that.

Finally, Bradford called for me over the radio and I was glad to get out of the SUV. "No joy on the visual. We do have three heat signatures. One maybe two in the back of the house on the first floor the other is on the second floor and moving around. I can't say which is which at the moment. If I had to guess I'd say your perp is on the second floor."

I nodded. "Okay, let's get into position."

Bradford dispatched three two-man teams to cover the sides and rear of the house, and four men to back us up at the front door.

I returned to the team. "Okay this is it. There's one upstairs and looks like two downstairs in the rear. We can't be sure who is who. It is likely the teacher is downstairs with her son. Jared, you take another officer and join the team that is already covering the rear. Everyone else with me."

We jogged quickly across the street. Logan stepped up to the front door and pounded.

"FBI, open the door!" We waited for any kind of response, but not for long.

Logan stepped aside and let the PD bust open the door. Not that he couldn't do it with the heel of his boot, but the PD had more body armor than we did, so why not? We rushed into the house. "FBI!" Logan and I rushed up the stairs, Stephanie led two PD's to sweep the lower front portion of the house. Jared should have breached the back door with his unit.

"FBI! Show yourself!" I called out at the top of the stairs.

I heard a scraping sound. I stopped and looked at Logan.

"Window!" Logan answered my unspoken question. He raced towards the sound of the noise, a room at the end of the hallway.

"Logan it could be a trap!" He had already crashed through the door just as our suspect was climbing out the dormer window.

"The suspect is going out the east second floor window, hold your fire! Agent in pursuit. I repeat hold your fire!" I ordered over the radio.

Logan tackled the suspect from behind and they both disappeared out the window. I rushed after them. Glass was all over the floor the curtains were laying on the ground outside. Logan had the guy in handcuffs and gave me a thumbs up. The PD was dragging the suspect away. I turned my focus back downstairs.

"Jared! Stephanie!" I called and I raced back down the stairs.

"Clear!" Stephanie called out.

"Do we have them?" I turned to the back of the house as soon as I reached the bottom of the stairs. Jared was wrapping a blanket around the shoulders of a woman who was holding a little boy and guiding her outside.

"We got them boss." Stephanie answered.

"Good work." I breathed a sigh of relief. I walked outside to check on Logan. Paramedics were arriving.

"You okay?" I asked him.

"Yeah, I'm fine," he said as he did a self-assessment.

"You know your head is bleeding." I informed him.

Logan reached up to check. "Must have cut it on some glass."

"Probably when you jumped out the window." I said, stating the obvious.

"Yeah that was probably it." He laughed.

I walked him over to let a paramedic look him over. The hard part was over now. All that was left was the paperwork. Lt. Bradford walked over and clapped me on the back.

"Congratulations Agent Craddock."

"Thank you for all your help." We shook hands and parted ways.

I walked over to Stephanie and Jared. "You guys did great work, congratulations on saving her life." I nodded in the direction of the ambulance where the teacher was being prepped for transport to the hospital.

"Thank you." They each said.

"Whose going with her to the hospital?" I asked looking at the pair of them.

"I am." Stephanie answered.

"Okay, good."

Stephanie smiled and took the keys from Jared to the SUV to follow the ambulance to the hospital.

"Guess I'm riding with you." Jared shrugged.

"Come on, there is plenty of room."

"Shotgun!" Jared laughed.

"You go ahead." I said to Logan. "I'll wait for the forensic unit so come get me later."

He nodded and pulled away from the curb. I pulled a pair of latex gloves from my pocket and headed back in the house to look around until the team got there.

Chapter Eleven
Kay

I worked the next couple of days to the point of exhaustion. I had a trip that would take me out of town for a few days and I needed to focus on convincing Bethesda Naval Hospital that my idea for an implant was a viable one. This trip was also going to allow me to see my grandfather. It had been far too long since I had seen him, and it was a rarity that we would both be in town at the same time. I was looking forward to having dinner with him.

This was one time I was going to take advantage of my position and use my driver, car and the company plane. I was packed and ready to go. Sherry made sure of that.

"Now I put your laptop and an extra charger in your bag. I know how you always lose them." She said handing me my messenger bag. I refused to adhere to the normal conventions of the business world. I didn't wear skirts or pumps on a regular basis. I didn't carry a fancy leather briefcase. Anyone who didn't like could take their business elsewhere. I was fortunate to have plenty with people who were more concerned with things like integrity and honesty than how much my suit cost.

I was wearing loafers, pinstriped slacks and a white blouse. I was more Katheryn Hepburn than Audrey Hepburn. Plus, I wasn't fond of showing off the scar on my leg. I was happy to have my leg, but it was a hideous scar and I didn't want the pity looks from people or the questions that would be inevitable.

"Sherry, I wish I could take you with me."

Sherry smiled.

"Then who would send you a replacement cable?"

"True enough, is there anything I can bring back for you? Anything you want from Maryland or Virginia?"

"A tall, handsome, rich man with a kind heart?" She asked.

"Girl, if I knew where to get one of those, we'd both have one." I laughed.

Sherry laughed too and hugged me. "You be careful in the big city."

"Sherry, Gates Point is a big city too."

"I know, but not like DC."

"No, not like DC." I agreed quietly. I grabbed the handle of my rolling suitcase and headed for the elevator.

"Ms. Dandridge."

Eddie my driver was waiting for me when I got off the elevator and took my suitcase.

"Hi Eddie, you are going with me to DC?"

"Yes, ma'am."

"You ever been here before?"

"Many times."

"Okay, good. You'll know more about how to get around than I will."

"Yes ma'am."

We drove to the Maguire Field airport.

"Ms. Dandridge, we'll be ready to leave in about fifteen minutes." Dennis Roach my pilot informed me as I exited the car.

"Thank you, Dennis. May we board?"

"Yes, ma'am."

Eddie and I got settled on the company jet while Chuck, the pilot, finished his pre-flight routine.

Eddie sat off by himself and I pulled out my phone. I sent my grandfather a text message and let him know I'd be arriving this evening. Although we weren't scheduled until Sunday for dinner, I thought I'd touch base in case he had some extra free time.

I could hear Dennis talking in the cockpit before he closed the door and we began taxing to the runway.

Flying wasn't my favorite thing, but Dennis did his best to make it a smooth as possible.

I laid my head back and closed my eyes. I could feel Eddie watching me.

When we leveled off, I opened them again and Eddie smiled. "You Okay?"

"Yeah, I'm okay." I said pulling out my laptop to do some work.

He nodded and turned to look out the window.

When we touched down at Regan National Airport, Eddie stood up first. "You wait with the plane while I go get the car."

"I can come with you." I protested half teasing.

Eddie just gave me his impatient look and nodded to Dennis as he descended the stairs of the plane. I sighed. I didn't like being handled.

Dennis smiled and ducked back into the cockpit.

I packed up my laptop and headed down the steps.

Eddie pulled up with a black town car with tinted windows. I smiled to myself. I still felt uncomfortable being chauffeured in cars like some kind of rock star. If Eddie had his way the thing was probably bulletproof too.

We drove off the airport property and onto the beltway. I was booked into a hotel in DC as it was central to everywhere, I planned to go this weekend. My appointment at Bethesda wasn't until Monday. So, I had the weekend to meet up with grandpa and maybe enjoy myself for a moment. I really wanted to go to the zoo and maybe a gallery. Something to completely take my mind off of everything.

We arrived at the hotel and Eddie dropped me at the door. I went in to get us signed in while he parked the car. I waited for him in the lobby.

"Here's your key card." I said as he met me near the elevators.

"Thank you. What floor are we on?" He turned the key card over in his hand.

"Fourteen. Should have a nice view."

"Hmmm."

"Why didn't you bring Wanda or one of the kids? They might have enjoyed it."

"It's a business trip."

"Eddie you need to relax a little. What does it say when the CEO is more relaxed than her employees?"

"That her employees are doing a good job, so she doesn't have to worry."

"Yeah except now I worry that you are working too hard."

"You don't fool me any Kay, I see those lines around your eyes, and you've had something on your mind for days now."

"Well you really know how to compliment a lady." I teased.

"Hmmpf."

The elevator opened and we found our rooms.

"Wanna have dinner later?" I asked.

"Yeah, okay."

"Unless you have plans. Which is fine."

"I don't have any plans." He reassured me.

"Okay, let's go down to the dining room about eight?"

"See you then." Eddie entered the room next to mine.

I had an hour and a half to kill.

I went in to explore the room. I never splurged on the big suites as it just didn't make any sense. I didn't have meetings in my room, it was just me. All I needed was a mini fridge and a TV for the most part. This room had a jetted tub though and I looked at it longingly. That would have to wait until after dinner. If I got in there now, I'd never want to get out.

I called downstairs and made a dinner reservation. Then ordered a bottle of wine to be delivered to my room later. If I was going to take advantage of that soaking tub, I was going to do it with a bottle of wine.

An hour and a half later I had a sense of Deja vu as Eddie and I were in the elevator again.

"Reservation for Dandridge." I announced as we approached the hostess stand.

"Yes ma'am."

We were seated near the window and there was a piano player on the opposite side of the room, the music was soft and allowed us to be able to hear each other without shouting.

After we ordered our dinner Eddie leaned in a little. "So, you want to tell me what's on your mind?"

"It's nothing."

"Kay I've known you since you were a little thing trailing along behind your father. I know when something is on your mind."

He had a point. I had known Eddie all my life. It was like an uncle to me.

I sipped the water and shrugged.

"That bad, huh?" He leaned back.

"It's nothing or it should be nothing."

"It's not, so it's something."

I knew I wasn't going to get out of this and more importantly Eddie would sulk the rest of the trip if I didn't tell him.

"I guess I'm just more nervous than I thought about this meeting at Bethesda on Monday. It's really important to me." I didn't want to go into the details of it and discuss survivors' guilt with him. But I believed that was part of what was driving me to get this implant option accepted and that Bethesda didn't believe it would work, I'd have little chance of getting any other hospital in this country to try it.

I concentrated on my food.

"What did you do when your father told you that you were too small to climb that big magnolia in the yard? You shimmied your way up the trunk to that first branch and climbed all the way to the top."

"Yeah, and then I got scared and he had to climb up and bring me down."

"Okay, what about when your mother didn't want you to leave Gates Point? You not only became a photojournalist, but you did it in the most dangerous places on earth." He stabbed the tabletop with his index finger. "And the fact that you have a Ph.D. and run a huge company all on your own, what does that say about you?"

"Eddie, you know I don't run it on my own, all the employees are part of the company but, if this doesn't work all those employees who have been working so hard to make this happen will be disappointed. I'll feel like I let them down." I didn't say what I was really feeling which was that I would have let my team down. Even though it was too late for Oliver, Chris, Micah and Devon, I was doing this for them.

After the plates were taken away Eddie reached across the table and took my hand.

"Look, I've never known you to shy away from a challenge. You stick your neck out for other people every single day. You take care of the company, the people the company serves, and you take wonderful care of all of your employees. Promise me you will take care of yourself too."

I covered his hand with mine. "I promise."

"Okay, good." Eddie leaned back in his chair. "Then I will be able to sleep tonight." He smiled.

I smiled back but I had my doubts about my ability to sleep.

I was looking forward to a nice bubble bath and a bottle of wine.

Chapter Twelve
Ethan

"You wanna get a beer or something after work?" Logan asked.

I thought about it. I really didn't want to go home because I know I would end up just sitting in front of the Kay's house all night again.

"Yeah, let's all go out and celebrate Jared and Stephanie!" I looked over to them.

"Yeah, that sounds great!" Jared was the first to join in. "How about it?" He looked at Stephanie.

"Well, I guess so."

"You guess so?" Jared pressed, "You got a hot date or something?"

"Not exactly."

"We can do it another night." I offered her an out.

"No, no, I'll text them and tell them I'll join them later." She picked her phone and started tapping.

"Great! Where are we going?" Jared asked.

I looked over at Logan.

"Sports bar?"

Stephanie wrinkled her nose. "Too rowdy."

"Okay...." Logan looked back to me.

"What about the Grill?" I suggested. "We'll go early enough to have dinner, on me."

"We're in." They all cheered.

"Good." I nodded. Well at least this would keep my mind occupied for a while. Distract me from Kay for a few hours anyway.

***

"Well, I'd better be going." Stephanie announced after we had finished dinner and I had lost track of the beer tab I was running. It didn't matter the team had been working hard and we needed to blow off some steam.

"Are you sure? Why not just tell your friends to meet us here?" Jared encouraged.

"Maybe next time." Stephanie smiled. "You sure I can't pay for something, Boss?"

"Absolutely, not. Go have fun with your friends and be careful!"

Stephanie waved and bounced out of the Grill.

"Come on man, it isn't that bad." Logan put his arm around Jared.

"What? I don't care if she doesn't know how to have fun." Jared shook him off.

"Yeah okay, then you can buy the next round." I said.

"Fine." Jared waived over the waitress. "Another round and I'll pay for this one."

"You got it." She gave him a sweet smile.

"Maybe she needs someone to walk her home tonight." Logan nudged Jared.

"She's not my type."

"Oh?" Logan looked at me and laughed. "The young man has a type. Do enlighten us."

The waitress returned. She was young with a complexion that said she spent her days at the beach. She had long dark hair in a braid and she clearly worked out.

"I like a woman with a lot of self-confidence."

"Looks like she has plenty of confidence to me." Logan said admiring the waitress's Daisy Duke shorts and low-cut t-shirt.

"She's trying too hard." Jared said.

"What do you mean? She knows her customer base. This is a Navy town and a port city. It is full of drunk guys are going to tip a girl who shows a little more of herself. I bet she pulls in a couple of hundred a night." I offered.

"So, you're judging her based on her occupation?" Logan challenged.

"No, but I know I wouldn't want my girlfriend being pawed by men every night." Jared replied.

"What century were you born in?" Logan laughed.

"You want me to believe you'd let your girlfriend work in a business like this, showing off her chest so men will tip her?" Jared came back at Logan.

"I didn't say that. I said I wouldn't judge her for doing it. Maybe she is a single mom and needs all the money she can make. Maybe she hates this job, but it pays. Or maybe she is putting herself through college. My point is you can't judge people based on their jobs." Logan took a long pull from his beer.

Jared looked over at the waitress.

"Didn't you ever have to work some crappy job to get by or were you born with a silver spoon in your mouth?" Logan was starting to get annoyed at Jared.

"Hey man, let it go." I said before the two of them ended the evening throwing punches.

"Maybe you're right, Logan. You're still an ass." Jared put the money for the round on the table. "See you Monday." He got up and walked out.

I shook my head at Logan.

"What?" He gave me a wide-eyed stare.

"Why do you always have to push his buttons?"

"Because, he is a punk kid and he needs to be taken down a notch every once in a while." Logan defended.

"He's a good kid and he's just young. He'll get there one day. You just had a head start is all."

Logan stared at the table. "I guess you're right. I'm sorry."

"Apologize to Jared on Monday." I instructed.

"Yeah okay."

It was nearly one in the morning when we finally left the Grill. I drove past the Kay's house slowly. I didn't stop. All the windows were dark. I went home and slept.

Chapter Thirteen

Kay

I managed to sleep in on Saturday morning. It was a wonderful feeling and I hadn't indulged in such luxury in a long time. I ordered breakfast from room service and sat by the window and looked out over the city. DC had a beautiful skyline.

There was a knock at the door.

"Yes, come in!"

Eddie was wearing jeans and a button-down shirt. "Have you eaten?" I asked.

"Hours ago." He smiled.

"Well, sit down and have some coffee." I offered.

"What are we doing today?" He inquired.

"Well I thought it would be nice to go to the zoo. It is a nice sunny day."

He looked at me with an impatient look.

"Well you don't have to go, seriously. I am more than capable of getting myself to the zoo and back."

"Like I'd let you go alone," he huffed.

"Are you mothering me? May I remind you that I managed to get to Afghanistan and back without your help." This was a reoccurring argument we had on a near weekly basis.

"May I remind you that, that little trip didn't work out so well."

I didn't mind the reminder of my 'experience' I really don't think the pandas are going to have RPG's, do you?"

"Should I change into shorts?" Eddie ignored my comment.

"God no! You might want to wear short sleeves, though." It was June in DC and I could already see the haze forming over the city from the heat, humidity and traffic.

He got up in a huff and went to change.

Eddie enjoyed the zoo even though he wouldn't admit it. He even bought a stuffed animal for his granddaughter and a toy for his grandson.

Sherry loves panda's so I bought her a panda necklace.

"What are you going to do tonight?" I asked Eddie on the way back to the hotel.

"Probably just sit in the car and wait for you," he sighed.

"Eddie, that doesn't make any sense. You said you are familiar with this area so go have fun. I'm not going anywhere until tomorrow evening. I can look after myself."

"Fine." He was resigned.

I didn't want to argue anymore. It was hot yet it felt hotter than Gates Point and frankly I didn't think that was possible. The heat here was vicious as it was an angry heat. Back home it was a kill you with kindness sort of heat. It snuck up on you slowly.

***

Tonight, was the night that I would go to my grandfather's house for dinner. The heat had not subsided, so I decided on palazzo pants and a loose-fitting blouse. We were stopped at the gate and checked briefly. No one can just drive into the Secretary of the Navy's home, not even his granddaughter. I didn't mind. I'd rather his security detail be safe rather than sorry. Eddie explained he would be back sometime later to pick me up. They wrote down the car's information and Eddie's license and waved us through.

"Kay, so good to see you!" Grandpa called stepping out of the front door as Eddie opened the car door for me.

"Grandpa!" I hugged him and kissed his cheek.

"Let me look at you!" He held me at arm's length. "You look so beautiful." He smiled.

"Thank you. You look handsome as ever."

"Eddie, good to see you." He reached over to shake Eddie's hand.

"You too, sir."

"She giving you any trouble?"

"Always." Eddie deadpanned.

"Hey!" I objected.

"She's a lot like her mother in that way." Grandpa added.

"I am standing right here." I pointed out.

"Well, I'm not sure about that but I believe she gets her stubborn streak from her father." Eddie continued to ignored me.

"Well, you're probably right there." My grandfather laughed. "You want to join us for dinner?"

"No sir, you two need some quality time together." Eddie gracefully declined.

"You're welcome to hang out in the guest house, there's cable and I'm sure we can scare up some dinner for you," my grandfather offered.

"That is too generous," Eddie objected.

"Don't be ridiculous. You're staying. I'll call the gate and let them know." My grandfather looked over at one of the security guards. "Jimmy, Eddie here is going to hang out and wait for my granddaughter. He is her bodyguard so take good care of him. Let him watch TV or something in the guest house, okay?"

"Yes sir." And just like that Jimmy and Eddie were gone in an instant. "Now then, come in and tell me what you have been up to." Grandpa got right to it.

"Well, just work, you know how it is." I hedged.

"Yes, I do that is why I worry about you." He squeezed my shoulder in a one-arm hug "Are you taking any time for yourself?"

"Yes, I went to the zoo today."

He turned and looked at me, clearly surprised.

"Yeah, I did. It was a lot of fun. I love watching all the animals."

"Eddie go with you?"

"You know he did. He wouldn't dream of letting me go alone in the big scary city."

"He is only trying to help."

"I know but it is something I am not used to. It feels like he is smothering me sometimes."

"He cares about you."

"I know. You care about me too and you don't follow me around."

"I would if I could." He laughed.

I rolled my eyes. "You probably would."

"You'll understand one day."

"What do you mean?"

"When you have kids of your own."

I stopped walking. "Are you serious?" I was shocked by his comment.

"Yeah, of course I am."

I wanted to tell him I didn't want kids. I didn't want to have a deep philosophical conversation about having children or not before dinner and I didn't want to start an argument either. "You're probably, right." I let it go at that and hoped he did too.

"When you have someone, you care for them more than life itself and you tend to do things like follow them around and make sure they are okay."

I immediately thought of Ethan. "I suppose but Eddie has his own children and grandchildren and he doesn't need to worry about me."

"He does and you should respect that and be grateful."

"I didn't say I wasn't grateful," I corrected.

"No, of course not, I'm sorry, I didn't mean to imply that you were ungrateful." He stopped to kiss my forehead.

We sat down in his study. I loved this room as it was like my grandfather's personality filled every corner. It was a dark, earthy room. With natural colors and textures. He had a heavy wooden desk that was well worn and had a few scars of its own. The furniture's was soft and comfortable. You sank down into the sofa and it was like getting a hug. The books were all shapes and sizes and everything from military history and reports to James Michener.

"So, tell me about your meeting on Monday." He asked as he sat down in a worn leather chair.

"Well, I'm meeting with the head of orthopedic surgery to talk to him about the prosthesis we developed and see if he would be willing to offer it as an option to patients particularly veterans before going straight to amputation."

"Do you think he'll agree?"

"I hope so, I mean it is patented and it has FDA approval, not that, that means a lot. They require it before they will use it in the hospital." I informed him.

"What do you mean the FDA approval doesn't mean anything?"

"I just mean that our standards for success rate are higher than the FDA, they allow a larger margin of error than I do."

"Honey, everyone does." He chuckled.

"And it already has a proven test case." I lifted my leg slightly.

"How has it been?" He looks sad for a moment. "Are you still in a lot of pain?"

"No, it only hurts when it rains or if I run too much on it. I do a lot of swimming these days and running indoors on a padded track."

"Well you look wonderful." He deftly changed the subject. Any discussion of my near-death experience was difficult for him. I was grateful that my mother hadn't been alive because she would have gone to pieces. It probably would have killed her. She was sensitive that way.

"So anyway, if I can get them to agree to use it that will open the door to other veterans and military hospitals using them."

"You're an amazing woman, Kay."

"Thank you." I blushed.

"I mean it. You took not just a bad situation, one of the worst possible situations and turned it into an opportunity to help others." He shook his head.

"Well, it was out of desperation. I really didn't want to lose my leg. At the time I had no idea if this would work and I wasn't going down without a fight." I stared down at my leg for a moment. "I didn't want anyone else to have to face that."

"I'm sorry you went through most of that alone."

"What?" I asked.

"I'm sorry I wasn't at the hospital when you were there."

"You came to see me." I defended him.

"Yeah, I wanted to be by your side. I didn't want you to be alone."

"Oh, that's okay. It was probably better that way. I had time to think and plan this out."

"Well, I'm grateful that it worked out in the end." He stood up to pour himself a drink.

We were venturing into uncomfortable territory. He told me that when I was injured Eddie had applied for a passport to come and sit by my bedside but by the time, he got it, I was about to be shipped back home to Bethesda. I have no doubt Eddie would have sat staring at me for the duration. As it was, he was with me in Bethesda quite a bit. I had sent him away and told him that I didn't need him staring at me twenty-four seven, so he came up and only stayed three days a week. He always brought me things I needed or wanted from home. I was still running the company as much as I could from my bed. Michael did a lot of that work for me too and I would be eternally grateful to them both. The trouble is that Eddie had not got past it. He still feels the need to be there in case I fall, and I love him for it. I needed him to let go a little. Between him and my grandfather it was worse than being a teenager with a new curfew.

"So, what about the rest of your life and what else are you doing besides working?"

I looked at him confused. "What do you mean?"

"Do you like camping? Do you sail on the bay, what are your passions?"

"Grandpa, I have a company with offices and manufacturing in three cities and I'm trying to start a new manufacturing branch. I don't have time for anything else."

"What do you do when you're not at work?"

"Sleep." I wasn't sure what he was driving at.

"I hope you're not serious."

"I'm very serious. Dinner with you is the closest thing I've had to a non-work-related event in years."

"Kay, that is not healthy. You have to take time for yourself."

"You're telling me to take time for myself. The man who invented the word workaholic?"

"That is not true, I do plenty of things for myself."

"Such as?"

"I play poker with some friends once a week."

"Are these friends from work and do you talk about work things?"

"Well yes."

"Then it doesn't count."

"Sure, it does we blow off steam and say things we can't say at work."

"Do you play golf, sail, camp?" I asked pressing the issue.

"No."

"I see." I drank some wine that he had silently poured and set in front of me.

He eyed me suspiciously waiting for my next comment. I just let hang there. He got the point.

"Well, speaking of poker, some friends are stopping by later tonight for a game and I thought you might want to join us."

"I smell a set up." I eyed him suspiciously.

"What kind of set up? I just thought you might want to play a hand or two of poker, maybe help you relax."

"And these friends, who are they?"

"Just some of the guys from work." He laughed. "You do remember how to play poker don't you?"

"Of course."

"Good." That seemed to decide the situation and he refocused on dinner.

An hour later. One of the security guards came in. "Sir, your guests are starting to arrive."

"Excellent. Thank you," he replied.

"I think I'll go upstairs and freshen up." I announced pushing away from the table.

"Okay, we'll be in the den when you come back down."

I nodded and escaped upstairs. I went to one of the bedrooms on the front of the house that gave me a view of the driveway. There were three cars with drivers so at least Eddie wouldn't be bored. . A man got out of the driver's side of the fourth car and walked to the front door.

He intrigued me. I couldn't see his face. He was tall and broad shouldered. I wondered who he was.

I went to the bathroom and put a cool cloth on my face and neck. If I was going to play poker with my grandfather and his friends, I needed to be awake and alert. I didn't know these men, but I knew how my grandfather liked to play. If he wasn't the Secretary of the Navy, he would probably be the best card shark in Vegas. He was a tricky one. I went down to the den to find four men and my grandfather with drinks in their hand.

"Ah, there you are. Would you like a drink?"

"No, thank you."

My grandfather nodded and set his drink down the table. "Gentlemen I'd like you to meet my granddaughter. Kay Dandridge." All the men were smiling in my direction, except one. "She'll be joining us tonight if that's alright."

"As long as she doesn't mind losing a little money." One of the men said. My grandfather gave me a small smile. "She's a good sport. Kay, this is Paul Miller, Secretary of the Army." I shook his hand and exchanged pleasantries.

"This is Richard Loftus, Joint Chiefs."

"Pleasure to meet to you." The man was about my grandfather's age with thick hair and incredibly straight teeth.

"You too, sir." I shook his hand.

"No sirs, here today." He laughed.

"This young man is Craig Nelson, we aren't allowed to know where he works." My grandfather joked.

"Mr. Nelson, a pleasure." I smiled.

"The pleasure is all mine." He said shaking my hand gently and giving me a wink.

"And last by not least, Director of NCIS, James McIntyre." The man who drove himself here. The one who wasn't smiling.

"Mr. McIntyre." I shook his hand.

"Mac."

I nodded. "Mac."

"Shall we?" My grandfather pointed to the table. We all settled in. My grandfather dealt the cards and the game started. I studied each man's face and hands. Looking for their tell. Everyone had one.

Mac's was the hardest. His expression never changed. So, I watched for other things. The way he arranged his cards. The way he held them. The way he looked at the others. I lost the first few hands. And Mac and my grandfather won a couple. I got the impression from the grousing of the others this was a normal occurrence.

It was time to shake things up a bit I thought. I stopped concentrating on the other players and focused on the cards for a while. I won three hands straight.

"Hey, what gives, is your granddaughter some kind of ringer?" Miller asked.

"What do you do for a living?" Loftus asked.

Mac studied me waiting for a response. "I'm CEO of Port City Industries."

"That doesn't tell me much. Do you go to Vegas on the weekends?" Loftus pressed.

"Don't be a sore loser, you'll have a chance to win your money back." I smiled. I lost the next couple of rounds. It was starting to get late and the men were getting antsy.

"I say we raise the stakes on this hand." Loftus announced. "A hundred dollars to start?" Everyone looked around the table and nodded.

I dealt the cards. I had a decent hand, but I would have felt better with a couple of aces. The betting continued and the cards went around the table. Everyone folded and it was down to Mac and me. I watched him just as carefully as he watched me. It was going to be down to the cards on this one. Finally, I called.

There was five hundred dollars at stake on the table. Mac laid down his cards, four of a kind.

"Not bad." I smiled.

"Let's have 'em." He demanded. The others around the table were watching intently.

"Straight flush." I laid my cards down. The other three was murmuring. Mac leaned back in his chair and smiled for the first time.

"Nice."

I gave him a little shrug. "Just lucky."

"I doubt it." He said still smiling.

"Nicely done, young lady." Miller congratulated me.

My grandfather gave me a wink and a nod.

"Well, listen. I've had a good time, but I should be going." I announced.

"So soon?" My grandfather asked.

"It's late." I said, looking at my watch.

"Okay, call me tomorrow?"

"Of course." I promised.

He gave me a hug and a kiss. "I mean it. I want to see you before you leave."

"Okay." I nodded.

"It was nice to meet you." I addressed the others. They all nodded and raised their glasses to me. Clearly, they weren't leaving anytime soon.

"Mind if I walk you out?" Mac approached me.

"Okay." I caught a glimpse of my grandfather smiling to himself as he watched Mac approach me. I shook my head. I knew he had a reason he wanted me to stay and play cards. I turned and headed for the door.

"You played very well tonight."

"Thank you. You did pretty well yourself." I smiled.

"So, I take it you don't live here?" He made inquiring small talk.

"No, I'm in town on business. I live in Gates Point."

"Beautiful city," he replied.

"I like it. Excuse me I need to text my driver." I pulled out my phone and sent Eddie a message.

"I'd be happy to give you a lift." Mac offered.

"No, Eddie is here on the property somewhere. He's probably playing his own poker game if I know him."

"Your grandfather teach you to play?" he surmised.

"Yeah, when I was a little girl." I laughed.

"He did a good job."

"Well, I've kept up with it over the years," I confessed.

"Not much else to do in the desert some nights," he ventured.

I looked at him with fear and curiosity. How did he know I had been overseas?

"Don't worry, your grandfather told me." He said reading my face. "How long were you there?"

"Four years." I wasn't sure I felt comfortable with this. "What about you?"

He looked at me with a little surprise. "Please, I can spot a marine from a mile away."

"Well, I want to thank you for your service."

"Why?" I looked at him confused.

"Because, even if I am a marine it still isn't every day you get to meet a Medal of Freedom winner."

My mouth dropped open. My grandfather knew I didn't like to talk about that and I sure as hell didn't go around telling people about it. I felt anger rising up in my chest. I could see the headlights of my car coming up the drive. "I can't believe my grandfather told you that."

"He didn't."

"Then how do you know." I wondered.

"I investigate people for a living." He said reminding me who he was.

"How did you know you would meet me tonight." I asked.

"That your grandfather did tell me." He smiled. "He told me you were in town and he asked us all if we would mind you sitting in on the game."

My anger quickly turned to embarrassment. It had been a set up after all. The car came to a stop and Eddie got out. Mac held up his hand to stop Eddie. He reached down and opened the door.

"It was a pleasure meeting you."

I slid into the back seat. "It was nice to meet you. I hope you have better luck in there." He smiled and closed the door.

Eddie back behind the driver's wheel. "Everything okay?" he asked.

"Yep, just tired." I sighed.

He nodded and pulled the car out onto the road to take us back to DC and our hotel.

Chapter Fourteen
Kay

I was looking forward to my meeting at Bethesda Naval Hospital today. I believed I had something that could truly help wounded service men and women. The new materials would improve prosthetics or maybe even replace them. It was essentially synthetic bone. It was pretty revolutionary, and I hoped that if used in field hospitals it might replace the need to amputate at all. I was also nervous.

I had once been a patient here after my surgery in Germany. They had been skeptical of Dr. Klaus' work. When I proposed using Dr. Klaus's new and still experimental internal prosthetic the doctors had been concerned my body would reject it and that I wouldn't be able to walk with it and that it was not practical as repairs and adjustments would require surgery rather than removing the artificial limb and making the necessary adjustments. They were all very valid points and ones I had very few answers for at the time.

Today, I hope to provide them with more answers and an alternative. I wasn't under any delusions this wouldn't be right for everyone. At least it was a choice they currently didn't have. Dr. Klaus was meeting me here. It had taken some convincing, but I managed to lure him away from his job at least part time to help me develop his work into something the medical community at large might be willing to accept. And since he was the only doctor who had successfully preformed such a surgery, I thought he should be the one to make the representation today. I would only serve as a prop. An example of the success that was possible.

The campus was impressive and had a rich history of treating presidents and being the flagship military hospital in the country. We were to meet in Building 17. It was one of the historic buildings on campus and impressive with over 400,000 square feet which housed administration and research activities. Dr. Klaus met me in the lobby, and we checked in and waited for Dr. Carr.

We spent two hours making the presentation and answering questions. Dr. Klaus brought a series of x-rays and MRI images of my leg over time, some of which had been taken during my stay here at Bethesda. They admitted they were impressed with my recovery and my mobility compared to traditional prosthetics.

"Can I offer you a tour of our orthopedic facilities?" Dr. Carr said more to Dr. Klaus than to me.

"Yes, that would be nice."

"Do you care to join us?" Dr. Carr turned to me. I knew he wondered if returning to the rehabilitation ward would be difficult for me.

"That would be lovely, thank you." I faked a smile trying to hide the fear and dread rising in my chest. I wanted to do this; I really did. I had come to terms with my injuries and my chosen treatment of my leg was a big part of that. Not having to put my leg on and take it off at night prevented the daily reminder of the physical trauma. It let me focus on the mental and emotional side of things. I wanted that for others as well.

We walked to the rehabilitation area; a place I had spent so many hours determined to return to as close to normal as possible. Many times, I had to be forced to stop working and return to my room for rest. I looked at the men and women here today and it felt like nothing had changed. I could see myself, Oliver, Chris and Micah working out together urging the others on.

Devon had a traumatic brain injury and his rehabilitation was in a different area. I tried to visit him daily, and despite the fact that he didn't remember me, my presence seemed to cause more harm than good. So, I stopped going to see him. I did spend time with his wife and when they were releasing Devon and allowing him to continue his treatments back home in Idaho, I made sure his wife had all my contact information and secured a promise from her that she would call if they ever wanted for anything. I sent cards and letters with no response. I got a Christmas card every year, that told me little.

Chris had more success and through him I learned that Devon would never be able to work again. He volunteered at local library helping out in various areas as part of a program his city offered. My only wish was that if he had to live like this, that perhaps he didn't remember the hell we all went through that day. I set up a college fund for his kids through a non-profit I started as soon as I got back to Gates Point. I sent a letter to his wife stating that I had submitted their names and they had been selected but never told her that it was really my organization that I had set it up just for them. I was afraid if she knew she would refuse the help and I knew they needed it. I then expanded the program to include children of employees of Port City Industries.

I made a mental note to touch base with the guys when I got back home. It had been a while and I needed to know they were okay. Dr. Klaus and Dr. Carr where talking as we walked but I really wasn't listening. My mind was filled with memories from the past. Visiting the rehabilitation center affected me more than I thought it would. The memory of my own struggles here and the days when I thought I'd never be able to walk normally again. The fear that I'd have to be fitted for a traditional prosthetic. What I remembered most was the pain I felt watching the men that had become my friends struggle with their own rehabilitation and the number of times they fell or couldn't complete a task.

Chris was the most painful to watch. He struggled with it physically and emotionally. Chris was a marine's marine. He was broad shouldered, muscular and fearless. He would do anything that needed to get done to accomplish the mission and he would just as quickly help a friend. I felt like I had let him down the most. Chris insisted that wasn't the case, that I had saved his life. It didn't feel like it. His life as he knew it was over. He wouldn't be a marine and now he had to use his strength to make up for the loss of his left arm and severe damage to his left leg. He had to learn to walk again, and how to distribute his weight to carry things. He had to explain to his kids why he looked like a robot. It broke my heart over and over again. I decided I needed to get out of here.

"Doctors, if you don't need me any longer, I need to head out."

Dr. Klaus looked at me with worry.

"Of course," Dr. Carr said extending his hand. "Thank you for coming today."

"No, thank you for taking the time to listen to our ideas. I'm sure we'll be talking soon." I forced a smile.

"Yes." He nodded.

"Dr. Klaus I'll talk to you in a day or so?" I said as we shook hands.

"Yes, of course." Dr. Klaus looked as if he wanted to ask if I was okay, but I turned away before he could. I took out my phone and called Eddie.

"It's time to go." I spoke into the phone.

"Yes ma'am."

I made my way back to the main entrance where Eddie was waiting for me.

He studied my face as he opened the door to the car for me.

"Everything alright?" He read the look on my face.

"Yes." I lied. I didn't want to talk about it. I slid into the back seat sinking into the cool soft leather. I closed my eyes and leaned my head back. I heard the driver's door close and felt the car start to move. Thankfully Eddie didn't press the issue by asking more questions. I just needed some time to relax and clear my head. I dozed off on the way back to the hotel.

"You sure you're alright? Eddie finally asked as we got on the elevator to our rooms.

"I have a terrible headache so I'm going to lay down. Maybe have a massage or something later. I won't feel much like going out, so you take the rest of the day off and go enjoy the city." I said taking out the keycard for the room and not waiting for a response.

"Okay, feel better." I heard Eddie say as I closed the door behind me. I was grateful he hadn't argued. I headed for the bathroom and the soaking tub. Then I called for a bottle of wine to be delivered and a fruit and cheese plate. I needed to relax. If this didn't work, then it would be time to take drastic measures and call for a massage.

I greeted the room service attendant with my wine in the fluffy bathrobe the hotel provided. It was luxuriously soft, and I had half a mind to just stay curled up inside of it the rest of the day.

I double locked the door. I took the wine bottle to the tub with me. After turning on my favorite chill music station I sunk down with just my head and shoulders above the water letting the bath salts help to relax my muscles. I took a sip of wine and closed my eyes. Yes, this is exactly what I needed.

The water started to chill and not wanting to ruin a good afternoon with cold bath water I got out and dried off. I had only had one and half glasses of wine and I was feeling better already. I put the robe back on and carrying the bottle of wine and the glass I padded back out to the sitting area of my room.

I sat looking out the window at the city and drank the rest of the wine in the glass. It was dusk and lights were starting to pop on outside.

My cell phone rang. I looked down and didn't recognize the number of a DC area code.

"Kay Dandridge."

"Kay? This is Mac."

I paused for a moment.

"Jim McIntyre, we met at the poker game."

"Of course, I'm sorry it's been a long day."

"Did I catch you at a bad time?"

"No, not at all, just watching the sunset from my hotel room window."

"That sounds...."

"Sad?" I laughed a little.

"I was going to say calming."

"Oh well, that too." There was a pause in the conversation, and I had to wonder why he had called. I assumed my grandfather had given him my number. "Was there something you wanted to talk about?" I asked.

"Uh, well. I was just wondering if you'd had dinner yet?"

"No, I haven't." Now that he mentioned it, I was starved as the fruit and cheese hadn't really been very filling.

"Would you like to have dinner with me?"

He sounded like he wasn't very practiced at dating. Neither was I. I wondered why he had chosen to ask me. Was it something my grandfather had asked him to do?

"That sounds nice so what did you have in mind?"

"Nothing fancy if that is okay."

"That is more than okay. I'd love nothing more than a place I could wear my jeans and sneakers." I laughed.

"You got it. Shall I pick you in an hour?"

"An hour would be fine. I'm staying at the Marriott in D.C.."

"Got it."

"Okay see you soon." I smiled to myself.

In an hour it would be close to nine o'clock. Mac must be a night owl like myself. I smiled. This could be fun. The trouble was Eddie. I changed into jeans, my white sneakers and an oversized shirt. I put on just a little eye makeup. I wasn't one to wear a lot of makeup not even to business meetings. They would have to accept me the way I am. I did wear heels because I could. It was a major accomplishment in my recovery that I taught myself to walk in heels again after my injury. So, I enjoyed it. I didn't do it every day, it was painful after several hours. When I was ready and a few minutes before Mac was due to pick me up, I walked over and knocked on Eddie's door. There was no answer. I was grateful to avoid the conversation and twenty questions.

I didn't want to text him if he was out having a good time. So, I left a message for him with the front desk that I had gone out with a friend for a while. He would get the message when he returned.

I walked over the lobby and sat down to wait. Ten minutes later Mac walked into the lobby wearing a USMC sweatshirt and jeans.

"Hello." I smiled.

"Hi." He looked nervous. "I thought you didn't want to dress up." I looked down at myself confused. "I'm wearing jeans and sneakers?"

"Well you have a way of making jeans and sneakers look better than they should."

I almost laughed. I saw his cheeks redden just a bit. So, I let it go.

"Thank you." I said accepting the compliment.

"Ready?"

"Yes." I nodded.

We walked to the door and he held it open for me. Then he walked over to a bright yellow charger.

"I love your car." I meant it.

"Thank you." He smiled, closed my door and then walked around to the driver's side.

"Do you like burgers and fries?"

"Love them."

"Or tacos?"

"Love them, too."

"Good I know just the place."

"Okay." I nodded.

The car started with a roar and he carefully pulled out of the parking lot and into traffic. We headed out of the city and into Virginia. I wasn't sure where we were exactly, but I could still see the DC skyline. We parked on the street and walked past a few shops to a little place nestled between a clothing boutique and a vintner. Both businesses were closed. You could easily walk past this place assuming it was closed too. He opened the wooden door and stepped aside to let me in. The place was eclectic to say the least. I still wasn't quite sure where we were. There was a counter like you might find in a diner with a window that opened to the kitchen. There were checked tablecloths on the tables and an interesting collection of mismatched tables and chairs. The booths looked like they had been repurposed from another restaurant and crammed into the space. There was a stuffed armadillo on display and pictures of historic buildings mixed in with pictures of the cook posing with celebrities and politicians who obviously had stopped in for whatever it was they served here.

"Is here, okay?" Mac pointed to a booth in the corner.

"Sure." I wasn't though.

I noticed a sign above the counter that said, 'Toni and Tiny's - Welcome." A moment later a heavyset woman appeared wearing jeans and a t-shirt that had a picture of an armadillo standing up holding a burger in one hand and a taco in the other. She approached the table with two glasses of water and a cup of coffee for Mac.

"Evening, Mac." She said sweetly.

"Evening Toni." He nodded.

"What can I get you drink, sweetie?" It took me a minute to realize she was talking to me.

"You have sweet tea?"

"Is there another kind?"

"No." I admitted.

She nodded and turned away. I noticed the back of her shirt said Toni and Tiny's on it too.

She returned a moment later with a menu and tea for me.

"I'll give you a minute."

"Thank you." I said.

This time she turned to look at Mac and she winked. He pretended he didn't notice.

"I take it you've been here before." I said.

He gave me a small smile. "Yeah, Toni knows me well enough to know what I like."

"What would you recommend?" I said opening the plastic covered menu. There was a slip of paper clipped to the top with daily specials listed.

"Well, they have the best burger in town and if you're into tacos, they can make them with anything you like, beef, chicken, fish."

"I think I'll go with a burger and fries."

He nodded. "Good choice."

A moment later Toni was back. "Have you decided what you would like?"

"Yes, I'll have the blue cheeseburger and fries."

"A girl after my own heart." She smiled and turned away.

I took a sip of the tea. It was in fact sweet tea. Someone knew what they were doing.

"So, you said you had a hard day." Mac stated.

"Oh yeah. Well it was good, but not easy." I tried not to sound like I was complaining.

"How so?" he asked.

"My company developed a new kind of prosthetic to replace damaged bone and we wanted to see if Bethesda Naval Hospital would consider using it or at least offering it to soldiers and marines."

His eyebrows lifted. "Really? You're a doctor?"

"Uh, well yes and no. I have a Ph.D. but I'm not a medical doctor."

"So, how'd you come up with the idea for the new prosthetic?"

"Out of necessity mostly." I hedged. I didn't think my injuries and their circumstances made for good first date conversation. If this was a date.

He nodded. "So, how'd the meeting go?"

"Well I won't know probably for another week or two. They did show interest. Where it really needs to be used is in the field hospitals. I figured if I can get the Naval hospital to approve of it, others might follow."

"So, no starting off small?"

I laughed.

"No, not with me. For something like this it's go big or go home."

He nodded and smiled. "I see." He sipped his coffee. "Don't you need government approval or something?"

"Yes, I have FDA approval."

"Well that seems like it would be the hard part."

I smiled. "You'd think so." I sipped my tea. It reminded me of home, and it was counteracting the effects of the wine I had earlier.

"So, what's different about your prosthetic compared to the ones they use now?"

I smiled impressed that he was paying attention. "Mine is more of an implant, it works with the body rather than replacing it."

He leaned back and studied me for a long moment. "That is interesting. Tell me more."

"Well, I don't expect that it will work in all cases. In some situations, if the tissue isn't completely destroyed and can be saved even if the bone can't be, this would allow the doctors to implant my product rods in place of the bone wrapped in simulated tissue. The simulated tissue would give the natural issue something to adhere to and repair itself where it can. It reduces the chances of the body rejecting the implant. The implant looks like the inside of your leg or arm for lack of a better term wrapped in muscle and other tissues."

"That sounds, incredible."

"Thank you. I hope it offers people an option anyway. Having an implant doesn't make it easier to learn to walk again or use your hands again, but, you don't have to remove your limb every night before you go to bed and I think that helps with the emotional and mental aspect of the healing process."

"Sounds like you have some experience behind you. How much research did you do?"

"A good amount, although not as much as I think the hospital would have liked but it's hard to get test subjects. Mainly because, the decision to use it has to be made before the affected limb is removed."

Toni came back with our plates before he could ask me anymore. I was worried I would have to tell him about my personal experience and I really didn't want to go into that. Although, I had a feeling he would understand.

The burger was huge, and the fries came on a separate plate. I removed the knife from the utensils wrapped in a paper napkin and cut it in half. It smelled heavenly. Toni had delivered a burger to Mac.

"Your usual?" I smiled nodded at his plat.

"Yeah." He shrugged. He then cut his in half as well.

We ate in companionable silence for a few minutes. After I had a couple of bites of my burger and a couple of fries, I was starting to feel normal again.

"Can I ask you something, and please don't take this the wrong way."

He raised his eyebrows at me and wiped the paper napkins across his mouth. "Shoot."

"My grandfather didn't put you up to this did he?" I regretted asking as soon as the words let my mouth. I had to know if this was some sort of pity date. He looked surprised for just a moment.

"Does your grandfather often arrange dates for you?" Touche`

"No, actually until this weekend I hadn't seen in a few years."

"So why do you think he would set you up on a date?"

"Well, before you and the others arrived at the house for the card game, he was quizzing me on my personal life." I was feeling worse by the minute for asking. "I'm so sorry, please can we forget I said anything?" I felt the heat rising in my cheeks.

He leaned back in his seat. "Sure, consider it forgotten."

I dropped my eyes to my plate, and I drug a French fry back and forth in the ketchup.

"You okay?" he asked, trying to get the conversation back on an even keel.

"Sure." I said not looking up. I put the fry down and picked up my burger. Before I took a bite, I looked up at him. He was watching me intently.

"So, are you working on anything interesting at work you can talk about?" I tried to change the subject. Then I bit into my burger to allow him time to answer.

"Oh well, I don't know if you would find it very interesting. We had a missing boy the other day. He was found safe, but it was intense for about twelve hours."

"Oh, that is terrible. I can imagine that was very stressful. What happened?"

"He got mad at his mother and ran away. Quantico is a big place and he never made it off the base."

"Still there are some places on base that aren't safe for a little boy." I said.

"You're right. Fortunately, he didn't wonder onto the firing range or anything. We found him in an empty building asleep with his camping gear."

"Smart kid, how old was he?"

"Twelve. His dad is deployed so he is having a rough time right now."

"I can imagine."

"Was your dad in the military?" Mac asked me.

"When I was very young yes, but I never really had issues with him being gone then. When he took over the family business, he was out of town a lot or worked late. However, he took me to work with him as much as he could." I smiled at the memory.

"And you're in charge of the company now?"

"Yes, I'm trying to add this new medical research and development division to it."

He nodded. "How long have you been in control of the company?"

"A few years. My father passed away and the company went to my mother, it was her family that started the company and then when she passed it came to me."

"That must have been quite an adjustment."

"You have no idea. I had to run it for the first year from Afghanistan. Drove the corporate lawyers crazy."

"Why didn't you come home right away?" he asked.

"I was under contract and I had an assignment to finish, it wasn't like I could just up and leave to run a company and at the time I wasn't really sure I wanted to run it. Things happen for a reason. And here I am." He seemed to know there was more to that story, but he let it go. "How long have you been with NCIS?"

"Fifteen years."

"Do you travel a lot for your job?"

"Not as much now as I did when I was a field agent then we traveled wherever our investigation took us. I also served as an agent afloat for a while."

"Sounds pretty exciting." I said meaning it.

"It can be."

"Now it isn't so much because you're in the office more?" I had a feeling he missed the action.

He studied me for what seemed like forever and I was starting to feel like maybe I had touched on a sensitive area."

"That's it exactly." He said as if saying it out loud made it better. His shoulders relaxed a little.

"I understand. I really do."

"I believe you do." He held my gaze.

"I do. You can't talk to anyone about it because you have to provide the leadership. You can't let them see you crack even if what you are feeling is the most basic human emotion. You've always got to be the person of strength and knowledge. They look to you and you have to provide them with what they need." I realized I was running on and cut my words short. I looked sheepishly at him. "Sorry, I tend to run on sometimes."

"No." His voice was hoarse. "That's it exactly."

I gave him a small smile.

"You can always talk to me." I shrugged one shoulder. "I mean if you want...need...to." I attacked my fries again. When I looked at him again, he was smiling.

"What?" I asked.

His smile widened. "I like watching the range of emotions that can cross your face in such a short amount of time."

I felt my cheeks heat up immediately. I was sure they were bright red.

"It's okay." He reassured me.

Toni appeared then staying me from further embarrassment. "Would you like a box for that?" She looked at the remains of my burger.

"No, thank you. I'm staying in a hotel I don't have any place to keep it, but it was delicious."

She smiled and nodded and removed all the plates. She came back with more coffee and then pie.

"Oh no, I couldn't." I protested. Mac was shaking his head no at me without Toni seeing him. I frowned at him. Toni put her hands on her hips.

"Don't tell me you ain't going to eat this homemade apple pie that I was up at four thirty this morning baking."

I wasn't sure what to say. Mac started nodding at me.

"Oh, well in that case, I'm sure I can, I mean I'd love some apple pie."

"That's better." Toni nodded and set the plate down. "You want a scoop of ice cream?"

"God no!" I let it slip out before I thought about it. I hated ice cream anywhere near my pie. I held my breath and waited for Toni's indignation to resurface.

"Okay then. Enjoy." She turned and walked away.

I let out a long breath and gave Mac a curious look.

"Sorry, I should have warned you." He said picking up his fork and attacking the pie.

"Yeah, that would have been nice." I said following suit.

We both laughed. We sat drinking coffee and talking until Toni started putting chairs up on top of the tables.

"I guess we'd better go." I said taking the hint.

"Yeah, she'll spray and clean us too, if we don't go."

I knew he was joking but I also didn't doubt she'd do it either.

As we walked outside the night was still warm and I really hated the thought of the evening coming to an end. To be honest, I was enjoying Mac's company way more than I thought possible. It has been years since I had dated anyone and these days, I was too busy to even consider it. But, Mac? Well he was different.

Mac opened the car do for me and we were nearly at the hotel when he broke into my thoughts.

"Penny for your thoughts," he said.

"Oh, I am so sorry. That was rude."

"No, it's not. I'm sure you have a lot on your mind."

"No, the idea was to spend time with you and have a conversation that didn't have to deal with work and here I've been drifting off in thought." I admonished myself.

"You can't just turn it on and off. No matter how much we might try work follows us home." He was right about that.

"Well, I'm afraid I don't have much practice at turning it off."

He kept his eyes on the road and I could see he was considering my words. We pulled in front of the hotel and he sat for a minute causing the valet to pause on his way to the car.

"I had a nice time at dinner, thank you." He said.

I felt terrible about drifting away and I doubted he had a very nice time at all. I felt the need to make it up to him. "Would you like to come up for coffee?"

He considered me for a long moment, and I thought he might say no. I was okay with that because I asked him on impulse and I honestly didn't know what I would do if he agreed.

"I really don't want this night to end." He admitted.

"Me either." I said staring down at my lap. "Come up. I promise to be fully engaged and have the most riveting conversations.

"Okay, since you put it like that." He turned off the car and got out. He looked at the valet. "Treat this car carefully as if your life depended on it. Which it does."

I laughed to myself as I waited for him to open the door for me.

Chapter Fifteen

Kay

Mac sat in the chair in the corner while I made coffee in the small pot provided in the room.

"Are you sure you wouldn't prefer room service?" I asked.

"No this will be fine, and I can do that for you."

"I've got it." I laughed. Once I got everything figured out and the coffee was brewing, I joined him in the living room.

"This is a nice room." He said looking around.

"It's one of my favorite hotel chains. "I don't come to DC often or at least I haven't in the past, but we do have facility in three locations. My office is in Gates Point and I try to visit the other locations a couple of times a year at least and I always try to stay in the same hotel." I was nervous and rambling.

"So, what does Port City Industries do exactly?"

"Well, we do a few things. We are in the manufacturing business mostly."

"And you do all of that here in the U.S?"

"Yes, we do everything in the U.S. No labor force or plants in other countries."

"Wow, that is pretty rare these days."

"It is and it is still a family business albeit a large one and some of our employees have been with the company for generations. I wouldn't dare take their jobs away just to save a buck on a bolt or something."

"That is very impressive."

"Yeah, it shouldn't be. It should be the norm." The coffee machine indicated it was done and I got up to get the coffee.

"Let me help." Mac offered again, standing.

"I've got it." I smiled.

He sat back down.

"So, what sort of things do you make?"

"We make components for various engines. Large engines. We have a lot of defense related contracts especially with the Navy for various components to ship engines. We don't make the whole thing; we just provide integral pieces. We then send them to the shipyards for the final assembly."

I returned and handed him a cup of coffee. I brought over the caddy of essentials from the counter sweetener, non-dairy creamer and stir sticks.

"And now you're branching out into the medical field?" Mac inquired between sips of coffee.

"Yes, to manufacture the components of a prosthetic and provide them to the hospitals. Same general idea, we will make the parts and someone else does the final assembly." I paused for a sip of coffee in an effort to control my senseless rambling. "That's the business side of it and I want to help wounded veterans." I added.

"You seem to feel pretty strongly about that; do you have someone close to you that was wounded in that way?" He wanted to know.

I blinked at him. I wasn't sure how to answer. "The short answer is, yes." I said deciding to be honest just not too honest yet.

"I'm sorry to hear that, I do too."

I looked at him in surprise. Although I don' know why I knew he had been a marine. So of course, he was bound to know people who had been injured. "Someone you are close to?"

"Yes."

He too was being vague. Fair enough. "I see."

"So, your idea wouldn't help someone after they lost their limb, correct?"

"Correct, the prosthetic is a replacement of the internal components of the limb so that from the outside everything looks normal, skin, hair etc. A replacement limb after the fact would be more of a robotics thing."

He nodded. "Do you have a degree in this field?"

"No, it was developed by a doctor I met. If it gets accepted and implemented, then I will hire Dr. Klaus full time and we will hopefully start helping more people."

He leaned forward in the chair.

"You mean you've already tried this on a human?" He looked surprised.

"Yes."

"Wow, how did it work?"

"Very well, actually." I smiled more at the secret that the success story was sitting in front of him.

"Are they able to use the limb normally?"

"Oh yes and you'd never even know they had an implanted limb. Well, except for maybe the scar."

"Amazing." He leaned back in his chair looking thoughtful.

"Well, yes, actually it was. It took some convincing of the doctors at the time."

"You must be very persuasive."

"I don't take 'no' for an answer."

He laughed. "I bet not."

I shrugged not willing to venture down this particular rabbit hole. "How's the coffee?" I asked hoping to change the subject.

"Not bad for hotel coffee." He smiled. He had a warm and charming smile that reached his eyes.

"Tell me a little more about you." I said.

"What is there to tell? I am a marine and I work for NCIS." He smiled.

"Okay, how long were you in the marines, do you see any combat, what unit were you in? Besides being an agent afloat and now the director what else have you done, how long have you been the director, and do you like it?" I sat back after my litany of questions.

He raised his eyebrows at me and sipped the coffee. "Okay, wow."

I smiled.

"Yes, I saw combat in the marine corps. I was a sniper."

I involuntary drew in a breath. A sniper. Those guys, at least in our unit, were hard core and our heroes.

"What?" He paused.

"I have a lot of respect for snipers."

He nodded. "Being the director is okay, but it really wasn't my idea. I got saddled with being the interim director and then your grandfather talked me into staying in the position."

I nodded. Grandpa could be very persuasive. "He wouldn't have asked you to stay in that role if he didn't believe you were good at it." I reassured him.

"Being good at something and enjoying it are sometimes two different things."

"So, tell him you don't like it."

"I have."

"And?"

"He laughed and told me to suck it up."

"That sounds like him. That is a front for what he is really thinking. If he told you that it was because he didn't or couldn't tell you why he needs, you in that role."

"Maybe." He sipped his coffee.

"So, what don't you like about it?" It was my turn to lean in and hang on his every word.

"I don't like sitting behind a desk all day. I miss being out in the field." I could see it in his eyes that he did truly miss it.

"Well, if you want, you're welcome to come over and kick in my door and demand coffee if you need the adrenaline rush."

He laughed a genuine laugh. I liked the way it sounded. "I could ruin a lot of doors."

"I think I know a couple of people who could probably fix them." I laughed.

"So, you're headed back to Gates Point." It was more of a statement then a question.

"Yes." Was all I could manage to say. I suddenly had the urge not to return but to stay right here in this hotel room with Mac and watch many more sunsets.

He nodded. He stared into his coffee and I got the feeling he wanted to say more was holding back.

"What?" I said softly.

"I wish you didn't have to leave so soon." His voice was a whisper like he was fighting not to say the words.

He stood up abruptly. "I should go."

I stood up too, surprised. So many thoughts and feelings flooded my mind. I didn't want him to leave. And what reason did I have for him not to stay? I was an adult I didn't live in anyone's shadow and I had feelings for Mac that I hadn't felt in a very long time. I suddenly had a flashback to a similar evening in the guest house with Ethan. He had stood up and left that night. But Mac wasn't married, and Ethan had been a long time ago.

"You don't have to go." My voice was a whisper now, too. What was I saying? Was I inviting him to spend the night? It was like I was having some sort of out of body experience. I heard the words coming out of my mouth, but I had no control over them.

He looked at me for a long time. I could see he was thinking my invitation. He stepped in close. "I don't want to leave."

"Then don't."

He leaned down and ever so gently brushed his lips against mine. Again, my mind was flooded with images of Ethan. I pushed them aside.

My head felt like a flash bag had gone off inside it. I saw only white lights. I couldn't see or hear anything else. I wasn't sure if I should kiss him. Images of Ethan flashed before my eyes. Mac must have felt my hesitation because he pulled away ever so slightly. He searched my face. I was breathless and couldn't speak. I wanted to kiss him.

Again gently brushed his lips against mine. This time the kiss became more passionate.

We stayed locked in an embrace for several minutes before he scooped me up carried me back to the sofa. He deftly reached over and turned off the lamp on the table and the room was light by the lights of the city at night.

"Kay you are so beautiful." He whispered.

I wanted to answer him, but he was nuzzling my neck and I wasn't able to form any coherent words. I moaned and kissed his ear.

I felt his hands slide down my arm, he stopped at my elbow and moved to my breast. It had been so long since anyone had touched me like this, I was trembling with the excitement of the moment.

"You okay?" Mac whispered.

"Yes." I managed to squeak out.

"Good." He growled and began unbuttoning my shirt. "Is this okay?"

"Yes." I breathed. I wanted him to stop wasting time with the buttons and rip my shirt the rest of the way open, but I controlled myself. I didn't want to rush it. I wanted this to last forever. I let my hands start to explore more of him. When I had worked my way to his jeans, he slowly stood up. I was afraid maybe I had gone too far and for a moment I panicked. Then felt his arms around me and lift me from the sofa. I concentrated on his neck and bare shoulder until he sat me down on the bed.

The room was dark, and I let my eyes adjust. The sound of clothes being removed let me know he was ready for me. I stood and slid my jeans off. I felt Mac's hands on my waist. My skin quivered at his touch.

"Kay." He sounded out of breath.

"Mac."

"I want you." He breathed against my skin.

I answered him by running my hand down his flat stomach until I reached what I wanted. Mac moaned.

"I want you." I answered him. He didn't waste any more time. He gave us what we both wanted. An hour later I lay clinging to him.

"You are an extraordinary woman." He whispered.

I turned my mouth to his and kissed him deeply. I felt his lips smile against mine.

"You're not sleepy?" he asked.

"No." I said as I rolled him on his back. "It's my turn."

The next morning the phone on the nightstand rang. I fumbled to answer it. "Kay Dandridge."

"This is your 6:30 wake up call, Ms. Dandridge."

"Thank you."

I rolled over to see Mac still sleeping. For a brief moment I had second thoughts about what we had done last night. Then I quickly erased it from my mind. I regretted nothing. I leaned over and kissed him gently on the shoulder.

"Mmmm, what time is it?"

"Six-thirty."

His forehead creased and he frowned. "I have to go to work." He mumbled.

"I have to go home." I let the disappointment show through my words.

He finally opened his eyes. "I wish you didn't have to go."

"Yeah, me too." I agreed.

"When can I see you again?"

"Well, I'm free this weekend." I thought about my schedule. Sherry was pretty good about not scheduling things on the weekends and if it meant I could see Mac again I'd have Sherry rearrange something if necessary.

"Really?" Mac looked hopeful.

"Yeah, are you?"

"Yeah," He smiled "I think I am."

I smiled down at him. "You're place or mine?" I asked.

He laughed. "Yours?"

"Sounds good to me." I smiled feeling excited at the prospect.

"I could drive down Friday night after work."

"Oh, that would take you hours! Friday night traffic is awful."

"I could leave early Saturday morning, and make better time."

"I have a better idea."

He sat up and studied my face. "Yeah?"

"Why don't I send my plane for you. You can meet Dennis at Reagan International."

"Your plane?"

I laughed at the look on his face. "Yeah, I have a company plane, I really don't use that much, and Dennis will be happy to have the flying time."

He thought about it for a moment.

"Is there some sort of problem?" I thought maybe some sort of conflict of interest with his job and my grandfather or something.

"No, I don't suppose there is."

"Perfect, then it is settled. I'll have Dennis fly in earlier in the day and he will be on standby for whenever you are able to leave work. I'll give you his cell number so you can give him a call and let him know when you are ready to leave."

"Okay." He agreed.

"Do you need a driver? I could send Eddie up with the plane?"

"Whose Eddie?"

"My driver from last night, you met him."

"Oh, I thought maybe he came with the car service or something."

I laughed lightly. "No, Eddie has been with the company for thirty years, he was my father's driver. He insists on accompanying me on trips. I don't use him or the company car at home. Drive him nuts. He is very traditional; doesn't think I should be driving myself around town."

"Wow." Mac looked at me.

"What?"

"Well, I know you told me about your company and all, I guess I didn't realize that it included all of this."

"Is it a problem?"

"No, it's not a problem. I've just never flown on a private plane or had a driver before."

"It does take getting used to, I have to admit."

"No offense to Eddie, but I think I can manage to get myself to the airport."

"Okay. No problem," I stood up "I'm going to take a shower, want to join me?" I gave him a devilish smile.

"Yes, ma'am." After the shower, Mac was dressed and headed to work.

"Text me when you land?" Again, flashbacks of texting Ethan when I had gotten home safely. I needed to stop this; I couldn't let something that happened six years ago ruin a potential relationship.

"I will." I smiled.

He kissed me deeply.

I didn't have any girlfriends that I was close to. I kept myself buried in work all the time. Michael, Eddie and Sherry were my closest friends. I felt the urge to call a girlfriend and tell her all about what had just happened with Mac and yet slightly sad that I had no one to call. The choices you make in life.

I was dressed and ready to go by the time Eddie knocked on my door. The hotel staff had already delivered my morning paper and picked up the dishes including the two cups Mac and I had used.

"You're up early." Eddie said as I let him in the room.

"Yep." I didn't elaborate that I hadn't been to sleep at all. "Did you have a good time last night? I asked.

"Yeah did you?" I turned to him with my eyebrows raised. "What do you mean?"

"You left me a message that said you had gone out for a while. Did you have a good time?"

I eyed him suspiciously, normally he would be peppering me with twenty questions about why I had gone out alone and who had I seen. "Yeah, I did." I smiled. "Are you ready to go?"

"Yes, I am." He nodded and spying my suitcase he picked it up and headed for the door.

I followed him out.

"Where's your stuff?" I asked once we were on the elevator.

"Already in the car."

"Oh." I watched the numbers change on the digital read out. I stopped by the front desk for a receipt and to return my room key.

Once we were in the air I sat back and thought about Mac.

I was exhausted by the time we got home. I had never been able to sleep on the plane very well despite the comfort it offered. There were too many memories of harried flights out of dangerous and unstable places to allow me to ever be able to relax enough on any plane to sleep.

I had Eddie drop me off at home. I'd go to the office tomorrow. For now, I needed some real sleep.

I woke up in the middle of the night. My timing was off. I was still tired, and my mind was racing. I was questioning just how well things went at the hospital and what would I do if they refused the idea of the implant. Honestly, the thought had never occurred to me until now. Then I started questioning my evening with Mac. What the hell had I been thinking? Why had I allowed myself to get in the situation to begin with? What would my grandfather think? I was a grown woman and if I wanted male companionship I was allowed.

I got up and paced. Arguing with myself was going to get me nowhere. I decided to venture downstairs for a warm toddy to help me get back to sleep.

I woke again before my alarm. I looked to the front window. The car I had seen before I left on my trip was back. I decided I would get to the bottom of this once and for all. If someone was up to no good, then they should know someone was watching them. I headed for the front door ready to give whoever it was a piece of my mind. But as I opened the door the car pulled away. I couldn't get down the steps fast enough to get a look at the license plate. But I noted is was a dark gray Dodge Hellcat.

I ate, dressed for the office and gathered my things including the gift I had bought for Sherry. I couldn't wait to see her face when she opened it. I drove to the office, happy not to have to make small talk with Eddie this morning. I wanted to be alone with my thoughts. My stomach was in knots. What if Mac did come down this weekend? Was I being ridiculous? Did I really want to be in a relationship? Mac didn't strike me as the love and leave 'em type of guy. But, was I ready for commitment?

"Good Morning, Sherry." I greeted as I came down the hallway.

"Good Morning. I'm so glad you're back."

I looked at her concerned.

"Did something happen while I was gone?"

"No, things just seem to run more smoothly when you are here. People seem to be afraid to make a decision when you're not here."

Hmm, that was something I needed to work on. I needed my staff to be able to make decisions and run things if something happened to me.

"Okay, well can you come in when you're ready?" I asked her and continued to my desk. I knew that would pique her interest and she would come in immediately.

"Do you need something?"

"Yes, I do." I opened the bag I sat down on my desk.

"I need you to open this." I handed her a stuffed panda holding a box.

She looked at me curiously and smiled at the panda.

"He is adorable!" She beamed. She eyed the box suspiciously. "What is it?"

"Open it."

She removed the box from the bear's lap and sat him on the corner of my desk. Then removed the gold ribbon from the box and opened it and gasped.

"Oh Kay, this is beautiful." She lifted the necklace with the panda charm. "Oh, and it's heavy. Is the real gold?"

"Of course."

"Oh no," she started shaking her head. "I can't take this, it's too much."

"You can and you will." I walked over taking the necklace and stepping behind her to put it around her neck. "Turn around, let's see."

When she did, she had tears in her eyes.

"Now that looks perfect." I said smiling. "Oh no, there is no crying. Why are you crying?"

She hugged me. Then stepped away. "You shouldn't have done this."

"Why not? You are my right hand. I get nothing done without you and you had to stay behind and handle the office. The least I could do was bring you something."

"People bring back t-shirts. Not gold necklaces."

"Do I look like 'people' to you?" I laughed.

"No, you don't." She laughed too. "Thank you so much."

"No, thank you. I might not always say it or show it but, I just couldn't do any of this without you."

Sherry wiped away a tear.

"Well, now that I have ruined my make-up, I suppose you want coffee."

"Absolutely." I smiled.

She made the coffee then gathered her bear and left.

I noticed later in the day the stuffed panda was sitting on the corner of her desk watching her work. I smiled.

The day was spent catching up on emails and I had a phone call with Dr. Klaus to discuss his opinion on how things went at the hospital.

By the end of the day I was ready to go home. I had no reason to be there. In truth I missed Mac. I was staring into space thinking about him and about Ethan when Sherry poked her head in. I didn't hear her until she was standing right in front of my desk.

"Kay, are you okay?"

"What? I'm sorry." I jumped startled at the sound of her voice.

"Are you okay, you haven't seemed like yourself all day."

"Really?"

"Yes."

"How can you tell?"

"The lines on your forehead and around your eyes."

"Gee thanks, are you selling Botox injections on the side?" I asked maybe a little harsher than I intended.

"You really aren't okay, are you?"

"Sure I am."

"I'm sure you not. Something is really bothering you."

I sighed and set back in my chair. "Yeah there is, but its personal."

"That's even worse." She got up and headed for the door. I thought she was going to leave now that she knew it had nothing to do with work. Instead she closed the door and returned to the chair in from of my desk with her folded her hands in her lap.

"Tell me everything."

"Why do you think there is an everything."

"Kay, I have worked for you for six years. Four of those years you've been in this office. I see you every day. I know how you sit, smile, talk. I know when you are angry, although that is rare, I know when you happy, which isn't that often and I know when something is bothering you. This is different. So, it has to be a man."

I was shocked. I made it a point to know about my employees, I knew that Sherry loved pandas, that her favorite color was pink, when her birthday was but it never occurred to me that anyone was giving me the same level of attention.

"What makes you think it is a man?"

"Because in all the time I have known you, you've never once mentioned a man and you've never asked me to make dinner reservations at a romantic restaurant or book a weekend getaway. You don't have any pictures in here of anyone I don't know, and I have never ever seen you like this so, it has to be a man."

She folded her arms across her chest and glared at me. "Tell me I'm wrong." She challenged.

I blinked at her in surprise and slowly looked around my office to see that she was right. I had pictures of my mother and father and company related photos and that was it, nothing personal.

"Okay, it's a man. Sorta."

"I knew it!"

She clapped her hands and bounced in the chair.

I smiled; her giddiness was contagious. I felt excited and relieved to have someone to talk to about this.

"Now what do you mean sort of?"

"Well, it's about two men, actually." I sighed admitting to myself I was still hung up on Ethan and being with Mac had only brought those feelings to the forefront.

"Wow! I wish I had problems like that."

"No, you don't." I shook my head.

"Yeah, just for one weekend."

"Okay, well let's see if we can pass you off as me and the problem is all yours." I laughed.

"So, what's the problem?"

"Okay, without getting too bogged down in details, I met a man the weekend of my mother's funeral. We spent two lovely evenings together drinking bourbon and listening to music. It wasn't the right time to start a relationship, you know?"

She bit her lower lip and nodded waiting for me to go on.

"Well, as you know I went back to my marine unit. Before I left, I told him that if it was meant to be, we would meet again."

"And did you ever see him again?"

"No."

"Never? He didn't try to contact you or anything?"

"No."

"Wow, that is really sad."

"Then the night before I left for DC, I saw a car parked out in front of my house. And at first, I thought it might be someone doing something illegal. But I've had this feeling all day that it might have been something else. That it might have been Ethan."

"Okay. . .,."

"So then on this trip to DC I met a friend of my grandfather's,"

Sherry made a face and wrinkled her nose.

"He isn't my grandfather's age." I said.

"Oh, well okay then."

"He was at my grandfather's house for poker night with some other people grandpa works with and he and I started talking."

"And then?" She drug out the words.

"He called me the next day and we went out to dinner."

"And?"

"One thing led to another and he might be coming down here to visit this weekend."

"Okay, so what exactly is the problem?"

"So the problem is that I've been thinking about Ethan, the guy from six years ago. Even when I was spending time with Mac this weekend, I couldn't help but think about Ethan."

"What does this Ethan do for a living?" Sherry asked looking serious.

"Ethan was an FBI agent when I met him."

"And this guy Mac, that works with your grandfather, what does he do?"

I was starting to feel a little uncomfortable under Sherry's scrutiny.

"He is the director NCIS"

"NCIS!" She raised her voice.

"Shhh, I don't need the whole office knowing."

"Sorry," she said, "are you kidding me?"

"No, why?"

"NCIS is one of my favorite shows."

"Sherry, he isn't on the show, this is real life."

"I know, I know, but still. How cool is that?"

"Well, I was thinking if it was Ethan in front of my house maybe I should look him up."

"And you think the car in front of your house was this Ethan?" Sherry studied me, "he is just an FBI agent?"

"Yeah,"

"I don't know I think I'd hold out for the Director."

"Sherry!"

"What? I mean if you haven't made up your mind which one to date, what's the harm?"

I shook my head. This is why I don't talk to people about my personal life.

Chapter Sixteen
Kay

My conversation with Sherry notwithstanding I couldn't stop thinking about Ethan. But, why go looking for trouble? If I sought him out that would imply, I was interested in a relationship and then how would I explain Mac. Although, Mac and I didn't have a relationship as yet. I needed to know if there was anything there for us. If there wasn't then I was free to see Mac without feeling the guilt I was experiencing now. Plus, if there wasn't anything there for us then why was he sitting outside my house. If, he was sitting outside my house, I reminded myself. I stared up at the ceiling. I needed to let this go and let life takes its course. I had other things that more pressing than my social life to deal with. I had a company to run, I needed to be ready to move on the expansion if the hospital came back with a positive answer. That would likely require another trip to DC this time with Michael to work out the details. Just then an email popped up on my screen from the Ohio plant, they were having a material shortage and needed some help.

The week was nearly a blur and on Thursday afternoon my cell phone rang. "Hello,"

"Kay, it's Mac.

"Mac, hang on a second please," I got up and shut my door. "Thanks, I wanted to shut my office door. How are you?"

"I'm good. I'm sorry I haven't called before now." Mac apologized.

"It's okay. It's been a busy week here and I'm sure you are busy too."

"Yeah, that is why I am calling. I don't think I am going to be able to make it down this weekend. I'm really sorry."

"Oh," I was surprised at how disappointed I felt. "We have a high-profile case and I'm getting pressure to get it wrapped up pretty quickly. I don't think I can get away."

"I understand, I do. I am disappointed, but these things happen." I reassured him.

"I know, I'm disappointed, too. Do you think it will do any good if I told SecNav I need the weekend free so I could go see his granddaughter?"

I laughed at the very thought. "No, I don't think that would be a good idea for either of us."

Mac chuckled. "Yeah I think you're right." He agreed. "I'll try to call, okay?"

"Okay."

We clicked off.

There was a soft knock at the door. "Yes?"

Sherry poked her head in. "Is everything okay?"

"My weekend plans just got cancelled."

"Oh no!"

"It's probably just as well. Who was I kidding thinking this would go anywhere with his schedule and mine and long distance, no less?"

"Hey, don't think like that. It will work out." Now it was Sherry's turn to be reassuring.

I had my doubts but didn't want to dash Sherry's hopes. "I hope you're right."

I worked late that night; I had no real incentive go home. And wondered if maybe I shouldn't develop a hobby or take a yoga class. Sherry had suggested we do something together a number of times and I had begged off. Maybe I should take her up on it and forget about men.

On a whim, I decided rather than drive straight to the back of my property where the driveway was located, I'd make a pass across the front of the house to see if anyone was parked out front. As I turned the corner the same dark colored car was there. I had a sudden thought that it could be something very different than what I imagined and possibly dangerous. But it was too late because anyone in that car had certainly seen me by now. I pulled parallel but not too close and put my window down. The dark sedan did the same. The streetlight was bright enough that I had no doubt as to who was sitting in front of my house.

"Ethan, would you like to come inside?"

After he recovered from the initial shock he smiled. "Yes, I would."

"Give me a minute to park."

"Yes, ma'am."

He rolled up the window and opened the door. I drove up the block and took two more right turns to my driveway. I drove into the garage and went straight into the house. I met Ethan at the front door.

I opened the door to find him standing there looking sheepish.

"How'd you know?"

I smiled. "I'd recognize you anywhere." I stepped aside for him to come in. "How'd you know I lived here?"

"I didn't, it's just the last place I saw you, so I took a chance."

"No fancy FBI database?"

"No, I'd never do that, besides I don't want to read about you on a computer. I want to get to know you in person."

I smiled. "How many nights have you been sitting out there?"

"Just a few times." He blushed. I raised an eyebrow at him.

"It only occurred to me recently that when I last saw you and where staying in the guest house that this might be your parents' home."

"You were thinking about me recently?" I said over my shoulder as I led him into the living room to sit down.

"Yes, and no."

"I turned to have him and was surprised he was standing so close to me."

"I have never not thought about you, but lately you've been on my mind more so than usual and then I thought I saw you in the crowd at the Mayor's Chamber dinner."

"You were there?" I asked surprised.

"Yes, were you there? Wearing a green dress?"

"Yes." I laughed.

"I know that had to be you. But I couldn't get across the room quick enough to get your attention and I never got a good look at y our face."

"Then why did you think it was me? "

"I heard you laugh."

"Laugh?" I was appalled, I suddenly wondered if I sounded like a braying ass and no one had ever told me.

"Yes, your laugh, it sounds like crystal wind chimes."

"And that is a good thing?"

"Yes, that is a very good thing."

There was an awkward silence and I thought he looked like he wanted to kiss me.

"Please have a seat. Can I get you anything to drink?" I offered taking a step back.

"No, thank you I'm fine." He sat down on the sofa.

I had a flashback to the last time we had been alone in a very similar situation. I sat next to him but not too close.

"So how have you been?" I asked tentatively.

"I've been okay." He nodded.

I nodded. I wanted to tell him that I thought of him every day and of how the memory of him had gotten me through the worst part of my life. I wasn't sure how to say it and I thought it might be a little much for the first conversation in six years.

"The last time I was here you were staying in the guest house; can I ask why?"

"I was home that week because my mother had passed away after a battle with cancer. I couldn't bear to stay in the house, too many memories and all."

"I'm so sorry. I didn't know."

"No reason why you should."

"That is why you were drinking alone at the club that night." He asked.

"Partly, yes. With my mother's passing and me being an only child, my life got complicated for a while and I wasn't looking forward to having to deal with all the legal aspects of that."

"I see." He nodded.

He didn't ask for further details and I wasn't quite ready to offer them. I was feeling very nervous for some reason. Like I was sneaking a boy in through the window or something. Like we were going to get caught at any moment.

"Why were you there that night?"

"My wife was out with her girlfriends again and she said she would be late. I couldn't stand the thought of going home to a cold empty house again. And because, I like Charlie Pickens music." He smiled.

"I heard that." I agreed.

The tension was so thick you could cut it with a knife. Suddenly I didn't know what to say.

"So..." We both said.

"You first." He said.

"I was just wondering how you have been?" I paused. "If feels like I haven't seen you in forever and at the same time if feels like only yesterday."

He smiled and nodded. "I know what you mean. I've been thinking a lot about you lately, not that I haven't thought about you the past several years."

I nodded and waited for him to answer my question.

"I've been okay." He shrugged.

I raised my eyebrows at him.

"I pretty much live on caffeine and don't sleep much." He continued.

"Why is that?" I was curious.

"I'm not sure," He paused and looked very uncomfortable. "I think it is because I was missing you. I wasn't totally sure that was the reason until tonight."

I felt my cheeks redden.

"What about you?" He asked.

I swallowed hard. I wasn't ready to answer and yet it was only fair that I did. I had asked him first. "Well, it has been an interesting few years."

"How so?"

"Well, after I inherited the family business, I had to try and run things from the Middle East. It was not my intention to be an absentee boss, but I was under contract and I needed to finish the assignment."

He nodded. "Makes sense."

"Yeah, but then," I stopped as I was afraid to tell him. It was a completely irrational fear but still it was there.

"Then what?"

"I was injured."

"Injured? Injured how?" His face paled.

"I was imbedded with a Marine unit and I went out on a patrol with them. We were attacked and..." I had to swallow hard. "We were all injured pretty badly. And one Marine was killed."

His face looked stricken. "How bad?" His voice was hoarse.

"It was pretty bad. I nearly lost my leg and I spent nearly a year in rehab."

He edged close. "I'm so sorry that happened to you, Kay. I wish I had known. I would have been there for you."

I loved that he was holding me and comforting me even now years later.

"I wish you had been there too. I was afraid to call and tell you, even though I wanted to. I didn't know your situation."

"I understand and I wish you had called as it wouldn't have mattered my situation. I would have been there."

I pushed him away gently, just enough to see his eyes. "You were there. When things were tough, I just closed my eyes and thought of you and remembered you and your smile."

He gave me a small grin.

"Do you want to talk about it?"

"Not tonight. One day I'll tell you all about it, but I thought you should at least know." I shook my head.

"Thank you for telling me and when you're ready to talk, I'll be here this time."

I smiled at him.

"You are the sweetest man." I reached out and squeezed his hand in mine.

He laughed. "You probably think I'm some kind of idiot or a stalker."

"No, I think it is romantic."

"Romantic? I've never been called that before." He laughed again.

"Well, then someone didn't know how good they had it." I looked into his eyes deeply, "am I to assume by the fact that you were parked in front of my house that you are no longer married?"

"No, I am no longer married." He gave me that lopsided grin I remembered so well.

Chapter Seventeen
Kay

Ethan and I stayed up talking all night. When the sun started to come up, I got up from the couch to make us breakfast. We sat in the kitchen eating omelets and bacon with toast.

"I wish we didn't have to work today." I said.

"Me too. Maybe we can have dinner tonight?" he suggested.

"That would be nice." I smiled. He smiled and took a bite of toast. "I'm sorry I kept you up all night, you'll be dead on your feet at work." I offered.

"Actually, I don't think so. I think I have more energy that I have had in a long time."

I rolled my eyes. "Really?"

"Yeah, really."

"Will you get any guff from your co-workers if you're late?"

"Well maybe just from Logan, but only because he is my best friend. And he probably knows more about you than I do."

"How so." That struck me as odd and a little creepy.

"Well, when I thought I saw you at the dinner party that was sort of my breaking point. I refused to look you up on online or anything because I thought that would be breaking our code or something. Logan researched you."

"Did he tell you what he found?"

"He tried but I refused to listen. I said I didn't want to know from a computer. I wanted to know about you from you."

I smiled. He made me feel like the happiest woman on earth. "That is sweet. And now I'm a little nervous about Logan."

"Don't be, he's a cool guy and I'm sure he deleted whatever he found."

"Well, whatever it was I'm sure it was boring. These days I spend my time in board meetings."

"Quite different than the Middle East."

"It is and I'm not complaining."

"I'm glad you're back."

"You'll have to come to the office one day let me show you around." I smiled thinking of Sherry and her reaction which made think of her comment about holding out for Mac. Mac, I had forgotten all about Mac. *Damn.*

"Everything alright?"

"What? Oh yeah."

"You looked like you drifted away there for a minute."

"Sorry just remembered something about work." I hedged. He accepted that answer and finished his breakfast. He left with a kiss on the cheek and a promise to call later about dinner. I stood smiling after he was gone.

Then my thoughts returned to Mac. Maybe, I was worried over nothing. I hadn't heard from him so this might be a non-issue. I had a feeling I was going to have to face this sooner or later. Until then I had a company to run and I needed to get on it.

I drove myself to the office again. When Sherry greeted me with her cheerful morning self, I matched her smile for smile.

"Morning, Kay."

"Morning, Sherry. Beautiful day, isn't it?" I walked straight into my office and looked out the window at the water. Sherry waited and then came in to make coffee. "Sherry, you know I really can do that. You don't have to do that every morning. I know you're busy."

"What are you talking about, of course, I have to do it. First, if I don't, you'll forget and be off to a meeting without any caffeine and I would feel sorry for the people you would be meeting with, and second, it is our girl time."

"Okay, well you have a point. This morning I've already had a couple of cups and we can have our girl time without the coffee." I smiled.

She eyed me suspiciously and came over to sit down in front of my desk.

"What?" I questioned her look.

"What's up with you?"

"What do you mean?"

"I mean you are not a morning person, not in the four years I've worked for you."

"With me, not for me," I corrected her.

"Whatever." Clearly, she was mentally rolling her eyes at me. "You have never once been rude or short with me, but you are not a morning person. What gives?"

"Nothing. I was just up all night and I'm already tanked up on coffee; I just already have a caffeine high."

"I'm not buying it." She crossed her arms.

I raised my eyebrows at her. "Okay, what's your theory." I stared at her hard using my best intimidating look.

"A man."

"What?" I lost my composure. How did she always know?

"Nothing else it could be."

"Unbelievable."

"You're right. It is unbelievable you haven't already told me everything, now get to it."

I had to laugh. "You should be handling some of my meetings for me Sherry, you're a tough nut to crack." She stared at me unamused, waiting "Okay, okay." I threw my hand up in surrender. "Close the door." Sherry eagerly returned to her chair and sat waiting for me to speak.

"I decided to drive around the block before I pulled into the driveway last night to see if the same car was parked out front."

"You didn't!" Sherry put her hands over her mouth. "So, what happened?" She whispered.

"The car was sitting right in front of the house."

"Then what happened?"

"I pulled up alongside it and rolled down my window. He did the same and it was Ethan, just like I knew it would be."

"Really? Did he say anything?"

I smiled. "He said hello and then I invited him inside." I paused, deciding how much detail to share after that. Sherry looked decidedly scandalized at this news.

"You did what? Well, you didn't waste any time."

"Sherry! It wasn't like that, let me finish."

"Okay." Sherry looked at me with suspicion. "Did you kiss him?"

"No, well yes, but not right away."

"So, what did you talk about?" she asked.

"Well, I don't know, everything."

"Did you tell him about your accident?"

"Yes, and no."

"Kay, there is a lot of yes and no's in this conversation?" It was beginning to feel a little like an interrogation.

"I only told him that I had been injured and it was bad. I didn't share any other details."

"Why not?"

"Didn't seem like first date conversation."

"Okay I get it." She nodded.

"I mostly told him about taking over the company and that sort of thing and he told me about what he had been doing for the past six years."

She nodded.

"I just have one question." She said.

"What's that?"

"What about the NCIS Director?" She nailed it.

"Yeah, I don't know."

"Well, don't you think you should let him know?"

"What do I say? Hi, how's it going? By the way I've reconnected with someone, so I won't be calling?"

Sherry gave me an impatient look. "You know that is not what I meant."

"I don't know what I will do about Mac, if anything. I mean it isn't like my phone is ringing and so it might be a non-issue."

"Do you really believe that?" Reality check.

I knew deep down I didn't. I knew this was the sort of mess I normally got myself into, so no need to think it would have an easy solution.

Chapter Eighteen
Ethan

Having Kay back in my life changed everything. I felt alive. I felt energetic. I stopped for my usual cup of coffee at the Island Cafe and took time to notice the people around me while I waited. A man was in the corner reading on a tablet and ignoring those around him. A table with four retirees laughing and enjoying each other's company. Several people in suits waiting impatiently for their orders. I smiled and tipped the barista and headed to the office.

"Morning." Logan said with a smile.

"Morning!" I returned the greeting and headed for my desk.

"You look," Logan paused. "relaxed."

"Do I?" I wasn't going to make it easy for him.

"Yeah, like maybe you got some sleep for a change?" he replied.

"Hmm." I tapped away at my keyboard.

"Morning all." Jared came in carrying a bag. "I stopped and got bagels."

"Good man." I smiled.

Jared did a double take when he looked in my direction, but he kept his thoughts to himself. I saw him look to Logan for an explanation. When none came, he set the bagels down in the kitchen and returned to his desk.

Stephanie was next, our resident morning person couldn't get under my skin with her exuberance today. In fact, I found her attitude refreshing to the cynical duo of Logan and Jared.

"Morning, Stephanie." I greeted her.

She rewarded me with a huge smile.

"There's bagels if you want." Jared announced.

"Oh, fabulous. I was running late so I skipped breakfast and I'm starved." She turned and bounced into the kitchen. "Anyone else?"

"Yeah I'll take one." I called out.

Stephanie smiled.

"Do you have a favorite?"

"No, I'm good with anything." I called back. A few minutes later she bounced back out of the kitchen carrying two small paper plates each with a bagel. She walked over and set one down on my desk.

"I added cream cheese, I hope that is okay."

"Perfect." I said nodding to her.

Logan and Jared exchanged looks. We all worked on our respective cases until noon.

"Why don't we all take a break and go out to lunch." I suggested.

They all looked up at me; it was Logan who scowled.

"Sure, what did you have in mind?" Jared asked.

"It's Friday and I thought we'd all go out after work." Logan suggested. I knew what he was doing. He had no such plans.

"Well, I thought all you young folks would have plans on a Friday night, so I thought we'd head over to the Dockside and have lunch." I smiled thwarting Logan's plan for digging up information.

"I'm in." Stephanie stood up and grabbed her purse. Jared followed suit.

I stood up and took my service weapon out of the locked desk drawer and put it on my hip. "You coming, Logan?" I asked.

I thought for a minute he might say no, but he stood up with some reluctance and joined us.

The Dockside was one of the best seafood restaurants in town if you weren't into the five-star scene. It wasn't fancy but the seafood was fresh, and the fishing boats were actually docked at a pier behind the restaurant. The place had checkered tablecloths covered in plastic. If you ordered a soda, it came in a can and if you wanted it in a glass you poured it yourself. The prices were right, and you could enjoy a cold beer with your meal if you chose. The owner used one of those old coolers that ran cold water through it to keep the bottles and cans extra cold. It was better than a draft beer.

We found a table in the corner and seated ourselves. The place was packed, and the waitresses were running back and forth their arms loaded with more plates than I would have thought possible for one person to carry.

"This might take a while, boss." Jared said looking around.

"No problem." I smiled as a waitress approached the table.

"Ya'll know what you want to drink?" she asked.

"I think we'll have sweet tea all around." I said, knowing that is what the crew usually ordered if we weren't drinking alcohol. Everyone nodded in agreement and the waitress left us with menus and went to retrieve our drinks. She returned a few minutes later with four glasses filled with ice and two pitchers.

"Ya'll ready to order?" she said, more as a greeting than a question. We gave her our orders and then I poured tea for Stephanie and myself. Logan and Jared each poured their own. L

"Are you doing anything this weekend, boss?" Stephanie asked. It was an innocent question, but I thought Logan was going to choke on his iced tea.

"As a matter of fact, I am." I smiled. Jared and Stephanie looked surprised but recovered quickly.

"That's great." Stephanie spoke first.

"What about you?" I said to no one specific.

"I'm going fishing." Jared offered.

"I'm going shopping with my mom." Stephanie smiled.

"Logan?"

He looked at the three of us. "Yeah, probably doing something. I don't know yet."

"You're welcome to come fishing with me. I'm going out on a charter and we've got room. A buddy of mine owns the boat."

"Yeah, I might do that." Logan said noncommittally.

"Good deal." Jared nodded and pulled out his phone and began texting someone.

Our lunch was served, and we all chatted about nothing in particular in between bites. Lunch took longer than I thought it would, so I had a few phone calls to return when we got back to the office. I took a break and sent a text to Kay. "Want to get together tonight after work?" I waited with bated breath that last night hadn't been some sort of fluke.

"Yeah, what did you have in mind?" she responded.

"Not sure, wasn't sure you would say yes."

She sent back a smiley face.

"How about a dinner and a walk along the seawall?"

"Perfect. Time?"

"Eight. Pick you up at your place?" I asked. I put my phone away and went back to work. It was six o'clock when Stephanie left, and Jared followed her half an hour later. I turned off my computer for the weekend and stood up. "I'm calling it a night."

"You want to explain yourself?" Logan asked.

"Is there a problem?" I asked not appreciating Logan's moo.

"No, problem."

"Then what's with the attitude today?"

"I've just seen how you've been the past few years and suddenly you're Mr. Personality and going out to lunch with us and now you have plans this weekend." Logan stood up. "I want to know what gives? No one does a one eighty like this without a damn good reason."

I was stunned.

"Okay, if you must know. I ran into Kay last night. I didn't get any sleep last night because I was at her house talking until this morning when she cooked us breakfast. I went home long enough to change clothes."

"Are you serious? Do you think this is a good idea?"

"Logan, I'm a grown man and I've dated plenty of woman and even managed to get married and divorced. I think I can handle this."

"You've dated plenty of woman before you got married but not in the past six years that I know about. I don't want this woman to send you back into a spiral."

"Look I appreciate that. I do." I took a deep breath, "You and I have been friends a long time. Kay is different."

He studied me for a moment. Then smiled. "As long as you're happy." He stood up and shook my hand. "See you Monday."

I nodded as we both walked out of the office together.

"Hey Logan." I called after him.

"Yeah?"

"Thanks, man."

He nodded and turned back towards his car. He was a good friend.

Chapter Nineteen
Ethan

I pulled up in front of Kay's house and rang the front doorbell. I felt a little nervous and I wasn't sure why. It wasn't like I hadn't just spent several hours talking to her about everything I could think of that had happened in the past six years. At least the highlights anyway. So why did I feel like this was a blind date? I knew what to expect, didn't I? I knew Kay, well enough not to be as nervous as a schoolboy.

I practiced some squared breathing I had read about in a magazine when she opened the door. All the air left me, and I couldn't speak.

"Hi." She smiled at me.

"Hi." I finally managed.

I stood starting at her unable to tear my eyes away from her. She was wearing a sleeveless dress with a neckline that was more suggestive than revealing. I didn't need much encouragement in that department. The dress came below her knees and she was wearing low heels.

She reached for a lace wrap and her purse. I stood just inside the still open door and watched as she draped the wrap around her shoulders. It was the perfect shade of blue to match her dress with hints of yellow.

"You look lovely," I said when my brain finally got with the program.

"Thank you." She smiled.

"Did you make the wrap yourself?"

"No, a friend of mine made it for me a couple of years ago." She laughed a small laugh, "and honestly this is the first time I've worn it."

"It's beautiful," I said staring just a little too long into her eyes.

"Thank you." She smiled sweetly. "What do you have planned for us this evening?"

"I thought we'd go over to the Garrison for dinner and then stroll along the seawall."

The Garrison was an old brick building that had served as a military administrative building during World War II and had long been any number of things. It's most recent use as a restaurant seemed to be a success. The building was three floors and the higher the floor, the more formal the attire. Tonight, we were seated on the third floor on the balcony overlooking the water.

"Oh, Ethan, this is a beautiful view. You know I have never been here before." She smiled.

"I'm glad you like it." I felt proud of myself for picking the spot.

I ordered wine before dinner.

"How was your week?" She asked.

"Better than most." I smiled. Thinking that she was the reason it has been better.

"Well that is good, many cases?"

"Well, no, we had a missing person's case and an investigation into civil rights violation by a local police officer. So, it's been busy enough. Plus, we have some ongoing cases." I didn't want to get into the details and talk shop all night. "What about your week?"

"Oh, just boring CEO stuff." She laughed.

"I doubt that seriously. Have you heard anything back from the hospital yet on your proposal?"

"No, not yet."

She looked troubled and stared at her wine. I had the strong sense there was more to that story, I wasn't going to push, and I didn't want to spoil the evening before we had even really got started.

"I had a few meetings about some of our other facilities and we have another company offering to buy us."

"Really, does that happen often?" I wouldn't have expected that.

"Yeah, once in a while it does," she replied.

"Are you considering their offer?" I asked.

"No." She said simply.

I nodded. I could see she felt strongly about the family business.

"Do you not want to be a photojournalist anymore?"

She looked up at me in surprise.

"No, I'm done with that life. I never expected or planned to run my father's business. Frankly, I'm surprised that he and or my mother didn't sell it. Now that it is mine, I have to take care of the people that work for me."

I nodded.

"Would they lose their jobs if another company bought them?"

"Probably. Another company would most likely move the manufacturing components to another country where the labor is cheaper."

"Why haven't you done that?" It seemed logical to me.

"Because, it is still a family business. Not just my family but the families of all the people who work for the company."

I had to smile. The defiance that showed in her face told me that she cared about her employees. It worried me as well because there were few companies like hers today and they were often taken over in less than friendly terms.

"Aren't you ever worried about someone forcing you to sell?"

"What do you mean?"

We were interrupted by the arrival of our meal and the more serious conversation was paused while we ate.

The waiter came to take our plates. "Would you care for dessert?"

"No, thank you," we said at the same time.

"Coffee, then?"

"Yes, that would be lovely." She agreed.

The second waiter quickly appeared with our coffee.

"So back to your question about selling or not selling the company," she said over the rim of the coffee cup.

"Yes."

"There have been attempts in the past when my father still ran the company to force a sale." She paused. "That is partially, why Eddie is so protective of me and has appointed himself my personal bodyguard."

"Do you think maybe you should have actual bodyguards?" I was suddenly more concerned for her safety.

She raised her eyebrows at me. "No, I don't need people following me around and getting in the way all the time."

"Maybe that is what Eddie does but trained professional bodyguards are almost invisible." I argued.

"Trained professionals are people I don't know," she said solemnly.

"What do you mean?" I was curious. She was getting into my world.

"I mean if I don't know them, I don't trust them, and bodyguards see way too much of my personal and professional life for me to not trust them. So no, that isn't going to happen." She explained.

I leaned back in my chair somewhat surprised at how vehemently she opposed the idea. I didn't want to argue on our first official date, so I didn't push the issue. I did make a mental note to come back to it at a more appropriate time.

"How about that walk on the seawall?" I asked, changing the subject.

She looked out over the water. "Sounds wonderful."

I quickly paid the check and we walked to towards the back of the restaurant to the pedestrian seawall. The water curved out towards the bay here and it was nothing but inky blackness with the moon dancing along the rippling waves. We walked in silence just breathing in the salt air and admiring the view.

We walked far enough away from the populated area to find an empty bench.

"Would you like to sit?" I offered.

She looked up as if she had forgotten I was even there. "Oh, yes."

We sat and I started to get that nervous feeling in the pit of my stomach again.

It was as romantic an evening as I could imagine. Dinner on the balcony of a very nice restaurant and a moonlit stroll. Most men would probably be kissing Kay by now. I was too nervous and too unsure of how she would respond. I wanted to savor my moments with her and not rush into anything. But I remembered how sweet her kiss was six years ago.

"There is nothing like the smell of salt air on a warm spring night." I said hoping I didn't sound too lame.

"You're right, nothing is as comforting to me as the smell of salt air, a warm breeze off the bay and even the smell of crabs; it all screams home to me." She smiled looking up at me.

"Kay, can I ask you something?"

"Of course." She smiled again.

"Well, it's something that has been on my mind lately and well I'm not sure..."

"Ethan, go ahead. It's okay, whatever it is."

"Well I, would you mind if...may I kiss you?"

She looked like she was in shock then she nodded ever so slightly.

I leaned in and she met me halfway.

She smelled sweet like vanilla and honey. And kissing her was everything I had dreamt it would be and more. It was like an electric jolt and fireworks exploding in my head all at the same time. When we finally broke away, I reached up and gently touched her hair. She closed her eyes and smiled, and I knew everything in my life would never be the same.

We sat for hours holding hands and watching the distant lights of the boat traffic on the water.

"I should probably take you home." I said when I caught her stifling a yawn.

"I really hate for this night to end," she said.

"I know, me too."

We drove back to her house and I walked her to the door.

"Would you like to come in?" she asked.

I wanted to say yes. I wanted to sit up all night with her, but I knew we needed to pace ourselves and not try to fit an entire relationship into one night.

"No, you go get some sleep. I'll call you tomorrow," I told her.

"Okay. I had a wonderful time tonight. Thank you."

She stood on her toes and kissed me again.

"No, thank you." I kissed her back. "I'll call you tomorrow and see if you're up to another date." I smiled.

"Please do."

She opened the door and I backed down the steps.

"Make sure you lock the door." I smiled.

She rolled her eyes at me.

"I will."

I turned back to my car. I felt like I was walking on air. There was no way I was going to sleep tonight as I was too pumped up. I drove home anyway, excited about the prospect of seeing her again tomorrow.

Chapter Twenty
Kay

I slept better than I had slept in a very long time. I woke up at nine the next morning and I couldn't remember the last time I had slept so long. I looked around the room. Sunlight was pouring in and I stood up to stretch. I had been a wonderfully perfect evening with Ethan. It was like something out of a book or a movie.

Despite the wonderful dinner I had the night before I found that I was starving this morning. I dressed in an oversized t-shirt and yoga pants and headed for the kitchen. I started the coffee and decided to make waffles.

My cell phone rang, and I nearly spilled my coffee trying to get to it fast enough in case it was Ethan.

"Hello?"

"Kay?"

"Sherry? Is everything alright?" Sherry had never called me at home on the weekend before unless it was something urgent for the office.

"Yes, of course. I was just calling to find out how your date went last night."

I smiled and sat back down to my waffles. I shouldn't have been surprised that Sherry wasn't going to wait til Monday to find out what happened. "Well, first we went to The Garrison." I started out.

"Ooh swanky, which floor did you sit on?"

"Uh, third floor balcony." I said timidly.

"Ooh la la." Sherry giggled.

"It was rather nice," I admitted.

"Oh yeah. That is one of the most sought-after spots in the city." Sherry assured me. "Did you have wine with dinner, too?" she went on.

"Of course." I answered.

"Oh man, I think I've died and gone to heaven."

"Sherry you need to get out more." It made me very uncomfortable that she was living vicariously through my love life.

"Who are you telling? Got any candidates?"

"Gates Point is a big enough place that surely there must be someone?" I pointed out.

"You'd think, so wouldn't you?" She sighed.

"Well, we'll work on it." I assured her.

"Never mind me, tell me more about your date."

"We had dinner and talked, then coffee." I recalled.

"Yeah, yeah!" Sherry urged.

"Then we went for a stroll along the seawall." It was a little, dream-like.

"A stroll in the moonlight, how romantic." She sighed.

"Yeah, it was. And then we sat down on this bench for a while watching the boats and he asked if he could kiss me."

"What?" This was what Sherry had been waiting for. "He actually asked before he kissed you? Wow, his momma raised him right."

I smiled. "Apparently so."

"Then what happened?"

"Well, we sat and talked and kissed a few more times. Then he brought me home."

"Did he spend the night?" She was persistent.

"No." I said, thinking that was a pretty personal question. But she was undeterred

"What? It's the twenty-first century and you're the owner and flipping CEO of a company. I don't think anyone would fault you for going after something or someone you wanted."

"I know. But, I went down that road with Mac and look where that got me."

"Okay, sorry. What happened?"

"He walked me to the door, we kissed good night and he promised to call me today."

"That's it?" Sherry said sounding disappointed.

"Yep, just your typical first date stuff." I said laughing to myself.

"Has he called yet?" She asked.

"No, not yet.

"Oh my gosh what if he is trying to call now and we are talking, I should let you go!"

"Sherry, I would know if he was trying to call while I was talking to you."

"Are you sure?"

"Yes."

"Well, just the same I'd better let you go."

"Okay, well I'll let you know what happens on our second date, if there is one."

"Oh, I'm sure he'll call." Sherry sounded sympathetic.

"I hope you're right." Up until this point I hadn't doubted he would call. Suddenly I was second guessing myself and thinking I might be overly confident. Yes, he had been sitting outside my house but that was before he actually had to spend an evening with me. Maybe, last night he decided I wasn't who he thought I was and decided not to call. I stared at the silent phone and lost my appetite. I threw away the remaining waffles on my plate and poured another cup of coffee.

I decided I needed to keep my mind off Ethan for a while and dedicated myself to doing the laundry and cleaning the house. I kept my phone nearby with the ringer turned up just in case. It was nearly eleven when my phone rang. "Hello?" I answered.

"Kay, it's Ethan."

My heart skipped a beat. "Hi, how are you?"

"Good, you up for a little adventure today?" He sounded excited.

"Sure, what did you have in mind?"

"I thought maybe you'd like to go spend the afternoon on the water."

It wasn't what I was expecting but I was up for it. "Okay."

"You don't get seasick, do you?"

I laughed out loud. "No, I don't get seasick."

"Okay, Jared and Logan, two members of my team are going out on a charter boat fishing today and I thought maybe you'd like to join in."

"Uh, I don't know."

"You don't like fishing. No problem, we can do something else," he back peddled a bit.

"No, I like fishing. I'm just not sure how your coworkers are going to like me tagging along on your fishing trip."

"Don't be silly, they'd love to meet you and Jared isn't happy unless he is surrounded by a crowd."

"Well, if you're sure." I wasn't but I was willing to go along.

"Of course, I'm sure." I could hear the excitement in his voice.

"When should I be ready?" I asked, gamely.

"I'm on my way."

"What, Ethan! I'm wearing yoga pants!"

"Perfect."

"No, not perfect! I have to go!" I hung up. I knew it wouldn't take him more than fifteen minutes to get to my house, I raced up stairs and started searching for something to wear. In a panic I called Sherry.

"Sherry, I need your help!" I was desperate.

"Oh, my God, what's wrong?"

"Ethan just called, and he wants to do deep sea fishing, I have no idea what to wear!" My voice was shrill as I was in full freak out mode. My panic and dismay was met with shrieks of laughter. "What. Are. You are laughing about?" I demanded. Nothing about this was funny.

"Something old that you don't mind throwing out because it's gonna smell like fish afterwards." She had a point.

"Okay, so jeans and a t-shirt."

"More like shorts and a t-shirt. It will probably be hot out there on the water with the sun beating down on the boat."

Shorts were not an option. "Have you ever done this before, Sherry?"

"Yeah I've been out a couple of times with my brother."

I nodded. "Okay, I think I have something." I heard a car door. "Gotta go, Ethan's here."

"Have fun!" She chimed.

I clicked off and stripped off my yoga pants and pulled on an old pair of jeans and ran for the door.

"Hi." I said, a little breathless.

"Hi." Ethan smiled.

"I was in the middle of changing, do you mind coming in and waiting a minute?" I asked him.

"I don't mind. You look fine," he called.

"I've been cleaning all morning in this shirt. I'm sure it smells like bleach or something."

"Okay," he shrugged.

"Make yourself at home." I bolted back upstairs. I had left my phone laying on the bed and it was buzzing. I had a text from Sherry. 'Try wearing a bathing suit under your clothes in case there is a chance for swimming.' If she thought I was going to strip down to a bathing suit in front of Ethan and his co-workers she was certifiable. I closed her message and slipped the phone in my pocket and found a more suitable t-shirt.

I found Ethan looking over some pictures on the mantel.

"Is this okay?"

"Yeah that is fine. You might want to take a spare pair of shoes though, sometimes the deck gets bloody from the bigger fish."

"Oh okay." Good to know. I ran back upstairs and was back in a minute. Thankfully, he was waiting for me at the bottom of the stairs.

"All set?" He asked.

"I think so." I said, doing a quick check.

"Okay, I told the boys we'd meet them at the marina."

"Who else is going?" I asked.

"You, me, Logan, Jared and Jared's friend who owns the boat."

"Does Jared or Logan have a girlfriend?" I asked, realizing I would be the only female on board.

Ethan laughed as he held the car door open. "Logan is too much of a loner and Jared is too much of a player." He got in on his side and started the engine. "There's a very good chance you'll be the only girl."

"Great." I forced a smile. Not that I didn't mind being around guys as the marines had certainly cured me of any inhibitions in that regard. It would have been nice to make a new girlfriend or two.

It didn't take long to get to the marina and I'm pretty sure Ethan probably broke a few traffic laws getting us there. We were greeted on the dock by Logan. "Glad you could make it." He said to Ethan.

"Logan, I'd like you to meet Kay." Ethan introduced us.

"Nice to meet you." I smiled and held out my hand.

"Glad you could join us." He smiled but the words sounded forced. Logan reminded me of Chris. He was definitely a marine, he wore his hair in a military style. He was broad shouldered. Bigger than Ethan. He also looked like he was less than happy I was there.

"Jared here yet?" Ethan asked.

"Here I am!" Jared appeared from the fly bridge.

"Jared Walker, Kay Dandridge." Ethan introduced us.

"Hey, great to meet you." He smiled. Unlike Logan, Jared seemed to genuinely mean it.

"Hi, Jared." I liked him right away.

"Anyone else joining us?" Ethan asked.

"No, I invited Stephanie, but she had other plans." Jared looked disappointed.

"Stephanie is another member of the team." Ethan explained.

"Oh, I see." I nodded.

"Well, that's okay, more beer for us, right Kay?" Jared laughed and handed me a can of beer.

"Right." I looked at it dubiously.

"What's a matter don't you like beer?" Logan said brushing past me as he climbed onto the boat.

"Beers fine, if that's all you got." I said without thinking."

"Would the lady like something stronger?" Jared asked.

"Beer's fine." I reassured him.

I looked over at Logan. He smirked and turned away. Ethan was watching the exchange and he didn't say anything but, I could tell he wasn't happy with Logan.

Jared leaned over and whispered in my ear.

"Don't pay any attention to Logan, he was born that way."

"No worries." I smiled and raised the can in a toast to Jared.

"Good girl!" He laughed. "Hey Nick, I think we're ready."

"Grab the lines, Jared."

"Can I help?" I asked.

"Sure, can you get the bow line?" Jared pointed to the front of the boat.

"No problem." Ethan and Logan both watched with interest. One with pride and the other with doubt. We were soon out of the no wake zone and headed to more open water.

Once we found our spot, Nick came down from the bridge to get everyone set up with poles and bait. It seemed that the men were well versed in this sport and didn't require any help. I suppose as the captain Nick had an obligation to ensure everyone was happy and safe.

I stood to the side and watched. There was a bit of trash talking between Ethan and Logan and I laughed quietly along the rail. I should have felt like the proverbial third wheel, but I was enjoying myself just observing the team in action together. They all seemed to know each other well and worked in concert with one another. When one of them hooked a fish, another would use the net to help bring it up onto the boat. I got a few pictures of them hamming it up with their catch.

"Hey Kay, check this one out, it's huge, I can feel it." Jared called.

I nodded and held my phone at the ready to take a picture when he pulled it aboard.

It was a very large bluefish. "Good job!" I called out.

Ethan passed the net over to Nick. "Come on over and take one of the poles." Ethan said rubbing my arm.

"No, you boys, go ahead, I don't want to get in the way."

"Don't be ridiculous. Come on." Jared insisted.

There was no use to argue so I followed him over to a chair and let him hand me a rod.

"Hey, she's a tiny thing, better strap her in." Nick advised. I didn't think of myself as tiny at five foot seven, but I was glad for the compliment.

Ethan nodded and strapped me in and started giving me instructions. "Now, for bluefish just troll so all you have to do is watch the line and wait for the hit. It's going to be hard so it might surprise you at first so be ready."

"Try not to drop the rod in the water." Logan said from behind his beer.

"I bet I can catch a bigger fish than you." I said stupidly at Logan.

He lowered his beer and smiled at me. "Really?"

"Yeah!" I boasted for some absurd reason.

Ethan and Jared stood slack jawed staring at me.

"Move over Jared." Logan said as he settled himself in to the chair next to me.

I watched him and then nodded when he had his line in the water.

"Ready to lose?" I asked, goading him.

"You tell me." He laughed.

I had no idea what I was doing but I was certainly tired of his attitude. My line got a hit first and Ethan wasn't kidding. The reel screeched as the fish grabbed my bait. I pulled back and started reeling him in. Ethan stood behind me giving me encouragement and directions on how fast or how slow to reel in the fish without losing him off the hook. Jared stood ready to help hoist it onto the deck.

By the time I landed the fish, everyone was shouting and whooping it up.

"That is a pretty big fish there, Logan." Jared chided.

"Beginners luck." Logan groused.

"Don't be a sore loser." I smiled.

"I haven't lost yet." He smiled back.

"More bait!" I called and Ethan was happy to oblige.

Even Nick was getting into it and went back to the bridge to check the positioning of the boat and see if we needed to move to get a better chance at catching something.

A few minutes later I got another hit. This one wasn't as big, and it wasn't a blue fish, so we took a picture of it and tossed it back.

"Don't worry, Logan. I understand fishing requires patience." I coached him.

"Fishing with you, maybe." He grumbled.

I laughed. Ethan wasn't finding our competition so amusing. I winked at him that everything was alright. Logan and I spent the next two hours locked in fishing combat. He did manage to catch some impressive fish but, in the end, mine just inched his out.

Nick said it was time to call it a day and asked Jared to pilot the boat back to the marina while he cleaned one of the fish and prepared it on the grill. It was ready as we docked, and we all sat enjoying our catch and drinking more beer.

"Good job, little lady." Nick said as he served me the grilled fish with corn on the cob.

"Thanks, it was really just beginners' luck. I've never been fishing before."
Logan rolled his eyes.

"Well, you can come fish on my boat anytime." Nick smiled and winked at me.

"Thank you."

"That was pretty bold challenging Logan like that." Jared laughed and raised his beer to me.

"Not really, everyone knows marines can't fish or swim worth a damn." I leveled my gaze at Logan.

Everyone fell silent and you could hear was the water lapping up against the boat. And then Logan started laughing. A genuine hearty laugh that you couldn't help but laugh along with him.

"You've got more stones than most people I know." Logan laughed.

I just smiled and sipped my beer.

"When you're not lowering your standards to drink beer what do you like?" He asked.

"I love a good single malt scotch." I smiled. "I enjoy a good bourbon, too."

Logan laughed again and slapped his thigh.

"I guess you're right boss, she's a keeper."

I glanced over at Ethan who was blushing under his five o'clock shadow.

"Is that right?" I said to him smiling.

He shrugged his shoulders. "What can I say?"

I smiled and nodded.

"Hey boss, that is like her sixth beer and she doesn't even look tipsy." Jared slurred his words ever so slightly.

"Yeah, she ain't no lightweight like you." Logan pointed.

"Piss off! You're just mad she beat you at fishing."

"She beat you too or didn't you notice?" Logan asked.

"Hey! You're right she did!" Jared suddenly looked offended.

We all ate and drank some more. We gave Nick the rest of the fish we caught and in exchange he didn't charge us for the fuel. I suspect he would get that back and then some more on the sale of this fish at the market at the other end of the marina.

The sun was setting, and we all decided to go our separate ways. Logan promised to get Jared home safely.

"That was a lot of fun." I said as we drove back to my house.

"I'm glad you liked it."

"Ethan you look worried, did you not have fun today."

"No, I had a great time. I'm just sorry Logan acted like a jerk," he grimaced.

"Oh, he was fine at the end, don't you think?" I observed.

"Yeah, I don't know what his problem was to start with."

"No big deal. As long as you like me that is all I care about." I smiled. I think the sun and the beer was starting to get to me.

Ethan looked over at me and took my hand. He raised it to his lips and kissed it.

"I like you a lot."

Chapter Twenty

Kay

Monday morning came too soon, and I knew I was going to have to answer a thousand questions from Sherry when I got to the office.

"Good Morning, Sherry." I smiled when I got off the elevator.

Sherry didn't look like her normal cheerful self.

"What's wrong?" I asked.

"Michael's waiting for you in our office. I already made coffee."

"Did he say what it is about?"

"That offer you had on the company last week," she answered.

"Alright." I had a feeling the guy from InDesign wasn't going to take no for an answer. "Morning, Michael. I trust you did not have a good weekend."

"No, not really," he said standing as I entered the room.

"Alright let's have it then," I said dropping my bag on the floor and sitting down behind my desk.

"They are upping the stakes." He said gravely.

"In what way?" I felt my shoulders tensing.

"Well, I got a call from their attorney and they intend to buy up our stocks," he said.

"Okay, well I own most of them so how is that going to help them out?"

"They are going to try to offer you way more than the stocks are worth, and the shareholders will have to vote," he went on to explain.

"Okay, so let them vote but they still can't buy my shares if I'm not willing to sell," I countered.

"Kay, this could get really ugly. I know you don't want to sell and I'm not suggesting that you do but I do want you to be prepared that this isn't just going to go away."

"What do we do? I can't let them take over this company and have all my employees lose their jobs."

"I realize that." Michael sighed.

What then?"

"I've been talking to some colleagues who have either dealt with InDesign before or have knowledge of their tactics. One of my friends used to work for the Security and Exchange Commission."

"And what does your friend from the SEC have to say?"

"He says they are dirty as hell but always stay just above the law. They haven't been able to touch them. He said it would be less hassle for you and everyone if you just sell to them."

"Seriously?"

"That is what he said."

"Well, no offense Michael, your colleague has the spine of a jellyfish."

"Hang on, that is only what he recommended." Michel defended, "He no longer works for the SEC and has his own firm and would be more than happy to work as a consultant for us to fight these guys."

"I don't know if I can trust a guy who recommends I should sell my company." I didn't have a good feeling about Michael's 'friend'.

"If you don't want to sell, he will do whatever he can to prevent that from happening."

"Do you trust him?" I needed to know. I trusted Michel and I was willing to give his friend the benefit of the doubt.

"Yes,"

"With your job?" I laid it out.

Michael went pale for a moment. "Yes."

"Then bring him in here. I want to meet him before I agree to anything."

"Okay."

"And Michael," I added leaning forward on my elbows. "We can play hardball too. Just because we aren't crooked doesn't mean we don't throw one hell of a punch. Got it?"

"Got it." Michael smiled.

I leaned back in my chair. I had no intention of selling my company or any part of it and I was pissed that I was going to have to go through this battle just to keep it.

"Oh, and Michael, call an emergency shareholders meeting. Anyone who isn't willing to fight with us, we will buy out ourselves."

"On it." And he was gone.

Michael left and I started searching my desk for a bottle of medicine. I had a migraine coming on.

"What are you looking for?" Sherry asked from the doorway.

"Migraine meds." I said rifling through my top drawer.

"Here, this is some over the counter stuff I have," she offered retrieving a bottle from her own desk.

"Thanks." I gratefully accepted them.

"What's going to happen?" Sherry fidgeted.

"We are going to fight like hell. These bastards might not take no for an answer, but they will be sorry," I said defiantly.

Sherry looked relieved and smiled. "I knew you wouldn't take this laying down."

"No, I'm not." I smiled. "Sherry do me a favor, no rush if you have time today. Can you research the number of companies that have gone from public to private?"

"Sure, thing," she replied. "In the last year or ever?"

"Ever. Thanks."

"I know this isn't the time to ask but I look forward to hearing about your weekend." She gave me a weak smile.

"When this blows over, I'll show you all the pictures. "I caught the biggest fish of the day!" I boasted.

"Good for you, girl." She smiled.

I went back to my office and poured some coffee. It was going to be a long day.

Ethan

My desk phone rang a little before noon. "Agent Craddock."

"Agent Craddock, this is James McIntyre, NCIS. We have a problem down your way, and I was hoping we could enlist the help of the FBI."

"Agent McIntyre, we'd be happy to help," I offered.

Logan looked up at me and raised his eyebrows.

"Actually, it's Director," he said knowing it would give me pause.

"Excuse me?" I asked.

"It's Director McIntyre," he clarified.

"Forgive me for asking but why is the Director of NCIS calling an FBI field office?" That made no sense, unless this was really important.

"I already spoke to your boss if that is what you are worried about and frankly, I don't have time to stand on ceremony. I have a missing NCIS agent and a dead sailor."

And there it was. "Okay, well what can we do to help?"

"This is a sensitive case, so I'll be there in a few hours to brief you."

"Yes sir, Director," I acknowledged.

"Oh, and I'll be bringing one of my agents along," he added.

"Yes, sir I believe he is on the phone with him now." I heard Logan say. "Yes sir, I'll tell him."

We both hung up.

"What's going on?" Jared asked.

"That was the Director of NCIS saying he needs our help with a case. They have a missing agent and a dead sailor," I said, half telling the team and half wondering where this was going.

"Why do they need us?" Jared continued.

"Not sure, but he said he was on his way down here to fill us in."

"The Director himself is coming?" Stephanie asked clearly surprised.

"Apparently." I nodded.

"Well, our Director just called and said to make sure we give them every courtesy and help them as much as we can."

"Wonder what is going on?" Jared looked from Logan to me.

"That is a very good question, Jared. Start looking into it. I hadn't heard anything about a dead sailor."

"They must be keeping it really quiet." Stephanie stated the obvious.

"We'll, find out as much as we can before NCIS gets here so we can be prepared." I instructed the three of them.

We all got to work. I sent Kay a text explaining I'd be tied up tonight and would call when I could. I had a feeling that might not be for a while.

Chapter Twenty-One
Kay

It was Thursday evening and I had barely heard from Ethan all week. I also hadn't heard from Mac. I knew Ethan's team had a big case they were working on, but he couldn't give me any details. I didn't need them. I had my own issues to deal with this week. I had made a tender offer to my other shareholders in the company. I wanted to take the company from public to private to try and protect it from the wolves at InDesign. I didn't care how much they were offering, and I knew they were willing to pay an outrageous sum to try and buy the stocks that weren't held by me. Going private would put the expansion into the medical arena nearly impossible but I was willing to give that up before I was willing to give up the company.

The tender offer had been met with mixed results. Some shareholders were willing to sell, and others were offended assuming that I didn't trust them to hold out against a takeover. At this point I couldn't be worried about feelings. I had employees and their families in three cities to worry about. It had been a long week and it was far from over.

I decided the least I could do was take a couple of pizzas to Ethan and his team on my way home. I called in the order to pick up and headed out of the office for the night.

"Sherry, go home."

"What about you?" Sherry looked up for her computer.

"I'm going to pick up a pizza and go home myself." It was a half truth.

"Okay then, I'll see you in the morning." She picked up her purse and coat as she headed for the elevators.

When I arrived at Ethan's office there were a lot more cars in the parking lot and I hoped I had brought enough pizza. Maybe they had other teams working late tonight.

I walked in the door and was greeted by Logan. "Kay what are you doing here?" I surprised him. That made me smile.

"It is always a pleasure to see you, Logan."

"I mean, we're a bit busy," he continued.

"So, I heard. That is why I am dropping off pizza," I replied, pushing my care package ahead of me.

"Thank you." Jared said as he stepped into the bullpen. "Is what Logan meant to say."

"I know it is, he just says it differently than other people." I smiled at Jared.

"We've tried retraining him and it just doesn't seem to work." He looked down and shook his head in mock dismay.

"Hey, you two I'm sitting right here." Logan growled.

"I brought three, I hope that is enough. One veggie for Stephanie, pepperoni for normal people and then a meat-lovers for Logan."

"That was very thoughtful." Jared smiled.

As sweet as Jared was, I could see tension in his face.

"Well, I won't keep you. I know you're busy." I turned to leave.

"Kay?" Ethan stepped out of what appeared to be a conference room. "What are you doing here."

I glanced over at Logan. "You're a bad influence on him."

He just grinned and shrugged.

"I'm not staying, I just dropped of a snack."

"Thank you so much." Ethan stepped over and kissed my forehead.

There was a coughing sound from behind Ethan. "Oh, I'm sorry." Ethan stepped aside.

I stood face to face with Mac. I felt the blood drain from my face and my knees felt weak.

"Kay Dandridge, James McIntyre, NCIS. We have a joint operation we are working on this week" I heard most of what he said, my mind was racing to find a graceful way to leave as quickly as possible.

"Really?" I said. My mouth felt like it was full of cotton.

"Ms. Dandridge it is a pleasure to see you again," he said, reaching out his hand.

I was sure it was anything but, I was certain he hadn't missed the kiss from Ethan. This is not at all how I wanted this to happen. I took his hand, weakly, hoping he didn't notice.

"You two have met?" Ethan looked surprised.

Logan's looked turned dark.

"Yes, I met Ms. Dandridge through her grandfather, and she managed to beat me rather badly in a friendly game of poker."

"It was just beginners' luck." I squeaked. I heard Logan make a noise that sounded like a snort.

"Well, I will let you all get back to work. I'm sure you're terribly busy." I started backing towards the door as quickly as decorum would allow.

"Okay, I'll call when I can, Kay." Ethan was saying.

"I understand. Not to worry, things are crazy this week in my world." I put my hand up to wave. "Enjoy the pizza."

Ethan smiled and turned back to the team. Only Mac stood watching me leave. I hated myself and I had no idea what to say or do. I wanted to say I was sorry, for what? I just held his gaze until I finally looked away and walked towards my car.

I wondered how long he had been in town and what if anything he might have said to Ethan. A million thoughts raced through my mind. I was second guessing everything. Should I have called Mac when I got back home and told him I met someone? I had no commitment to him. Still I hadn't intended to hurt him if he was even hurt? Maybe he didn't care. I was going to drive myself nuts with this, I needed to relax.

I put the car in the garage and went in the house for a nice hot bath and maybe a little splash of scotch. I took my phone with me in hopes that Ethan might text me later. An hour later, the bathwater was cold, and I needed another scotch. I went downstairs and poured another drink. Then I decided to just take the bottle back upstairs with me. I was in the mood for a movie to help me forget what an ass I was making of myself.

I needed to talk to Ethan, and I needed to explain things to him before Mac did and gave him the wrong impression. But I wanted to talk to Mac, as well. I checked the time. It was nearly midnight. Surely, they weren't still working. Maybe Ethan was sleeping at the office or maybe he was just too tired to call when he got home. I laid back on the bed and tried not to think about it. I pressed the button for another movie.

Chapter Twenty-Two
Ethan

It was nearly one o'clock in the morning and too late to call Kay when I got home so I sent her a text with a promise to call her the next day. I didn't get a reply, she was probably already asleep. At least I hoped she was. I missed her and I felt very uncomfortable not knowing how she was doing. I had a bad feeling in my gut, and I couldn't shake it. I laid down across the bed trying to chase the thoughts from my mind. When I opened them again it was six in the morning the sun should have been up instead there was a strange light in the sky like there were too many clouds for the sun this morning and it cast a gray pallor over everything. It reminded me of the color of worn gravestones, and it sent a chill down my spine. I'd been working too late and getting too little sleep and my mind was starting to go to some dark places.

I showered, changed, and headed back to work. Mac met me in the parking lot.

"Couldn't sleep either?" he asked.

"No, not really." I returned his look.

He nodded and we walked into the office. I liked Mac but he didn't have to be here. He had his team from the Navy base. Plus the agent he brought with him from D.C. Mac was a marine and he had a man missing. He wasn't going back to his office until that man was found. I had to admire his grit and his ethics.

Logan came in a few minutes later, looking like the rest of us felt. "Did you even try to sleep last night?" I asked.

"No, why did you?" Was his reply.

"I passed out in my clothes and woke up this morning." I answered.

He nodded and headed to the kitchen to make coffee.

I walked around turning on all the computers and monitors and bringing everything to life so we could get started for the day. I felt like we were getting close to something, but I wasn't sure what. I wasn't holding out a lot of hope for the missing agent. There hadn't been a ransom demand or any contact from anyone, so I didn't believe it was a kidnapping. Although, I hadn't ruled out that he had been taken, I feared it may have been for purposes of revenge rather than a means to an end.

I sent Kay a quick text knowing she was usually up by now. No reply. I wondered if she was upset about something. Surely, she knew Logan well enough to not pay any attention to him and I hoped he hadn't offended her last night when she stopped by. Although, she didn't seem like herself and she seemed in a hurry to leave. I frowned at my phone.

"Everything alright?" Logan asked returning with a cup of coffee.

"Yeah." I said stuffing the phone in my pocket.

The forensic team popped in on the screens about nine o'clock. "Agent Craddock, I think we may have something."

"Okay, what?" I asked not feeling particularly patient this morning.

"According to the GPS records from his phone it appears that Agent Foster made a couple of trips out to an old hunting lodge recently and when we investigated the lodge, we found the property traces back to this man."

An image flashed up on the screen.

"Do you know who that is?" I asked Mac.

"Yes, I do."

We all waited.

"That is Walter Simmons, a former NCIS agent. He was fired ten years ago and is believed to be working for the highest bidder these days."

"Doing what?" Logan asked.

"Computer hacking."

"Why would Agent Foster contact him?" I asked.

"Because Agent Foster was investigating Simmons." Mac and stared down at the floor as if he was trying to see something not there.

"So, they set up a meet?" Logan asked.

"I don't know. I didn't see anything in the case notes that indicated he set up a meet." Mac looked worried.

"I've looked through them all I didn't see anything." Stephanie offered confirmation.

"Alright team, let's go." I said. "Send me the directions to the cabin and meet us there."

A moment later my phone beeped with a notification that the directions had been received. We all headed out to the parking lot. It was going to be a two-hour drive to get out to the cabin in the mountains. Logan drove, while Mac, his case agent and I discussed what he knew about Simmons.

Stephanie was riding with Jared and working the laptop for any information that might help us. "Stephanie, I need to know if this place is going to be booby-trapped or something."

"On it, I'll have to be a lot closer to do us much good. I need to see if there is a Wi-Fi system or anything on site," she replied.

"Understood, stay on it." I nodded.

We finally found the place. It was well hidden among the mature trees and some overgrowth. The place looked like it was a hundred years old. We all stepped out of the vehicles and looked around.

"Everyone move very carefully. We don't know if this is a trap or not." I ordered. "Stephanie you got anything?"

"I'm not picking up any wireless signals," she whispered.

"Okay, what about cell phone signals?" I wanted to be damned sure we weren't going to get blown up walking up on the porch.

"Nothing. That just means that if there is someone up there either they don't have a cell phone, or it is turned off."

"Stay alert," Mac called out and started advancing forward.

I motioned for Jared and Logan to take the back. Stephanie and Mac's agent covered the sides and Mac and I headed for the front door.

My eyes swept the ground and the steps to the porch and I stepped up gingerly.

"Hello! FBI anyone home?" I called out.

"NCIS! Open the door!" Mac yelled.

We both waited. No response. He nodded and we both flanked the door.

"FBI and NCIS, anyone home?"

Again, no response so I knocked and yelled again. Three times, no response. I nodded to Mac as I reached for the door handle and pushed the door open. The stench from inside escaped out the door as soon as it was open.

"Ah!" I used my arm to cover my mouth and nose. I entered and Mac followed in behind me.

Logan and Jared breached the back of the cabin and were backing out from the stench. I held my hand for them to stay back. The cabin wasn't that big, and we didn't need to be tripping over each other. Mac and I found the source of the smell in the back bedroom. Agent Foster was tied to a chair with a gag in his mouth.

We called the cabin clear and instructed everyone to stay out and let the forensic team come in and do their work. Once outside Mac and I stood taking in deep breaths of clean air.

"I'm sorry about your man." I said to Mac.

"Thanks." Mac's face was grim.

"Now we just have to find out who did it."

"Yeah." He agreed.

My cell phone rang. "Agent Craddock."

"Is this Ethan?" A woman's voice asked.

"Yes, this is Ethan Craddock, who's this?"

"My name is Sherry; you don't know me. I work for Kay Dandridge."

Her voice was shaky, and she sounded upset. The hair on my arms stood up. "Sherry, what's wrong?"

"Kay mentioned you were friends and you worked for the FBI," she said, making it clear this was not a social call.

"That's right, what's wrong? Has something happened to Kay?"

"I'm not sure, well yes, I am. I'm sorry to bother you. Kay didn't come to work today. She isn't answering her phone and when Eddie went to the house, she wasn't there but her car was in the garage." The words came in a rush.

"Okay, slow down, Sherry. Did Eddie see anything else at the house? Was the door open or anything like that?"

"I'm not sure," she said, her voice cracking.

I could tell Sherry was on the verge of crying. Frankly, I was surprised at how calm I sounded because my adrenaline was pumping hard. I turned back towards the cabin.

"Hang on, Sherry." I held the phone away from my face. "Logan! Keys!"
Logan jogged over.

"Everything okay, boss?"

"No, I need the keys to the SUV. You'll have to ride back with Jared."

"No problem." He handed me the keys. "Anything I can do?"

"Not right now." I looked at Mac. "Sorry man, something's come up and
I gotta go."

"No problem." Mac turned back to the task at hand.

I started jogging to the SUV. "Sherry, you still there?"

"I'm here," she squeaked.

I could tell she was crying. "Listen, I'm two hours away but I am driving
back right now. Can you have Eddie meet me at Kay's house?"

"Yes, of course."

"Okay, then I will come see you at the office. Are you sure she just didn't
take the day off?" I needed to check.

"No, Kay has never taken a day off in four years and if she wasn't feeling
well, she would have called me or something." A sob escaped her lips. She was
starting to come apart.

"Hang on, I'm on my way." I assured her.

I turned on the sirens as soon as I hit the interstate. I don't think I have
ever driven so fast in my life. I had a bad feeling. I thought it had to do with
the case we had been working on and I had been right when we had found
Agent Foster dead which is what we all feared. But Kay was missing? My
mind was reeling, and I couldn't let anything happen to her. I knew I couldn't
live without her. The six years I had been without her had been dark times
for me, but those days wouldn't compare to what my life would be like now
if something were to happen to her.

In front of Kay's house there was a faded gray Malibu with local
government tags. I assumed the local police had already arrived. I presumed
the man standing on Kay's porch was Eddie.

"Eddie?" I showed my badge.

"Yes, sir. You Ethan?" He, too, was clearly shaken.

"I am." We shook hands. "Eddie, did you touch anything in the house?"

"Only a few doors," he said.

"Okay, do you remember which ones?" I asked fishing latex gloves from my pocket.

"Yes, sir."

"Okay, good." I let my hand fall of his shoulder trying to be comforting. Kay had told me how much Eddie cared for her as if she were one of his own children. "Are the local police inside?"

"Yes." He nodded towards the street as a marked police car pulled up. The officer took note of the Malibu and walked up on the porch.

"Is the detective here?"

I looked to Eddie.

"Yes."

"Did you call it in?" The officer asked Eddie while taking out a small notebook and pen.

"No, Ms. Dandridge's secretary called the police after she had me come over to check on Ms. Dandridge and I found she wasn't here."

"And what about you?" The officer directed his attention to me.

I pulled out my badge. "Agent Craddock."

"What's your interest in this?" he inquired.

I thought about my response. I had no jurisdiction here and I didn't want to ruin the chance of being involved if there was something to investigate.

"Ms. Dandridge has information she shares with the FBI."

"So, she's a witness for you?"

"No, not exactly." I hedged.

"And informant, then?" he pursued.

"Something like that." I didn't want to outright lie, and I wanted my options open.

The officer looked frustrated. "So how did you find out about Ms. Dandridge this morning?"

"I got a phone call from her secretary as well," I told him.

The officer nodded and made notes. Before he could ask any more questions and I dug myself into a hole that I couldn't get out of, the detective stepped out onto the porch.

"Well, it seems like Ms. Dandridge was popular."

I didn't like his attitude.

"Ms. Dandridge is important to a lot of people, Detective."

"Oh, I see. Does that mean the FBI is taking over this investigation? If you are, good luck. I have other things to do today." He started for the steps.

"Where are you going? Aren't you going to do something to find Kay?" Eddie demanded.

"You've got a hot shot FBI agent here, what do you need me for?" The detective asked.

I pulled my cell phone from my pocket. I didn't want to make this call, but I was angry. While I punched the speed dial number for Chief Corey, Eddie followed the detective down the steps.

The officer who had been all business before now looked apologetic. I walked down the steps and held out the phone. It was on speaker.

"This is Chief Corey, which of my detectives am I talking to?"

"This is Detective O'Reilly, Chief." The detective looked decidedly pale.

"I understand you just handed a case over to the FBI because you are too busy?

"Did you just tell Agent Craddock if he wanted the case he could have it and good luck."

"Well, I..." he stammered.

"Be in my office in half an hour and bring Agent Craddock with you," the Chief ordered.

"Yes, sir. Agent Craddock is in charge of the investigation until further notice."

"Yes, sir." O'Reilly gave me a contemptuous look.

"I'll see you soon Chief." I said taking the phone off speaker. I clicked off the call and put the phone back in my pocket.

"Officer...?" I searched for his name tag on this uniform.

"Officer Spivey, sir."

"Office Spivey, can you please secure the scene until I return. No one goes in or out. Got it?" I demanded.

"Yes, sir." He acknowledged.

I turned back to Eddie. "Go back to the office and stay with Sherry."

"Okay." Eddie was reluctant but he walked to his car and left.

I turned back to the Detective, "Shall we?" I glared.

He mumbled something and headed for his car.

I climbed into the SUV and drove to police headquarters.

The chief called us in one at a time. I went first.

"Ethan, you want to explain to me what is going on?" He asked trying to get a handle on the situation.

"I got a call from Ms. Dandridge's secretary telling me she was missing and that she hadn't shown up for work and couldn't be reached by text or phone call."

"And why would she call you?" This was going to be a problem.

"Maybe she thought the FBI investigated kidnappings?" I hedged.

"It's possible but that isn't the reason is it?" He saw right through it.

"Probably not." I admitted.

"You going to tell me the reason?" he pressed.

I thought about that answer carefully before answering. "Jim, we've been friends a long time and that has earned you the right to hear the truth."

"I would hope so," he agreed.

"Kay and I are friends," I began.

"Close friends?"

"Not as close as I'd like to be, but yeah, I guess you could say close friends." I was honest.

"You know the FBI doesn't have jurisdiction on this case, at least not yet," he clarified.

"I know that."

"Still Detective O'Reilly was out of line and our friendship affords you some latitude."

"Thank you." I was feeling a little better, I had hoped Jim wouldn't toss me off the case outright, which he had every right to do.

"I'll assign another detective and tell him this is a joint investigation. Please understand that I will recommend that you back off if there is no FBI jurisdiction and you cross the lines of our friendship. Understood?"

"Thank you." I said and shook his hand.

"Send that idiot O'Reilly in here, would you?"

I nodded on my way out.

I could hear Jim's voice on my way out into the hallway.

I drove back to Kay's house. Some of the neighbors were starting to gather on the sidewalk. The garden district was an old historic neighborhood that had once been home to the captains of local industry and companies like the shipyard, Sunray Bank, the Point Herald newspaper. The architecture of the homes reflected the heyday of a bygone era. Some of the homes were still owned by family members like Kay's. Everyone who lived in the garden district even if they lived in the smaller carriage houses took pride in the history here. The streets were beautifully maintained by the garden club as well as the parks and the cemetery which was also on the historic registry. The homes were well maintained, and it was a quiet area where the neighbors knew each other and watched out for each other.

I climbed out of the SUV and walked over to the small crowd and introduced myself. "Your neighbor Kay Dandridge is missing, and we believe she disappeared sometime last night. Did anyone see or hear anything?" There were several heads shaking with people talking among themselves.

"Does anyone here live next door?" I asked.

An elderly lady stepped forward. "I do."

"Thank you," I smiled at her warmly. "Would you mind if I asked you a few questions?"

"No, I suppose not."

I led her away from the small group. "Have you lived here long?"

"My whole life. I was born in a house three streets over."

I smiled. "Then you are the exact person I need to talk to." I smiled again. "Would you care to sit down?"

"I love to but not in that thing." She pointed to the SUV. "Why don't you come inside?"

I nodded and followed her down the sidewalk to the house on the west side of Kay's property.

Kay's property was so large that the houses were not close together and I suspected there was little chance that this woman could have seen Kay's house through the row of evergreen trees that provided privacy between the two lots.

"Let me see your ID again." She said before we ascended the steps up to her porch.

I smiled and showed her my badge and the photo ID that went with it.

She nodded approvingly. "You care for some tea?"

"That would be nice." I smiled again. "I'll just wait here on the porch." I indicated the chairs and the swing.

She nodded and went inside.

I sat down and looked out at the property. Even on the porch she likely didn't have a good view of anything over at Kay's house.

She returned with a tray that held a pitcher and two glasses. "Here let me help you." I stood up and took the tray.

"Oh, thank you, you're such a gentleman."

I smiled. I learned a long time ago, if you treat people like they are your own neighbor they will tell you things they wouldn't if you try throwing your badge around.

She poured iced tea into each of the glasses.

"Hmm, that is excellent." I said enjoying the sweet tea.

She nodded.

"Now Ms., uh" I realized I didn't know her name.

"Ms. Fowler," she provided.

"Ms. Fowler, do you know Kay Dandridge?" I asked gently.

"Oh yes, I've known her family since before she was born." She smiled.

"Do you talk to Kay regularly?" I went on.

"Oh yes, absolutely. She comes over a couple of times a week to check on me. She is such a sweet thing. She takes me shopping sometimes on the weekend. I can't drive anymore, and I have most things delivered these days. I still like to get out and Kay takes me anywhere I want to go."

I smiled. I was surprised not by the fact that Kay was kind. I knew she was a good person with a good heart, but it was surprising to me how little I knew about her when I felt like I knew her my whole life.

"Have you spoken to her recently?"

"On Wednesday she called me in the afternoon, and she said she would be working late but wanted to know if I needed anything." Ms. Fowler shook her head. "She is such a sweet person, young people aren't like that these days, she had good home training." Ms. Fowler nodded.

"Do you know of anyone that would want to harm her?"

"I can't think of a soul. She takes care of everyone, not just me and she helps whoever she can. One of the young families a few streets over in one of the carriages houses fell on hard times. The husband died young of cancer and left his wife with two little boys."

"What did Kay do for them?" I asked.

"Well, the mom had been a stay at home mom and needed a job. So, Kay got her a job at her company with flexible hours so she could get the boys to and from school and then Kay set up a college fund for each of them," she told me.

"Have you seen anything odd lately, anyone hanging around that looked out of place?"

"Besides you?"

I stared at her dumbfounded for a moment.

"Oh yes, I saw you parked across the street." She laughed. It was the laugh of a young woman and it belied her age.

I felt a little embarrassed. "I assure you I mean no harm to Kay."

"Oh, I know. I mentioned it to Kay, and she explained it all to me." She gave me a sly wink.

I was tongued tied.

"Now that you mention it. I thought I saw someone standing in the path between here and Kay's house."

"The path?" I was curious. I had never noticed a path between the houses.

"Yes, there is a garden path that Kay put in so that we can get to one another's house more easily than we can from the street."

"Can you show me?"

"Of course, follow me." She led me through the house, which was as big as Kay's if not bigger and out the back door and into the garden. There was a place where one of the trees had been removed and a little gate installed. The path was paved and level. No chance of footprints.

"It used to be oyster shells, but Kay was afraid I'd fall and break a hip or something, so she had it paved."

I laughed. "That sounds like her." "Okay, Ms. Fowler you stay here." I instructed and I walked down the back steps to see if anyone had stepped off the path and left a footprint. I walked slowly examining the area looking for any signs at all. I didn't see any, but I would let the forensics unit check the area just to be sure.

I walked back to the back porch.

"Anything?" Ms. Fowler asked.

"No, I'm afraid not," I told her

"Damn," she said.

Her words surprised me, and I smiled. "Do you have cameras?" I asked looking up at the house.

"Oh yes, I forget about those things, come this way." She suddenly became very animated.

She nearly danced with excitement and I followed her back into the house.

"Kay installed these things and she checks them when she comes over. She says it won't stop anyone from breaking in, but it might help catch the people if they do break in."

"She's right. Do you have many break-ins over here?"

"No, she said you can't be too careful. I asked her if I should have a gun, but she said no." Ms. Fowler looked disappointed.

"That is probably for the best." I reassured her. "Do you know if Kay has a gun?"

"Well, I've never seen it, but I would suspect she would."

I wondered why she thought that but didn't ask. That could wait. "Anything else you can think of that seemed out of place this week?"

She looked at the floor in thought. "No, I can't think of anything."

"Okay, I'm going to have some people from the local police department come over and look at your cameras, is that okay?"

"Anything to help Kay." She was very concerned for Kay's wellbeing.

"Thank you. And if you ever need anything just call me. I live over in the carriage section."

"Oh, I knew you were a good boy." She beamed when I told her I lived over in the section of the garden district that had once been where the higher paid blue-collar workers of the shipyard and some of the middle management types had lived back in the twenties and thirties. My house had once belonged to one of the apprentice school instructors. Like I said, we all take pride in our section of the city.

I used the front sidewalk to walk back over to Kay's house. By now the forensic unit had shown up and a new detective seemed to be in charge. I approached him slowly and held up my badge.

"Ah, Agent Craddock, I was told to expect you." He held out his hand. He was much younger than O'Reilly, close to Jared's age mid to late twenties.

"I'm Detective Charlie Cavanaugh."

"Have you been inside yet?" he asked

"No, not yet."

"Come on in." He waved and led the way.

"You can call me Ethan." I said as I walked around the first floor inspecting every room looking for signs of an intruder. "Was the security system active when you came in?"

"No." Detective Cavanaugh shook his head.

I inspected the control panel by the door and then proceeded upstairs. There were no signs of a struggle and the only thing that looked out of place was the empty scotch bottle. I bagged that and the empty glass.

"I assume your forensic team is going through everything," I said.

"Yes, I've been instructed to make sure your team is included in the findings," he reassured me.

"Do you mind if I have one of my team members join you? She has a lot of experience with missing persons cases," I asked, hoping I could get Andria on this case.

"We'd appreciate the help. We're stretched a little thin right now," he told me.

"Okay. Thank you." I took the evidence out to the car and then pulled out my cell phone.

"Forensic Unit."

"This is Agent Craddock, is Andria there?" I waited until I heard the phone click.

"Ethan?"

"Andria, I need you over at 9 Westover Street with a full kit," I told her.

"What? I thought you were out in Nelson County with the rest of the team." She as surprised.

"I got pulled back for another case. This one is urgent, a possible missing person. Can you meet me here?" I hoped.

"On my way," she said.

It took Andria thirty minutes to get to Kay's house.

"Okay," she said upon entering the living room. "What are we looking for?"

"Well the occupant of the house lives alone and didn't show up for work today." I said trying to not let my anger and stress show.

"We don't know if she left of her own accord or not, but we do know she is not answering her cell phone and she didn't let anyone know she wouldn't be at work today."

"Okay, got it." Andria went to work introducing herself to the team that was already there and began helping them search for clues as to what happened to Kay.

I was certain the house was in good hands, so I left go to Kay's office and talk to Sherry.

***

The headquarters for Port City Industries was impressive, and I took the elevator up to Kay's office.

An attractive woman about Kay's age was sitting at a reception desk. Her eyes were red from crying.

"Excuse me. I'm looking for Sherry?" I offered.

"I'm Sherry," she said with a frightened look on her face.

"I'm Ethan, we spoke on the phone."

"Oh!" She looked relieved and got up and walked around the desk.

"I'm so sorry to have bothered you, I just didn't know who else to call. This isn't like Kay, even if she needed a day off, she would have told me."

"I'm sure she would have." I said in a comforting voice, at least I hope I sounded comforting. "Is there somewhere we can talk in private?"

"Kay's office?" She pointed to the closed door next to where we were standing.

"Yes, that will be fine," I said. I stepped inside and looked around. I don't know what I was expecting frankly but somehow it wasn't this.

"Has anyone else been in here this morning? Or last night?" I asked looking around the office. It was well appointed with very few personal effects. The pictures were of employees, company awards. There was nothing of the woman who normally occupied this office.

"No one comes in here without my knowing it. If I'm the last one to leave, I lock it. If Kay is the last one out, she locks it. She and I are the only ones with keys."

"What about janitorial staff?"

"They come early in the morning and Kay puts her trash can outside the door if it needs to be emptied."

"Okay, so no one else has a key. Are you sure?"

She looked thoughtful. "Eddie might." She looked stricken that she didn't know the answer.

"That's okay, I'll check with Eddie later."

"He would never do anything to hurt her, she treats her like one of his own children. He worships her."

"I don't believe Eddie would do anything to Kay." I tried to reassure her.

"Is there anyone that might hold a grudge against her?" I motioned for Sherry to sit down. "Has she fired anyone lately that might want to get back at her?"

"No, the last person she let go was three years ago or more and that was Elliot," she told me.

"Who is Elliott?" I didn't remember Kay ever mentioning anyone by the name.

"He was the corporate attorney when her father ran the company and he and Kay didn't really see eye to eye. Elliot was old school and didn't like Kay's new ideas for the company. Michael was his junior attorney, so she encouraged Elliot to retire and then she promoted Michael to the lead corporate attorney."

"And was Elliot bitter?" I asked.

"I don't think he was happy, but I wouldn't say he was bitter. He received an excellent retirement package and I know they still exchange Christmas cards."

Sherry was wringing her hands in her lap. She was nervous about something.

"Okay, so not Elliott, anyone else? Has she talked about anyone new lately, anything stressful here at the office?"

"Well, there is this company that is trying to buy us out. They are being really aggressive about it, too," he said, looking a bit secretive.

"What do you mean, aggressive?" I was surprised to hear this; Kay had only mentioned there had been an offer and she didn't intend to sell.

"When did this start?" I wanted to know.

"Last week, I think."

"What else can you tell me about it?"

"Well, not too much. Kay said she would never sell, and she had me researching companies that are traded publicly that went private."

"Can they do that?" I was surprised.

"Oh yes, it can be done, it requires Kay to buy out all the other shareholders," she said with wide, honest eyes.

"Who currently owns the majority of the stock?" I thought I knew.

"Kay does and before that her father did. There are about ten other shareholders in the company and I know she made them offers this week."

I could see she was very thorough. "Do you know if any of the sales have gone through?"

"I'm sorry, I don't." She shook her head. "Michael would know, you should talk to him."

"Michael?"

"Our attorney, the one that replaced Elliott." Sherry smiled.

"And do Michael and Kay see, eye to eye?"

"Oh yes, Michael and Kay are very close, professionally I mean." She added quickly.

"He was the one she called after the attack."

"I'm sorry, what attack?"

Kay had never mentioned Michael. I was beginning to realize I still had a lot to learn about Kay.

"Oh, maybe I shouldn't say anything. If Kay hasn't told you about it yet."

"Why? Sherry, what attack?" This was from left field.

"It was back right after her mother passed away and she was still working overseas."

So right after I had met her, putting the timeline together in my head.

"Ethan, I really am not sure I should be the one to tell you this story." She was very protective of Kay's privacy.

"She told me she was injured while she was in Afghanistan, but she didn't give me any details. Sherry, was the attack something that might have anything to do with her current disappearance?"

"I don't think so. The attack wasn't aimed at her personally. It was part of the war and she was embedded with a company of marines and was injured when they were attacked." "Well, Kay was one of the first ones hit and she nearly died but she still managed to save the rest of them. Imagine a bunch of marines getting saved by a photojournalist!" Sherry laughed. "They gave her the Medal of Freedom and everything!" She beamed.

"She was awarded the Medal of Freedom by the President of the United States?"

"Oh yes, everyone was quite proud of her."

"How did she take it?" I had a feeling Kay wasn't quite so proud.

"She threw one heck of a fuss and said she didn't want it and said she didn't deserve it." Sherry shook her head. "It was quite the scene and she and her grandfather didn't talk for a while after that."

"Her grandfather?"

"Yeah, he insisted she accept the medal and she refused."

"I see. So, what did Michael have to do with any of this?"

"Well, Kay wasn't sure if she was going to make it or not. She called Michael over to Germany where she was in the hospital to draw up papers to deal with the company and other things in case she died."

"And is that when she retired Elliott?"

"It was right after that yes, when she came home."

"Well, I'll lknow more after I speak to Michael."

"Oh dear, I just realized I don't think he knows Kay is missing. He has been in meetings all morning."

"Is that normal?"

"Well, yes and no. His meetings usually don't start until ten because he and Kay block out time each morning to talk."

"About what?" I was curious.

"Oh, anything really." She waved her hands and sighed.

"I make the coffee you see, and when Kay arrives, she and I sit down together and go over her schedule for the day. Then Michael comes in and they talk about anything of a legal nature and then they both start their meetings for the day. Sometimes they are in the same meetings."

"And today?"

"Well, everyone's schedule has been off this weekend because of the takeover of the business, so Michael wasn't scheduled to be here this morning. He is meeting with the bank."

"Okay, do you have access to his calendar? Can you tell me when he will be back? I'd like to talk to him and find out more about this take over thing."

"Sure." Sherry got up and went back to her own desk.

"He should be back here within the hour."

"Okay, can you tell me the name of the company wanting to take over Port City?"

"InDesign, is the name of the company."

I took out my cell and called Stephanie.

"Boss, you okay?" she sounded concerned.

"Yeah, I'm fine, but we have another case," I told her.

"When it rains it pours." Stephanie recited.

"No kidding. Listen get everything you can on a company called InDesign and their take over strategy or any companies they have bought out. Do a deep dive, okay?" I instructed.

"Sure, no problem."

"Thanks." I said, then hung up.

"Ethan?" Sherry poked her head back into Kay's office.

"Yes?"

"Michael is here."

Sherry stood aside and a middle-aged man dressed in a suit that probably cost as much has my car walked in and gave Sherry a questioning look. He was what most women would probably consider attractive.

"Sherry what's going on?" he asked looking from me to her.

"Mr. Nichols? I'm Agent Craddock, FBI." I stepped forward and offered my hand.

"FBI?" He shook my hand.

"When was the last time you talked to Kay?"

"Kay, oh my God, what's happened?"

"We don't know that anything has happened yet." I motioned to a chair. "Please sit down." Sherry quietly closed the door.

I sat in the chair next to him and turned it, so we were facing each other.

"Has something happened to Kay?" he asked directly.

"No one seems to be able to find her," I told him.

"And that involves the FBI?" He was understandably curious.

"I'm a friend of Kay's so I'm helping out for the moment."

"Oh, okay. Let me think." Michael put his head in his hand. "Yesterday. I talked to her yesterday."

"In person or on the phone?"

"Both."

"When was the last time you talked to her? Was it after work? In person?"

"It was on the phone and she was here in the office."

"What did you talk about?"

"A company is trying to buy us out and we are fighting them. I have been interviewing consultants to help us fight the take over."

"Were you aware that she tendered an offer yesterday to the other shareholders?"

"Yes," He looked at me curiously.

"And how'd that go?"

"Well, it was met with mixed reviews, but I think they all agreed in the end."

"Why is that?"

"Because they care about the company too and I think that will prevail over greed," he analyzed.

"You think their stocks would go up with this new company?"

"No, but I think the new company will offer them more for their shares than Kay can."

"I see." I didn't understand the details, but I was getting the gist.

"Anyone of the shareholders upset enough to do her harm over the offer?"

"Absolutely not!" he declared.

"You seem pretty sure."

"I know all of those people and they've been around since her father ran the company. They are loyal to Port City Manufacturers and Kay?"

"I hope you're right." I paused, "What do you know about this InDesign company?"

"Well, they are a bit sketchy. I can't prove anything. No one seems to be able to. But they don't have a reputation for being the most transparent company. I have a friend that used to work at the SEC, and he investigated them several times. They were always too smart to get caught."

"Do you think they would harm Kay?"

Michael looked thoughtful. "Well if they found out about the tender offer, they might as she is the largest shareholder. And if she isn't able to follow through on her offer to the others then they wouldn't have anything stopping them from taking over the company."

I had suspected as much.

"Mr. Nichols, you need to consider the possibility if they have harmed Kay you could be in danger as well."

He looked at me in surprise. "Do you really think so?"

"I'm not sure of anything yet, so we can't rule it out."

I took out my cellphone and called Logan. "Logan, it's Ethan."

"Hey man, what is going on? Why'd you take off like that?" Logan asked.

"Kay is missing, and we think she may have been kidnapped," I told him.

"Are you serious?" He was dumbfounded.

"Yeah, I've been to her house and Andria is there now. And I'm at Kay's office now. Listen, I think the corporate attorney may be in danger as well. Can you come get him and take him to a safe house?"

"On it. I'll be there soon."

I clicked off.

"It is going to take a few minutes for my agent to get here. He has to open up the safe house and then come and get you."

"Agent Craddock, I appreciate your concern, but it is going to be very hard for me to work from a safe house. If we just stop our efforts to fight back against InDesign they will take over for sure, in fact, that may even be their plan. With Kay out of the way they may think it would be easier to take over the company."

"Alright, I'm listening." I sat back down.

"I think maybe Sherry should hear some of this."

I nodded for him to bring Sherry back into the room.

Michael got up and pressed a button on Kay's phone. "Sherry can you join us?"

A moment later the door opened and Sherry came in with a pad.

"Have a seat," I said.

"Okay, so at the moment the facts are this...." I started.

"Kay is missing from her home. She disappeared in the last twelve hours or so. We have no idea who took her or why if she was even taken."

Sherry started to protest so I held up my hand to stop her. "We suspect that her disappearance has something to do with the attempt to take over the company."

I paused and looked at the two of them. They both nodded.

"If we follow this assumption then Michael, like I said before, you could be in danger as well."

"Why?" Sherry asked.

"Well, if our assumption is correct then the kidnappers may believe a takeover will be easier without the CEO and major shareholder of the company." I continued. "And if they know or believe that Michael has the ability to act on behalf of Kay, then logically, they will need to remove him from the picture as well."

Sherry gasped.

"I'd like Michael to stay in a safe house and I understand your concerns about effectively being able to fight this take over while in a secure location."

"So, what do we do?" Sherry asked.

"That is a good question." I agreed.

"Well, I can tell you if we lose this company before we find Kay, she will be devastated. We can't lose the company." Michael protested.

"We have to find Kay." I argued. "And as an FBI agent she is my only concern."

"As a friend?" Sherry asked.

Michael looked from Sherry to me, clearly confused and interested where this was leading.

I sighed. "As a friend, I'll do everything I can to help ensure that those who can save the company are able. But," I raised my hand before Michael could speak. "My first priority is keeping you safe and finding Kay."

"Understood," Sherry said.

"Does that mean I don't have to stay in a safe house?" Michael asked.

"No, it means you will stay in the safe house and when you leave the safe house you will have an agent with you at all times."

Michaels shoulders slumped.

"Don't even think about arguing." I looked him in the eye.

"Wouldn't dream of it." He gave in.

Sherry reached over and squeezed his hand. "It's for Kay."

Michael nodded. "I know."

"Ethan!" I heard Logan calling out in the outer office. Sherry jumped up and opened the door.

"In here," she said. Logan walked in and assessed the situation."

"Whose going with me?" he asked, all business.

"He is." I pointed to Michael.

"What about Sherry?" Michael asked.

"Me?"

"She's Kay's assistant. She knows everything."

"Honestly, I don't believe Sherry is in danger. And if they wanted to use Sherry for leverage, they would have taken her first, not Kay." I said. "They aren't wasting any time which shows how desperate they are," I assessed.

Michael nodded.

"Sherry are you scared, and do you want protection?" I looked at her directly.

She swallowed hard.

"No, I'll be fine," she said bravely as she lifted her chin slightly.

I nodded to Logan to take Michael.

"Okay, come with me," he said to Michael.

After the two of them had left I turned back to Sherry. "I honestly don't believe you're in danger but give me your address and I'll come by tonight and check on you. If you see anything that is just slightly out of the norm, you call me, okay?"

She nodded and took my card.

Chapter Twenty-Three

Ethan

I headed back to the office to see if Andria had learned anything new and to talk to the IT gurus and see if there wasn't some way, we could let Michael work from the safe house. I also put a call in to Detective Cavanaugh to update him on what I had learned over at the Port City offices. I also told him that I had moved Michael to a safe house and offered him the opportunity to provide the protection instead of the FBI. He declined.

I was going to have to be able to justify using the safe house in this situation but if my hunch was right it wouldn't be a problem.

Mac was still there when I walked in. I had forgotten about him after the phone call from Sherry. I owed him an apology.

"Mac, hey man. I'm sorry about leaving like that earlier," I began.

"We had everything under control by then, no problem." Mac looked at me his brow furrowed. "Is it something I can help you with?"

"I wish you could but there isn't an NCIS interest that I know of yet."

"Doesn't matter, you helped us. I'm sure I can find a way to help you."

"Thanks, I'd appreciate that. It's actually not even my case. It belongs to the local police and the only reason I'm involved is I called in a chip with the GPPD Chief." I shrugged I wasn't going to turn down free help, especially to find Kay.

"What do we have?" Mac jumped right in.

"Possible kidnapping."

"Possible?"

"Not sure yet, and don't really have a clear suspect only a hunch."

Mac leaned on a desk and crossed his arms. "Why don't you start from the beginning"

"Well, the..." I couldn't bring myself to say, victim. "The missing person is Kay Dandridge."

Mac shot up off the desk. "Kay? Why didn't you say so?"

I had forgotten in the heat of it all that he had met her. "Yeah, she didn't show up for work this morning and her secretary got worried. She tried calling her and got no response. The chauffeur went by the house..."

"Eddie?"

I was curious to know how he knew Eddie, but I let it go for the moment. "Yeah, when he didn't find her home and the car was still in the garage, the secretary called me."

"Well, I'd have to say your hunch is probably right." Mac rubbed the stubble on his chin absently.

"Her secretary called the local police and it's their case, like I said I called in a favor so it's sort of a joint investigation.

Mac nodded. "Have you contacted her grandfather?" Mac asked.

"No, I really don't know what to say. I haven't any evidence of foul play."

"You said you had a hunch, what is it?" Mac pressed.

"Well, according to the staff, the company is in the middle of fighting a takeover. Some larger company has offered to buy out Port City and Kay refused. She had made a move to take the company from being traded publicly to private as a means of fighting the buyout and I think they took her to stop that from happening."

"That is a good hunch. It is also possible this has something to do with her grandfather. A means to get at him."

"Why would someone do that?" I wondered turning to Mac.

"Because her grandfather is the Secretary of the Navy?"

I looked at Mac dumbfounded.

"She didn't tell you, did she?" he deduced.

"No." I said hoarsely. I was thinking about what Logan had tried to tell me before when he researched Kay online and I stopped him. "Why wouldn't she tell me?"

Mac shrugged. "I only know because he's my boss. I don't think she tells people a lot about herself. Have you two known each other long?" he asked.

"Yes and no." I said not sure I wanted to get into the details.

"Well, let's not dismiss your hunch because that is the simplest answer and the closest to home. I'm going to call SecNav and see if he's had any threats lately that might indicate someone would take his granddaughter. I'll also have my tech guys check the chatter and see if they come up with anything."

"Okay, sounds good. I left my forensic team at her house and I need to check in with them and see if they left any evidence behind."

Mac looked around. "Are all these phones secure?"

"Use mine." I pointed to my desk.

"Thanks."

"Andria, it's Ethan. Did you find anything at the house?"

"Not much. Nothing I can identify yet anyway."

"No prints?"

"Plenty of prints, I'm just weeding through them to see who they belong to. So far, I've identified Kay Dandridge, Eddie Green, and you."

"Well, keep trying." I ran my hand through my hair. "What about traffic cameras, phone calls, anything?"

"It takes time Ethan, you know that. We are working as fast as we can."

"I know. Thank you. Are the local police any help?"

"Yeah, they are actually over at traffic ops looking at the traffic cameras for any sign of Kay Dandridge and the techs here are going through the footage on the neighbor's cameras."

"Okay, thanks."

I clicked off and called another number. "Greg, it's Ethan Craddock."

"I've been expecting your call, Andria told me what was going on," Adam replied.

"It's a high priority. We have a co-worker of Kay Dandridge who could be at risk at a safe house. Is there a way he can work on his laptop and phone from there without someone being after to track his location?"

"Sure, the laptop is easy. The phone might be a little harder though, if someone is really trying to find him," He explained.

"Okay, let's say he really needs his phone."

"I suppose I could port his number over to one of our phones that can't be tracked and let him work that way."

"Okay, let me know when you get a chance to get someone to set that up over at the safe house. Call before you go in, Logan is there," I warned him.

"Got it." He clicked off.

I went to one of the desk phones rather than using my cell to call Logan. "Logan, Ethan. In a little while Adam or someone from IT is going to come out there to switch out Michael's phone and work on his laptop so he can work from there without being traced. Try not to shoot them when they show up."

"You tell them to call first?"

"I did."

"Then I'll do my best."

I laughed. "How's Michael doing?"

"He isn't particularly happy with the arrangement, but I think he is more scared than pissed so he is living with it."

I smiled. I'm sure any complaints Michael had fell on deaf ears with Logan.

"Okay, I'll try to come by later. I'll have Jared relieve you."

"Okay." And he was gone.

Mac hung up the phone his face grim.

"Everything alright?" I asked.

"Well, SecNav wasn't all that thrilled to hear his only granddaughter was missing, especially since she was snatched out from under my nose." I didn't make that connection, but I let it go.

"It's not your fault," I assured him, thinking she was snatched more from under my nose than his.

"It will be if we don't get her back in one piece." He shook his head.

"We will," I said, more for my benefit than his. I had to believe that we would. I had been operating on autopilot all day, doing what I knew had to be done. In a sense treating it like any other kidnapping case because if I didn't the cold fear that was sitting in the pit my stomach was going to take over and I couldn't let that happen. I couldn't let anyone else run this investigation. I had to be the one to find Kay.

Jared came into the kitchen where I was pouring myself a coffee preparing for an all-nighter. "Boss, I'm getting ready to head over to the safe house and relieve Logan."

"Okay, are you taking anyone with you?" I asked.

"Yeah, one of the locals is going with me."

"Okay, just be careful. We don't have any leads or suspects yet, so we don't know who or what we are looking for," I cautioned him.

"Got it."

I handed Mac a mug of coffee.

"So, did SecNav give you any leads that might help?" I asked trying not to think about how much I was learning about Kay from this case.

"No, he said he hasn't had any new threats. Just the same old standing ones," he explained.

"Could there be something there?"

"Only if someone was smart enough to know they are related. This is one of the reasons they have taken great pains to not let anyone know the relationship." Mac explained.

I nodded, it seemed extreme, but I could almost understand.

"She saw him recently, so could anyone have seen her with him?" I was trying to cover all the basis.

"No, she came to his house, which I assure you is extremely secure."

"And that is where you met her?" I asked trying to sound casual and failing miserably.

"Yeah, SecNav has a weekly poker game. Me and a few others go over and lose a few bucks. This week he called us ahead of time and said his granddaughter was visiting and did we mind if she sat in on a few hands."

"Did anyone have a problem with that?" I tried to stay on track with the case.

"No, you play at his house, his rules."

"So how did the game go?" I was curious.

"Well, she won." Why am I know surprised?

"Anyone a sore loser?"

"No, the others folded before it got too risky and it was just down to her and one other person."

"Who?" I asked.

"Me."

"How much did she take you for?"

"Five hundred."

"Ouch."

"Not really. She returned it."

"Returned it?"

"Yeah, she said she was playing for fun and didn't want my money. I tried arguing which didn't go over so well. So, in the end I took my money back."

"And that was it?"

"We sat and talked for a while and had a drink. That was pretty much it. I haven't seen her since she was in DC." He told me.

I felt pangs of jealousy in the pit of my stomach and I didn't like it. It tasted bitter and I had no reason to doubt Mac at his word. But I felt like he was holding something back. He had a good poker face, but I got the impression there was more to him and Kay than he was telling me. If I was right, it would explain her reaction the night she dropped off the pizza and saw Mac here.

Chapter Twenty-Four
Kay

I thought I was having a dream induced by too much scotch and too many B movies, but when my head hit the floor with a thud, I realized it wasn't a bad dream at all. I tried to focus, but my vision was blurry. I'd never had this problem with scotch before and I hadn't really had that much. I could hear sounds like maybe someone talking but it sounded distance and garbled. I tried to move but I felt like I was moving running in mud, my limbs were sluggish and slow to respond. My brain was screaming loud and clear. Get up! Move! I tried with all my strength to do just that. Thoughts of Ethan filled my mind. Why was it in a moment of crisis I always thought of Ethan?

Things began to fade in and out and I felt like I was moving effortlessly like I was flying or something. I opened my eyes, and everything was dark around me. I couldn't see anything. I concentrated on listening. I could hear a hum of some kind. I shook my head to try and clear it. Big mistake. The world began to spin in the wrong direction and then nothing.

I came to again and this time there was some light and I could at least see my hand in front of my face. I could hear voices shouting but I couldn't understand the words. My head felt fuzzy and I managed to sit up. My hands and feet were not bound, that was a good sign.

I sat still for a moment and looked around trying to let my eyes adjust and try to figure out where I was. I was thinking more clearly this time and it was obvious I had been drugged and brought to wherever this place was. I put my hands on the floor and it felt like metal. I looked up and the light that was coming in was through little round holes high above my reach. I stood up and touch the wall behind me and it felt like corrugated metal. I felt around some more. I was in a box. A metal box. Great. I felt around and found what had to be the door and pushed just in case this was some mistake and I had crawled in here for shelter or something. No. The door was locked or jammed and either way I wasn't getting out. I started to yell for help. No response. The voices had disappeared, and I could hear a distant hum again but this time it was different. There was another noise too, but I couldn't quite place it. I put my ear to the seam of the door and listened. It sounded like water slapping up against a bulkhead or something. I began pounding on the walls. First the back, then the sides, and finally the front. I kicked and screamed and waited. Nothing.

I sat down to try to think about the situation and figure a way out of this mess.

Okay, clearly someone had put me in here, so who and why?

I stood up and pounded on the walls some more and I shouted upward towards the holes near the ceiling.

I had no idea how long I had been out or how long I had been in this box. Surely someone would have noticed I was missing by now. I had no phone. That would have been too good to be true. If I had wondered in here on my own, Again, I tried to think who or why someone would do this.

I thought about my grandfather and wondered if I was leverage for someone who wanted something from him. He received threats all the time. Maybe, someone had finally figured out the connection between us and kidnapped me. I hoped my grandfather was refusing to comply with whatever demands some terrorist group or psycho individual was asking of him.

I prayed that he was okay and unharmed.

Then I thought about anyone who might want to hurt me and the only thing I could think of was the buyout proposal; was InDesign so desperate to have my company that they would kidnap me? Would they demand that the shareholders turn over their shares to them? That wouldn't help. I still had more shares than the rest of them. Besides, basic greed would solve that problem they would offer them more than I did for the tender offer and get control of forty-eight percent of the company. What they needed were my shares. Maybe they planned to kill me thinking that would be the best way to get the company. Maybe, they thought with me out of the way Michael would cave in. Even Michael didn't have the authority over my shares. He didn't have the authority to sign for me in such matters. He did have power of attorney but not over everything. That had to be it. InDesign must think that if they got rid of me then they would take over the company more easily. They hadn't done their research well enough because it wasn't as simple as that. Even in the event of my untimely demise, it wouldn't make taking control of the company any easier. I hadn't been ready to die in Afghanistan and I wasn't ready now. I just needed to figure this out. I began searching the ridges and cracks for anything sharp I could use to on the screws I found in the wall. Maybe it would help weaken the doors or something. I sat listening to the sounds of the water. I was clearly out in the bay maybe even the ocean. I could smell salt air, but I didn't hear any gulls. I feared I may be too far offshore for anyone to see me and no idea where I might be drifting to. I was beginning to lose hope. I had no way to signal anyone and no way to know where I was or what was happening around me. I was starting to feel real panic in the pit of my stomach.

I sank down to the floor and closed my eyes. I tried not to think about all the things that could go wrong but in the back of my mind I knew I could very possibly starve to death in here or worse drown if I was hit with a big wave that capsized whatever this container was sitting on. I tried to refocus to think about something else. I concentrated on Ethan. I thought about his smile. How he was so gentle, and kind yet was a no-nonsense, take no shit kind of guy at the same time. I began to cry. I prayed Ethan would find me in time. I prayed that I hadn't survived being blown up in the Middle East to come home and find Ethan all over again just to die before we ever really got to spend any time together. I started to examine my life. What had I accomplished? Not much. Sure, I took a few photos and shared the real story about war and its effect on soldiers and marines. I took over my family's company, but I hadn't been there long enough to do the things I wanted to do. My thoughts circled back around to my situation and I screamed for my own end, my own death and unfinished life.

Ethan

"Where are we?" I demanded walking into the bullpen.

All eyes lifted from computers, print outs and reports to stare at me. I know my voice had been harsh, but I was getting desperate. We had absolutely nothing to tell us where Kay may have been taken and by whom.

"I've been looking into InDesign with some help from Mac." Stephanie started. "The man who made the offer to Port City and met with Michael and Kay was Todd Bannister."

"Is he the head of the company?"

"More or less, yes. He's the face of the company. InDesign itself is operated by a board, but as best I can tell, the names of the other board member are fake. InDesign seems to be a shell for something or someone else. I haven't gotten that far into them yet."

"What about closer to home, do they have anything like this linked to them in the past?"

Logan spoke up next. "Nothing that can be tied directly to them. They are smart and they cover their tracks very well. Four years ago, they tried to buy out another company and at first the company resisted but, before the deal could be settled either way, the owner of the company died in a car crash."

"Now that is interesting." I felt hopeful.

"Yeah, there were no witnesses and the physical evidence led to a rental car, which was rented with a stolen credit card." Logan looked just as frustrated as I was.

"Anything else?" I began to pace the room.

"A few years before that, they bought a company after the CEO died of a heart attack." Logan looked down at his notes. "Nothing suspicious about the death according the coroner's report and the local police. The company was poised to go public and it was predicted their stocks would skyrocket.

InDesign bought them the next day and promoted the second in command and the company rebounded nicely. InDesign sold the company a year later and made a huge profit."

"Convenient." I said.

"Yes, but nothing to prove that it was anything more than a lucky break for InDesign."

"Was Todd Bannister with the firm then?"

"Yes, he was."

"Okay, so if they follow the same MO, then they aren't going to outright kill Kay, they are going to make it look like an accident of some kind. So, we need to be on the lookout for any Jane Doe's that show up at hospitals or morgues and trace this guy Todd Bannister for the last 72 hours. Who has he talked to? Where did he eat, where did he sleep?"

"We aren't going to be able to get any warrants based on the information Logan just gave us." Jared pointed out.

"That's true, but you don't need a warrant to find him and follow him on traffic cameras." I stated what I felt was the obvious. Jared nodded and got to work. "Also, ping his cell phone see if we can tell where he is or was. No phone records, just location."

Mac and I were debating the merits of trying to get IRS records on InDesign or Todd Bannister himself when Jared called out.

"Boss, got something!"

"Bannister was at one of the industrial parks along the water."

"What was he doing?"

"I don't know yet but it's in our time window."

"Okay, you stay here keep digging, Mac, Logan." I said heading for the door.

My heart raced. It was the closest thing I had to a lead and we were working against the clock. It had already been twenty-four hours since Kay went missing and we were no closer to finding her than when we started.

"Boss, you want me to drive?" Logan asked.

"No." I needed the distraction and to concentrate on something else for a little while.

We drove in silence to the Brookline Industrial Park, which was home to several seafood processing plants, boat works, and other businesses. It was a tough place with the fishermen and dockhands. They weren't very trusting of police much less the FBI. Jumping out of the SUV and flashing our badges wasn't going to get us very far.

"Keep it low key, guys." I advised as we got out of the vehicle.

We were getting a lot of looks as dockhands crossed our paths and I looked for anyone that was more interested in us the anyone else. Halfway down the dock, I found him. He was a short man with a pencil mustache, wearing jeans and a black t-shirt. He wasn't dressed like the fisherman with the typical white rubber boots. He was cleaner, with no fish scales, blood or stains on his clothes. He watched us intently and I had the sense that he wanted to talk to us, but he didn't want anyone to know. He made eye contact with me and held it before slipping in between two warehouses.

"Stay here." I said over my shoulder to Mac and Logan.

I walked casually in the direction I had seen the man disappear and then slipped between the buildings. The two buildings cast dark shadows and it took my eyes a minute to adjust. I put my hand on the butt of my gun just in case this was an ambush. I found the man leaning against the wall behind a stack of wooden pallets.

"You want to talk to me?"

"You're here about that woman, aren't you?" the man asked nervously.

"Yeah, I am, what can you tell me?"

"I don't want to go to jail."

"Is there some reason why you should?"

The man began to sweat, and he looked around nervously. I didn't want to lose him. Right now, he was the closest thing I possibly had to Kay.

"Just tell me what you know and if you're implicated, I'll do what I can to help you."

"Can you do that?"

"Yeah I can."

"You with the FBI or something?"

"Yes, I am. You want to see my badge?"

"No, not here."

He looked around nervously again. "This man came here late yesterday. He paid a lot of money to tow a barge offshore and leave it."

"You a tugboat captain?"

He nodded.

Now I understood why he was so nervous. Tugboat captains are a very tight knit group and you don't want a reputation of being a snitch or worse. If found out, he would be drummed out of his job and blackballed.

"And you saw a woman?" I pressed, trying to re from a ship sitting on the barge and I saw these two other guys drag her onto the barge and lock her in there."

"You say drag, was she hurt?"

"I didn't see any blood or nothing, but she couldn't walk on her own." He shook his head.

"Okay, can you tell me where you released the barge?"

"Yeah, I can give the coordinates."

"Would you be willing to come to my office and help us find it on a map?"

"I can't be seen talking to you." His eyes shifted left and right while we talked.

"I understand. I typed the coordinates he recited into my phone."

"Here's my card. It has the address of my office so when you leave here come straight there."

He shoved the card quickly in his pocket and left. I sent the coordinates to Jared and Stephanie back at the office and asked them to start mapping them. Then I walked back out to the SUV. Mac and Logan were waiting.

We all got in the SUV without a word and I drove out of the park and pulled over.

"You get anything?" Logan asked.

"Tugboat captain was paid to drop a barge offshore with a storage container aboard. He says there was a woman inside."

Mac took out his phone "I'll ask the Coast Guard to start searching. Do you have the coordinates?"

"Yeah, thirty-six degrees north by seventy-four degrees west."

Mac repeated the coordinates. He listened and acknowledged whatever information was shared. "Those coordinates are nearly one hundred miles offshore."

My heart sank. "We need to map the currents and see where she could have drifted to in the past twenty-four hours."

"Well, the currents would be pushing her north and further out to sea." Mac said matter-of-factly.

"If she is in a container, she'll be protected from the sun though." Logan offered.

"Hopefully, there is a way for air to get into that container." Mac answered Logan's optimism with a dose of reality.

I glanced over at him.

"Sorry." Mac looked back down at his phone.

"We need to know what we are dealing with and how we can best help her." I said.

"Well the temperatures shouldn't be too bad, and she will have shelter from the wind, and she should be dry." Mac offered. "Her biggest problem is drinking water."

He was right; it was doubtful that Bannister had been thoughtful enough to give her any especially if he wanted to get rid of her. I was confused by the method he was using.

"What I don't understand is, why this? Of all of the other instances where his opponents have come to a bad end, they all looked like accidents." I glanced over at Mac and in the rearview mirror at Logan. "How do you explain this as an accident?"

"Maybe he is hoping she isn't found, and no explanation will be needed." Logan offered.

I nodded. That was probably true.

Mac's phone rang. He listened more than he spoke. Then he clicked off. "They are sending the helicopter up to search."

His face looks grim. "What's the catch?" I demanded.

"There's a storm brewing off the coast so they have to send the chopper up now because they may not be able to later. "

My grip on the steering wheel tightened. A storm might capsize the barge and the container would sink like a rock to the bottom of the ocean.

"Where are they sending the chopper from?"

"North River." Mac named the large Coast Guard station in the southern portion of Gates Point. The name was a misnomer as it was in the southernmost part of the city. I made a U-turn sending other cars swerving out of the way.

"What are you doing, Ethan?" Logan demanded.

"We are going to North River."

No one said a word as I turned on the lights and sped in the opposite direction. We pulled into the parking lot of the operations building and I barely had the SUV in park before I bailed out and ran for the door.

"Ethan, wait!" Mac called behind me.

I rushed through the door and was stopped. "I'm Agent Ethan Craddock." I showed my ID. "I need to be on that chopper!"

"What chopper?"

"The one that is headed out to see to look for a missing barge."

"Sir, that Chopper left five minutes ago."

"Damn!"

Logan and Mac joined me.

Mac showed his ID. "May we join your staff in the communications room to see if they find our kidnap victim on that barge?"

"Yes, sir. This way."

The room was dim with the glow of monitors and communication panels that provided most of the light.

"Hey Mac, I'm surprised you got here so fast."

"Damon, it's good to see you again."

I watched the monitors and tried to determine which one was for the chopper that had just left. "Lt. Commander Damon Pincus, this is Agent Ethan Craddock and Agent Logan Watson of the FBI." We shook hands. "What can you tell us about the chopper, has it found the barge yet?" I asked not wasting time with small talk.

"No, yet. Come over here and I'll show you the situation."

I followed the Lt. Commander to a map that was lit up to show the ocean and wind currents.

"Using the coordinates Mac gave me, we believe our starting point is here. Now given the weight of the barge and the fact that it has no power of its own, we believe it should be about here." He placed his finger on the map.

I concentrated on that one spot and prayed that he was right, and we had found Kay. "What do we do now?" I asked.

"We wait." Lt. Commander said.

"That isn't going to be easy." Logan muttered.

I stood never taking my eyes off the screen.

A voice crackled over the speaker. "Command, we have a visual."

I held my breath.

"Rescue One, are you able to repel down to the barge?"

A blurry image of the barge appeared on the monitor. The wind and the wake from the helicopter made it hard to see. I could make out a tan colored box sitting in the middle of the barge.

"We will attempt to rescue." The voice announces through the static.

I watched as a man repelled down to the barge and approach the box. His body camera showed there was a lock. He called for tools to be lowered down to him. It seemed to take an eternity for the tools to be lowered. I watched as the weather was deteriorating and willed them to hurry up. I hated the fact that I wasn't the one cutting my way into that box and pulling her out. I felt helpless and trapped and I started to pace. Logan came up next to me.

"They're going to get her out." He said quietly.

I wanted to tell him it should be me. I knew he understood how I felt. Mac was standing off the side with his arms crossed over his chest. I could see his jaw muscles working.

The pilot and the rescuer were talking to each other. The pilot was getting antsy about the weather.

"I'm almost in!" The rescuer was shouting.

I turned to Lt. Commander Pincus. "You can't allow them to leave without her!"

"They will do their best, but I can't risk the safety of my crew and equipment in this storm."

"Rescue is what you do, right? Doesn't that apply to people stuck in a storm or do you just rescue people on sunny days?"

"Ethan, come on man." Logan grabbed my shoulders and steered me out into the hallway.

I could hear Mac as I left the room. "Nick, he's just upset."

"I get it. He's got a temper." I heard the Lt. Commander say.

"Yeah, he does seem to be a little worked up, but his man will deal with him."

Out in the hallway I shrugged away from Logan. He remained silent waiting for me to calm down. I paced up and down the hallway a few times trying to bring my anger under control. "I'm good, man." I said attempting to go back in the communications room.

Logan shook his head. "I don't think so, Ethan."

I stopped short and looked at him. "Are you really not going to let me back in there?"

"I will let you back in there when you have calmed down a little more, I don't think you're there yet."

"Logan, we've been friends a long time."

"Yes, we have." He didn't disagree. "And so, you really think you can stop me if I want to get in there?"

"Yes, I do." He shifted his weight. "I'm not going to get physical. You need to hear me out." He looked me dead in the eyes.

I narrowed my focus to him. "Let's have it and make it quick." I said.

"Think about what you are doing. You're too close to his and no one can blame you for that. Shouldn't we notify GPPD? It's their case? You're not thinking clearly, and you need to take a step back."

"I should be on that chopper and I should be on that barge getting her out of that box." My anger was rising, and I turned away from Logan so he wouldn't see the emotion.

"Dude, I get it. I really do." He said quietly. "Do you think she isn't going to love you because you aren't the one pulling her out that box?"

"I should have protected her and if I couldn't do that, then I at least should save her." I felt myself starting to come apart.

"I think you need to dial down the macho stuff and just concentrate on being there for her." Logan's words slapped me in the face. I stared at him for a moment. He was right of course. I apparently was acting like a complete ass.

"You're right." I whispered and walked past him to go apologize to the Lt. Commander. I heard voices shouting as I came back into the communication center. "There is no time to send the basket, we go now!"

I watched in horror as the rescuer on the barge grabbed Kay's limp body and wrapped his arms and legs around her without benefit of a harness as the helicopter pulled up and started the wench to reel him in.

The room was completely silent as a wave swamped the barge and is listed to one side and the container slid off into the ocean. I prayed that he held onto her as they were both hoisted into the air above the raging sea. I prayed the chopper made it back to land safely. I didn't even care where they landed just so long as they did.

The whole room let out a collective sigh of relieve when the pilot announced they were safely back aboard the chopper and they were starting medical treatment. They would be headed for trauma hospital.

Lt. Commander Pincus turned to me and held out his hand. "Thank you," I said shaking the proffered hand "And I apologize."

"It was a tense moment. We were all feeling the pressure." He reassured me and slapped my shoulder.

I left Mac to talk with the Lt. Commander a moment and I walked outside to say a prayer of thanks. Logan walked past me to the SUV and stood next to the driver's door making it clear he would be driving us to the hospital. I tossed him the keys and waited for Mac.

"Thanks for all your help." I said as Mac exited the building.

"Anytime." He smiled. "Hospital?"

"Hospital." I smiled.

Chapter Twenty-Five
Kay

I felt whatever boat I was on start to rock a little more than it had been, and I heard the wind whistling through the holes in the container. This was not going to be good if a big storm was brewing. I had no idea what type of vessel I was on or if it and this container would survive a storm, although I suspected the idea was not to survive it.

Panic began to set in again and this time I let it. I was desperate and I could barely see anything. I began pushing on the walls and the door looking for any weak spots. I threw my body up against them all in a desperate attempt to knock something loose. I screamed until I was hoarse. I was pretty certain I was alone on this vessel. I hadn't heard any sounds of an engine or people working. I was certain I had been set adrift. My mind was racing in circles. I thought of Ethan and I was overcome with emotion again at the thought of never seeing him again. Then I thought of Mac, he meant so much to me as well. And I was truly sorry that things weren't working out the way I thought they would with him. I was conflicted I loved them both in their own right. But it didn't matter now. I was probably going to die out here. I had a little room in the container so I ran and charged the door hoping once again my efforts would be rewarded.

I was wrong.

I fell to the floor in pain. My shoulder was on fire. I laid there crying and screaming silently. I kicked at the door as hard as I could and then the world went black.

***

I opened my eyes. And my shoulder didn't hurt as bad, but everything was a sickly green and too bright. I closed them again.

I woke sometime later; the light wasn't as bright, and I could tell someone was in the room with me. I tried to move my head.

"Ssshhh, take it easy. Don't move around too fast." I heard Ethan say.

Despite my lips being dry and cracked, I smiled at him. "Hey."

"Hey," he said drawing circles on the back of my hand with his thumb. "You had me a worried there for a while."

"Me too." I said my voice cracking.

He nodded. "You're going to be okay now. I let you down before, but it won't happen again."

I watched his jaw tighten.

"Let me down, how?"

"I wasn't there to prevent this from happening."

"You couldn't have known." I squeezed his hand. "You're here now."

He nodded. He looked like he wanted to say something but didn't. "Listen to me, Kay. Nothing and no-one is going to hurt you now. Logan is standing outside the door and he isn't letting anyone in without a pat down."

I laughed a little.

"I have to go take care of some things, and there are some people here to see you." He kissed the back of my hand. "I wouldn't leave if it wasn't absolutely necessary."

I nodded. "It's okay but take Logan with you. I would feel better knowing he has your back."

"No need to worry about me. I'm covered."

He smiled and stood up still holding my hand like he didn't want to let go.

"Sir?"

I lifted my head a little to see Jared standing in the doorway and Mac at the foot of the bed.

"Mac?"

He smiled. "I'm glad you're going to be okay."

"What are you doing here?" I asked getting my bearings.

"Checking on you."

"Did my grandfather send you?" It seemed like a logical question.

He was silent for a moment. "No."

Again, I felt guilty for asking him. "Mac, can you stay a while?"

"I can't right now, but I'll come back later, okay?"

"Okay." I nodded. That was comfort enough for now.

Ethan squeezed my hand again. "I'll be back a little later," he said.

"Okay." I nodded to Ethan as well.

I was surprised when Mac turned and followed Ethan out. I didn't have time to think about it long because as soon as they had left the room, Sherry came bursting in.

"Oh Kay! Are you alright? How do you feel?" she asked. The questions running together.

"I'm okay," I assured her.

"Are you sure, do you need anything? How about some ice chips?"

"You don't need to fuss but some ice chips would be nice."

"I'll be right back." She swooped out of the room only to be replaced by Eddie.

"Kay?" he said tentatively as he stepped inside.

"Come on in, Eddie."

I was hoping this wasn't going to last long as I was already starting to feel tired.

"I know you need your rest, but I just wanted to see for myself that you were alright," he said gently.

"I'll be fine, I've been worse." I gave him a weak smile.

"I know, but a person can only take so much."

He had a point. "I know, I'll be fine," I told him.

"Carolyn and the girls sent these." He walked over and placed a vase of flowers that he had been holding on the windowsill.

"Thank you, those are beautiful. Please tell them I love them," I smiled.

"They wanted to come see you, but I told them to wait until you are stronger,"

"They are welcome anytime, Eddie. Just like you."

He smiled. "I wish I could have done something to prevent this."

"There isn't anything anyone could have done." I tried to reassure him.

"Do you remember what happened?" he asked.

"Not really. I stayed up late watching old movies and I guess I had too much to drink because I fell asleep and the next thing, I knew I woke up in the back of a van."

"You didn't see any faces of the persons who took you?"

"No, not that I can remember."

Eddie nodded.

"How did you know I was missing?" I asked him.

"When you didn't come into work on time, Sherry tried to call you and when you didn't answer she sent me over to check on you."

Sherry stepped back into the room.

"You two are my heroes." I smiled.

"Oh no, Ethan is the real hero." Sherry stepped around Eddie to sit down next to the bed.

"Oh?" I was intrigued.

"I called him after I called Eddie." Sherry began "The local police showed up and that was a real mess at first. Ethan and the detective got into it and Ethan had him thrown off the case. That detective was pissed, I can tell you."

I was more than intrigued. "Really?"

"Yes, and then Ethan and his team, oh and Mac, started investigating even thought it was really up to the local police." Sherry whispered.

"They were looking at traffic cameras and everything and that is how they found you." Sherry leaned back in the chair nodding.

"Traffic cameras?" I asked.

"Yes, just like on TV. It was a good thing too, because there was a storm coming and if they hadn't found you in time..." Sherry started to sniffle.

"They did find me." I said weakly. I was trying to remember but I couldn't.

"Yes, they did." Sherry squeezed my hand. "And you're a lucky woman."

"Is everyone else okay, did anyone else get hurt?" I needed to know.

"No, Ethan put Michael in protective custody, I think they call it," she explained.

"Why? Do they know who did this?"

Sherry looked uncomfortable and looked around the room. Then she leaned over and whispered. "They think it was Todd Bannister from InDesign."

"Are they sure?"

"Ethan is." Sherry insisted.

"Don't take this the wrong way but are we sure Ethan is thinking clearly right now?" I was getting concerned about him.

"How can you say that after everything he went through?" Sherry protested.

"I'm sorry, you're right. I guess my brain is still foggy." I didn't want to have an argument with Sherry and I also wouldn't expect her to understand.

Her demeanor changed and she gave me a sympathetic pat on the arm. "I'm sorry, I've kept you too long. You need to rest."

She stood up.

I tried to look drowsy. "Sherry, you're my best friend. Thank you." I said reaching for her hand.

She smiled and then a tear escaped down her cheek. "I love you, Kay and if you need anything you call me okay?"

"I will, I promise."

She seemed to have forgotten my questioning of Ethan's judgement and she and Eddie left. I closed my eyes, I was exhausted. I thought about what Sherry had said about Todd Bannister and if it could actually be true.

I drifted back to sleep.

***

There was debris flying and I couldn't hear anything. I knew I should be able to hear something. I could see the mouths moving on the marines as if they were shouting but I couldn't hear the words. My leg felt like it was on fire and I was frozen and couldn't move. Oliver was waving at me to get down, but I couldn't for what seemed like an eternity. He was running towards me then a cloud of smoke blocked him from my view and when I saw him again, he was lying face down on the ground. I wanted to scream. Maybe I did but I couldn't hear anything. I looked around and when I could hear again, everyone one was down on the ground. No one was left standing. There was rubble and debris all around me and no one was moving. I looked beyond the space we had been occupying.

There used to be walls but now there was nothing. There had been furniture, a table and some chairs. Now there were only sticks. The marines that had been standing just a few moments ago were all bleeding and hurt and I just stared at them.

***

I woke with a start, drenched in a cold sweat. I think I must have called out.

"Hey, there. You're okay. I've got you."

I was startled to hear someone's voice. Every other time I woke up from that dream I had been alone. The voice was new, and it scared me as much as the dream itself. I flinched.

"Kay, it's Ethan. You're safe. It's me, Ethan."

"Ethan?"

"Yeah, it's me." The voice was so calming.

"I didn't remember an Ethan on our team in Afghanistan. It took me a minute to realize where I was. Thousands of miles and six years away from that day. The day the world around me blew up.

"Oh, yeah. Ethan."

His face came into view. "You okay?" he asked.

"Yeah," I told him.

His face told me he knew I was lying but he didn't press for any more information. I rested back against the pillow and started to shake.

"Kay?" He leaned over me. "Are you sure you're alright?"

"Yeah, just give me a minute." I tried to will away the images that still clouded my vision.

Ethan pulled the blankets up closer to my chin. I felt him sit down on the side of the bed.

"Can I do anything?"

I shook my head. I reached out my hand to his. He took it gently and sat silently until I stopped shaking.

"You need the nurse or anything?

"No."

"Okay." He didn't argue. He just sat holding my hand until I fell back to sleep.

When I woke he was gone. Logan sat in the chair next to the bed watching me. I wasn't sure if I was comforted by his presence.

"Hi," I said.

"Hi, do you need anything?" Was his short reply.

"No. Where's Ethan?"

"He had something he had to do." He was a font of information.

"Why aren't you with him?"

Logan frowned. "Because he told me to babysit you." Great.

"And where do you think I am going to go?"

"Nowhere, but it isn't about where you are going, it is about who might be coming." And there it was. The elephant in the room.

"You still haven't caught him yet?" I asked.

"It's complicated," he replied.

I could see I was going to get nowhere with Logan, so I nodded. "Still, you should be with him to have his back."

"I couldn't agree more." I knew where Logan's loyalties were.

"Then go!" I commanded.

"I can't because if I leave you and something happens to you, my life won't be worth living."

"I doubt that." I rolled my eyes.

"Then you don't understand or appreciate how Ethan feels about you." He bit the words off. Clearly, he wasn't happy to be here, and he wasn't happy with me.

"I seriously, doubt that ever stopped you from doing something you thought was right."

He stared at me as if considering my words. For a moment I thought he might get up and leave.

"Ethan and I have been friends a long time and if he has asked me to guard the one thing he holds most dear in this world, then that is what I am going to do," He glared at me, "No matter how annoying she is."

His words both shocked and stunned me. "What's your deal anyway? Why do you dislike me so much without knowing me?"

"You're right I don't know you, but I know your type," he generalized.

"My type?" I laughed. "And pray tell, what is my type?"

"I know you were a photojournalist and you were imbedded with a marine unit." His eyes narrowed, "I don't know how you pulled that off. But people like you get people like me get hurt."

"Were you injured because of a photojournalist?" I asked using my most innocent voice.

"No."

"Then your statement has no basis in fact, and you can guard me from outside the door."

I closed my eyes. I didn't believe my presence had gotten my marine corps team injured. The fact was, they had been injured and they were alive because I found a car and drove them all back to base. I was the reason they were alive. It didn't feel like I had done anything brave or that I had been strong despite my own injuries. I did what needed to be done at the time to simply survive. While I don't believe any of those marines blamed me, I still felt sick about what happened. Logan's words made me question if we had been targeted because I was there or whether it was because I was female or a journalist. But I had no idea. I closed my eyes and the images returned. The blood, the screaming, the smoke and dust. It was nothing short of a miracle that we got out of there alive even if most of us weren't in one piece. I tried to block it out, but with nothing to distract me here I couldn't. I pressed the button for more morphine and hoped that in sleep I might find relief from the images.

I selfishly prayed that Ethan would be back when I woke up. Then I let the drugs carry me into the blackness.

Chapter Twenty-Six
Ethan

It was hard for me to leave Kay in the hospital. I wanted to stay there and tell her how sorry I was. How I planned to spend the rest of my life making things right. And protecting her. Todd Bannister had turned this case into one with FBI jurisdiction written all over it. And I was hot on his trail. I was still working with the local police and letting them handle the local aspects of the investigation, interviews of witnesses, even talking to Kay about what she knew if anything. We still had Michael in protective custody, and I left Logan to guard Kay, not trusting anyone else. I knew he was not happy about missing out on the action, but he was the only person I trusted to keep Kay safe. I was filled with self-doubt, thinking maybe I should let Logan handle the investigation while I sat with Kay. Somehow, I felt like I had to do this in order to be worthy of her, again.

I went back to the office to check in with Stephanie and Jared.

"Where are we?" I announced myself.

"We are trying to track Bannister, but it isn't easy," Stephanie said.

"Why?"

"He stopped using his credit card a couple of hours ago and his car just parked at the airport. I don't know if he has bought a ticket or not."

"We don't have actual eyes on him?" I demanded.

"The agents that were following him lost him in traffic and are coming into the airport now." Stephanie answered.

"We are assuming that he is headed at least out of the area and possibly out of the country?" I put my hands on the edge of her desk and leaned in to look over her shoulder at the computer monitor.

"Yes, sir."

"Do we have access to the cameras at the airport?" I pointed to the computer; my patience had been worn thin.

"Not from here." She shook her head.

"Call the agents out there and tell them to get with airport operations or the police or whoever controls the damn cameras out there. I want to know where he is going." I was not going to let him get away.

"Maybe he is traveling with someone who is purchasing the tickets," Stephanie suggested.

"Possible." I entertained the idea. "Or maybe the airport is a decoy and he just dropped his car and picked up a rental. It's hard to trace a rental." I stepped away from her desk and started pacing.

"We have no way of knowing if he called ahead or not but check any outgoing cars from the airport shortly after Bannister's car entered."

"On it." Jared said as he spoke to the agents out at the airport.

"What would be his reason for staying?" I asked out loud, not expecting an answer.

"Well, he couldn't have done all of this alone. He had to have help. Maybe he is doubling back to meet up with his partner in crime." Stephanie suggested.

"That's possible." I was deep in thought wondering who could he have been working with to kidnap Kay? Was he coming back to finish the job? A thought slowly started to take form in my mind.

"Jared? Who is at the safe house right now?" I asked.

"A couple of Mac's agents."

"Where's Mac?"

"Dunno," he replied.

I turned around expecting to see him sitting at a desk in the corner or something. He wasn't. I pulled out my cell phone and punched Logan's number.

"Logan." His gruff voice barked into the phone.

"It's Ethan, listen we've lost Bannister. Keep an eye on Kay because he might be coming back for her."

"You got it." Logan said as he clicked off.

"We've got camera access!" Jared called out from his desk as he snapped his fingers at Stephanie to get her attention and point to the computer.

Stephanie began typing and clicking something on the screen. Jared was still talking to on the phone.

"Got something!" Stephanie called out. "He did get into another car."

I returned to stand behind her looking at the black and white images on the screen. Bannister made it a point not to look up as he drove off the airport property past the cameras mounted at the exit ramp that led to the interstate.

"Can you track him? Can you get me a location?" I demanded.

"Working on it." Stephanie said without taking her eyes off the screen.

"I didn't see anyone else with him, did you?" I asked.

"No." Was all that she said. She was concentrating on the images on the screen.

"Maybe he is using an alias?" Jared offered.

"There are too many maybes." I began pacing again. We were missing something. I couldn't figure out what it was.

"He has to have someone helping him. We know he didn't put her on the barge himself. What do we have on the people who were with him at docks?"

The clicking of keyboards was fast and furious in the office. The phones started to ring.

"Agent Craddock!" I barked into a desk phone.

"Agent Craddock, this is Agent Mercer at the safe house and we're taking some fire. I've called the local PD for back-up."

"How many?" I asked.

"At least three that I can see," he reported.

I started snapping my fingers to get Jared and Stephanie's attention. They both looked up.

"We're on our way!" I slammed the phone down.

"The safe house is under fire!" I ran for the door trusting Stephanie and Jared would follow.

When we got there the Gates Point police were there. It looked like the shooting had stopped. We all approached the scene cautiously.

"Who's in charge and where are the agents?" I called out.

"You Craddock?" A police sergeant asked.

"Yeah."

"This way." He motioned for me to follow him.

I could hear more sirens in the distance. I found the two NCIS agents on the floor and one was unconscious. I checked his pulse. He had been shot but he was alive. A Gates Point officer was administering first aid. I knew the sirens must be the EMT's. The second agent was propped up against the wall and conscious.

"What happened?"

"It was Nichols. He was part of it."

"Michael Nichols, the man you were protecting did this?" I was stunned. The agent nodded.

"Jared!" I yelled standing up and looking around.

"I'm on it."

I saw Jared step outside and start talking into his phone. "What else can you tell me?"

"They opened fire through the windows. Nichols ran to the back of the house and opened the back door."

The agent coughed. The EMTs pushed their way in.

"He let them in?" I was having a hard time believing all of this.

"Yes, then he just opened fire on us. We returned fire and I think we got at least one of them. It all happened so fast."

"I understand, it's okay." I tried to reassure him. "Did you hear them say anything about where they might be going?"

"No, they didn't say anything once inside the house."

The EMT's stepped between us and started assessing the agent.

"I'll call Mac and have him meet you at the hospital."

I don't know if the agent heard me. It looked as if he had slipped into unconsciousness.

My mind was full of thoughts of Kay. I pulled out my phone and called Logan. No answer.

"Dammit." I ran out the door. "Jared, I'm headed to the hospital."

"I'm coming with you!" He and Stephanie jumped in the SUV.

"If these guys are headed there, they might be meeting Bannister and you'll need back-up." Jared explained.

I nodded and started the engine. I redialed Logan but still no answer. I tried Mac, nothing.

"I have a feeling we might be too late already." I said out loud without realizing it.

"You try Logan?" Jared asked.

"Twice, no answer. Same with Mac."

Stephanie frowned. "I'll keep trying." She offered.

I drove like a bat out of hell to the hospital. We skidded to a stop. There were no obvious signs that Bannister or anyone else was there.

We got out of the SUV. "Don't draw any unnecessary attention and stay alert."

They both nodded and followed me as I led the way to Kay's room. We stepped off the elevator and I didn't see Logan in the hallway.

"Be ready." I whispered.

We all put our hands on our weapons and walked as casually as we could towards Kay's room. A nurse looked up from her station.

"Can you tell me how Kay Dandridge is doing today?" I asked.

"Oh, she is much better, and she's had several visitors today." The nurse smiled brightly.

"Any visitors in there with her now that you know of?"

"Not that I know of."

"Thank you." I motioned for Jared and Stephanie to flank the door to her room.

The door was closed which I thought was unusual, especially since Logan was not at his post outside the door. I used my foot to push the door open. I swept my gun back and forth in the room, then stepped inside. Jared and Stephanie followed me in one at a time. I turned to the bathroom and it was empty.

"Clear." I called out.

"Over here, Ethan." Jared answered.

I turned to see Logan face down on the floor and bloody.

"Is he...."

Jared was checking his pulse. "He's alive, just unconscious."

Stephanie shouted out the door. "We need a doctor in here now!"

Nurses and staff came running. I pulled one aside. "Where is the woman that was in this bed?" I demanded.

"I don't know." She sprang into action seeing Logan on the floor.

"Do you have cameras in the hallways?"

"Yes."

"Get your security team up here now!" I barked.

Logan was coming around.

"Logan, what the hell happened?"

He looked at me. His eyes rolled around in his head.

"He may have a concussion; we need to take him now." One of the nurses pushed me aside.

A uniformed security guard and a doctor showed up. "I need to see footage of this room."

"Come with me," I followed the guard down the hall to the stairwell then downstairs to the security office. He sat down at the computer and began stabbing at the keyboard.

The video showed two orderlies entering Kay's room. Then a doctor pushing a gurney. Several minutes went by that I assumed involved a fight with Logan, then the orderlies and the doctor appeared in the hallway pushing Kay on the gurney. A few seconds later Mac strolled down the hallway and entered Kay's room. He immediately came back out and ran down the hallway after the doctor and orderlies.

"Where does that hallway lead?"

"A number of places, let me pull up the other cameras and see if I can tell which way they went."

"Great, do that!" I turned away and punched in Mac's cell number. He hadn't answered before. I prayed he did this time.

The phone rang three times. "This is McIntyre."

"Mac, its Ethan, where the hell are you?"

"Ethan, thank god, listen they've kidnapped Kay...."

"I know," I cut him off. "I'm at the hospital. Where are you?"

"I'm not sure, and my cell service is cutting in and out," he said.

"Tell me which direction you're heading." I ran out of the security office back towards Kay's room looking for Jared and Stephanie. I met them in the lobby.

"Hang on Mac." I looked at Jared. "Do you have your laptop? Can you trace Mac's cell phone?"

"It's in the SUV," Jared ran for the door and Stephanie and I followed.

"Mac, Jared is going to ping your cell so we can come to you. Tell me what you see?"

"We crossed a bridge and a tunnel about fifteen minutes ago and I think we are heading south." He replied.

"How fast are you going?"

"About sevent,."

Where were the state troopers when you needed them?

"Okay, stay on the line, we're coming to you." I got in the SUV and let the phone sync so I could drive.

"Mac, can you still hear me?"

"Yeah. Ethan, I see a sign that says North Carolina in ten miles."

"Good, I know where you are." I turned to Stephanie.

"Already on it." Stephanie was working her phone to call the state police for both Virginia and North Carolina.

"Got him!" Jared called out.

I glanced over at the laptop screen. I knew we'd never catch up to them before they reached the state line so hopefully the North Carolina highway patrol could intercept them.

"Yes, there is a female victim in the vehicle she was kidnapped from a hospital, condition unknown at this time." Stephanie was speaking rapidly into the phone.

"Description of the vehicle?"

"Mac, what are they driving? Can you see the license plate?"

"It's a white work van. No windows in the back. Looks like a Ford, plat number is PRD, I can't see the rest...,"

Stephanie repeated partial license plate and description of the van to whichever agency she was talking to.

I turned on the emergency lights and sped up. "Mac, we're trying to catch up. Stay on the line if you can."

"You got it."

We drove in silence. I wanted to concentrate on the road to make sure the other drivers got out of the way. After several minutes I could hear sirens through the phone.

"Mac what is happening?"

"State police have set up a roadblock at the border."

"Keep me posted, Mac." We were probably only ten miles from Mac's location.

"They've stopped." Mac's voice came through the speakers.

I heard his tires screen and the door open and close.

"Mac!" I yelled. "Mac!"

"They've stopped at the ramp from the Carolina expressway." Jared confirmed.

As I focused on getting us there as quickly as possible, the speedometer inched closer to ninety miles per hour. I hard Stephanie whisper my name, but I ignored her.

"Mac!" I shouted again. I couldn't hear anything anymore. My heart was racing, and I hated not knowing what was going on, once again. I wasn't there when Kay needed me. My fear turned to anger. Within minutes we arrived. I saw the lights of both the Virginia State Police and the North Carolina Highway Patrol.

Shots were being exchanged but I couldn't see where Kay was. I turned the SUV sideways as close to Mac's car as I could get to provide additional cover from the bullets.

"Mac." I put my hand on his shoulder. "What's the status? Where is Kay?"

"They stopped when they saw the roadblock and bailed. I think Kay is still in the van. The three suspects ran over there." He pointed to where the firefight was being concentrated. I needed to know if Kay was in the van and if she was alright.

I pointed to Jared and Stephanie.

"Cover me."

"Where are you going?" Jared asked.

"The van."

"But..." They started to protest.

I didn't give them time to argue. I crouched low and ran towards the back of the van. I was exposed to the suspects, but I needed to get to the van. I threw open the back door and saw Kay laying in a heap on the floor. Her eyes where closed and she was very pale. My heart dropped like a stone.

A bullet hit the side of the van but thankfully it didn't come all the way through. I grabbed Kay in my arms shielding her with my body as much as

I could and ran for the SUV. Jared, Stephanie and Mac fired continuously towards the place where the suspects were hiding. I felt a thud in my side like I'd been hit with a two by four and knew a bullet had found its mark. I stumbled but kept going. I got back to the SUV and fell to my knees placing Kay on the ground. The gun fire stopped.

"Kay, Kay can you hear me?"

There was chaos all around me, I was only slightly aware of it. I was focused on Kay. She was breathing but she wouldn't wake up. I wasn't sure if she was drugged or injured.

"Kay!"

I felt hands on my shoulders pulling me away. I shrugged them off, but they pulled again this time harder.

"Ethan." It was Mac's voice.

"Let the EMT's take her. They can help her."

I didn't want to let go of her, but I knew she needed help. I sat back resting against the tire of the SUV.

"Ethan, let them look at you." Stephanie said.

"What?" I snapped.

"You've been shot, let them look at you." Stephanie insisted.

"I'll be fine," I insisted.

"Don't be an ass."

Her voice caught me off guard and I blinked at her.

"Get your ass in that ambulance and get checked out." She demanded.

I don't know if it was the shock of Stephanie yelling at me or the truth of her words, but I got up and did what she said. "Is she going to be okay?" I asked the EMT who was closing the door to Kay's ambulance.

"We'll know more when we get her checked out." He shut the door and the ambulance drove away. I laid back on the gurney in the ambulance and closed my eyes. I felt like I'd been here before.

Jared jumped in the back with me. "Let's go!" he said to the driver. He sat near the back and out of the way.

"Looks like you'll need a few stitches and probably have a broken rib."

I nodded. "Wouldn't be the first time." I looked down at Jared. "How's Kay?"

"We don't know yet," he answered.

"Any word on Logan?" I asked.

"He'll be alright. They drugged him with a sedative so he'll be out for a while but should be okay." Jared smirked.

I smiled. I should have known he wouldn't have let them take Kay without one hell of a fight. Drugging him would have been the only way to stop him.

"Now we just need to make sure you're okay." Jared added.

"I'll be fine. I've had worse."

He nodded.

"What about the suspects?" I tried to focus on Jared and not what the EMT was doing.

"They are all dead." Jared nodded.

"Bannister too?" I asked.

"Yeah." Jared nodded again.

"Michael Nichols?" I secretly hoped he was for betraying Kay the way he did.

"Him too."

I nodded and closed my eyes. Well at least this madness would stop now. I just needed Kay to pull through and I hoped there weren't any more surprises. "Call the DC Office and put them onto Bannisters company," I said.

"Stephanie is already on it. I imagine they'll be shut down by the end of the day."

He was right. I was lying in a hospital bed watching images of an FBI led raid on Bannister's corporate offices. Computers and boxes of files were carried out of the building and loaded into vans. A few people were being marched out in handcuffs. I smiled. It was almost a perfect ending if you didn't count the gunfight, kidnapping, and high-speed chase.

Chapter Twenty-Seven
Kay

The night was hot and humid, and the air was heady with the scent of Gardena. I sat on the front porch taking it all in. I loved summer, the heat, the humidity, the heat lightning and the lightning bugs. I loved it all. I had lost track of time and wasn't sure how long I had been sitting there when the headlights shone up the street. I sat very still watching until they stopped in front of the house. I smiled as I watched Ethan step out of the car. The leaves in the trees began to rustle just then, as if the trees were as happy to see him as I was. I waited until he walked through the iron gate and was at the bottom of the steps before I rose.

"Kay, don't get up!" He rushed up the steps to help me sit back down.

"Ethan, I'm not made of glass. I can get up and down."

"Humor me." He sat down next to me. "How are you feeling today?"

"I feel fine. I'm going back to work on Monday."

"What? No, please Kay, give it a few more days."

"Ethan, I've been gone for too long already and I'm going out of mind staying home with nothing to do.

"I know, but I don't want you to push this, you've been through a lot."

"Yes, well..." I let it go. "What about you? You were shot..." I countered.

He looked sheepish for a moment.

"You didn't waste any time going back to work." I reminded him.

"That's different."

"How so?" I pushed.

"I've been shot before. How many times have you been kidnapped?"

"I don't see the relevance; it is like apples and oranges." I argued.

"You're right, being kidnapped twice and nearly killed twice is much worse." He stood his ground.

I could see there was no point in arguing. "How was your day?" I attempted to change the subject.

"Long. I didn't like not being able to see you. You know that, right?"

"Ethan, you have to stop blaming yourself. There was no way to know it was going to happen. You can't watch me twenty-four hours a day."

"Yeah, well that doesn't mean I don't wish I could."

"Me too," I smiled. "Are you hungry? Have you eaten today?"

"Not really."

"Not really, so you're not hungry or you haven't eaten?"

"I haven't eaten." He admitted.

"Come in. I have some dinner staying warm in the oven." He followed me inside and sat down at the kitchen table.

"I can do that," he said.

"Ethan, I swear if you don't sit down and stop treating me like a china doll, I'm going to do something drastic." I shook the serving spoon at him.

"Like what?" He looked amused.

"I don't know, maybe bungie jumping or something."

"I'd like to see that." He knew I was afraid of heights.

I put a plate in front of him and sat down. "How's Logan doing?"

"It's hard to say, he was a grump before the attack at the hospital." Ethan observed.

"He did his best. He knows I don't blame him, right?" I said.

"Doesn't matter, he blames himself."

"Seems to be a trend." I muttered. I watched Ethan eat with some satisfaction. I had been ordered to stay home for at least a week. I decided to use the time to try and improve my cooking skills.

"Maybe I should talk to Logan," I mused.

"You can try. If anyone can get through to him it might be you."

"Maybe I'll stop by tomorrow with some brownies or something."

"He'd like that I'm sure." Ethan nodded between bites.

"What about you?"

"I'd love just seeing you." He smiled and I thought about how much I had grown to love him.

"Mac called today." I noticed he bristled slightly at the mention of Mac's name.

"He just wanted to know how I was doing."

"I bet."

"Ethan, I've told you there never will be anything there." I was a little sadden by the whole affair. Mac was very special, and I would always have a place in my heart for him. But he helped me understand that my heart always belonged to Ethan.

"You sure Mac knows that, right?" Ethan held my gaze.

"Yes, I was very clear with him that while I appreciated everything he did while he was here, you were my one and only hero."

Ethan rolled his eyes.

"You want more?" I said taking his plate.

"No, I'd better not this late at night, I'll never get to sleep."

"It is terribly late so why don't you stay here tonight." I nearly bit my tongue off. The words had come out without my thinking about it.

"You meant that?" He cocked a hopeful eyebrow in my direction.

"Yes," I couldn't take it back now.

"I could sleep on the sofa." He offered.

"Don't be ridiculous. This house has enough bedrooms." I laughed.

He didn't sleep on the sofa or any of the guest rooms.

We went upstairs together. I felt awkward at first, but I knew Ethan and I were meant for each other. We slowly undressed and climbed into bed. As much as I would have been happy to make love with him, we were both tired and I'm sure despite his bravado his ribs were still sore. I was happy to fall asleep in his arms with gentle sweet kisses.

***

The next morning baked brownies. I made enough for the whole office and a separate plate just for Logan. Then drove to the FBI field office.

"Excuse me, Logan?" I said entering the office.

"Kay?" He looked surprised.

"Is there somewhere we can talk?" I asked.

The color drained from his face and he glanced at Ethan. I'm sure he was looking for help. I had told Ethan what time I would be stopping by in case they were busy.

"Why don't you two go into the kitchen? I think here is fresh coffee." Ethan offered.

That was clearly not the answer Logan was looking for.

I smiled sweetly. "Thank you, that will be perfect."

Logan stood and pointed the way to the kitchen. He immediately went to the coffee maker which allowed him to turn his back to me.

I began unpacking the bag I was carrying. "I brought these for you I know it isn't much. I was trying to think of a way to say, 'thank you'".

That got his attention. He spun around to face me. "Thank you for what?"

"For protecting me in the hospital."

"Hmmpf." He wasn't buying it.

"You put up one heck of a fight." I nodded to his hands which were still bruised.

He looked like he wanted to argue but held his tongue.

"Will you sit with me?" I asked pulling out a chair.

He reluctantly took a chair opposite me and for good measures spun it around, so he was leaning on the back of the chair.

"Listen," I started. "I know things didn't go exactly to plan but what you did was amazing. You risked your life to protect me. I can't even think of enough ways to thank you for that. I am so glad that you are okay."

He blinked and just stared at me. "I didn't protect you or save you." His hands were in tight fists.

"Yes, you did because you delayed them taking me long enough that Mac was able to follow them and bring Ethan and the rest of the team to me before things went too far." I paused and reached across the table. I didn't touch him instead I laid my hand open and up turned in front of him.

"You made it possible for me to be saved." I tried to reassure him.

He looked at me and then at my hand. He slowly released the grip he had on the back of the chair and put his hand in mind. I was surprised at how big it was. It was rough with manual labor and I wondered what he did in his spare time.

I smiled at him. "I baked you some brownies." I stated the obvious.

He smiled then, a small smile. "I like brownies."

"Great!" I took my hand back and unwrapped the plate and pushed it towards him.

He carefully selected one and bit into it.

I waited for his appraisal.

"These are pretty good," he said around a mouthful of brownie.

"Are you surprised?"

"A little." He smiled.

I nodded. "Don't blame you, I was surprised too." I laughed.

Jared popped his head in, "Can I come in and get coffee or is this a private party? Whoa! Brownies!"

Jared started for the table.

"Paws off, these are mine!" Logan growled.

"Not to worry." I pulled another plate of brownies from the bag, "I brought some for you and Stephanie too."

"Thanks!" Jared smiled and accepted the plate.

I turned back Logan. "I mean it, you're my hero." I whispered.

Logan stared at me and if I didn't know better, I believe he blushed a little.

He simply nodded.

I stood up and he did as well. I walked over and gave him a hug. I expected him to stand there with his arms at his side, he surprised me by gently wrapping his arms around my shoulders and leaning down to whisper in my ear.

"I'm glad you're alright." I stepped back and nodded. "Me too." Then I turned to leave.

Ethan winked at me on my way out.

"Hey Ethan, Logan is putting moves on your girl." Jared called out.

"Shut up or I'll punch your lights out." Logan threatened.

I heard Jared laughing as I closed the door behind me.

Next stop my office.

I hadn't mentioned to Ethan that I planned to stop by the office today. I wasn't going to work all day although I did feel the need to check in with everyone. Especially, Sherry.

"Kay, what are you doing here? You should be resting at home." Sherry greeted me.

"If I do anymore 'resting' I'm going to lose my mind." I smiled back at Sherry.

She fell in step behind me as I walked into my office. "How's everything going?" I asked surveying my desk for mail or papers to sign.

"Well, it's been a little odd, not having you around and I just can't get over Michael."

"I know, me either. I trusted him so completely." I said sinking into my desk chair.

"What are you going to do?" she asked.

"Well, we have to have a corporate attorney and you can bet I am going to vet the heck out of them before I bring them on board." Sherry nodded.

"Does Ethan know you're here?" Sherry blurted out.

"No, why. Should he?" I looked at her directly.

"No, I guess not." She blushed. "I just worry you're doing too much."

"I'm not staying all day. I just need to get back into control of this company before anyone else tries to take it over."

"Okay, well, let me get you the mail," she offered.

Sherry left and came back with a small box.

"What is all of this?"

"I think just about every employee sent you a get-well card. I didn't want to overwhelm you, so I was holding them until you felt better." Sherry explained.

I looked inside the box. "Are you serious?"

"Yeah"

"Holy cow! There are a lot of envelopes in here."

Sherry nodded smiling. "I know."

"Well, I guess I better start opening them."

"I'll leave you to it." She returned to her desk.

I reached in the box and pulled out a handful of envelopes. I was so touched by the outpouring of well wishes by the employees that I was brought to tears a few times. Some of the letters were from the children of employees who had benefited from a scholarship program. It was nearly eight o'clock when I got to the last one. Tomorrow I would start replying to them all.

"Kay?" I heard Sherry shuffling things at her desk.

"Yes?"

"It's getting late so we should probably call it a day." Sherry called out.

"Okay, you're right." I began tidying up the cards and letters.

Just then my phone buzzed with a text from Ethan.

"Leaving work, up for company?"

Crap.

"Um, sure. How long before you can come over?" I clicked.

"About fifteen minutes," came his reply.

"Can we make it thirty?" I countered.

"Sure. Everything okay?"

"Yep, everything is fine." I gathered my things and Sherry and I walked out together. "See you tomorrow." I said to Sherry

"Are you sure that is a good idea? You're not supposed to be back until next week." She reminded me.

"I'm just going to start replying to all the cards and well wishes." I told her.

"I can do that for you," she offered.

"I know but it wouldn't be personal then."

Sherry looked at me dejected.

"You can help, how about that?" I suggested.

"Okay, I don't like it, but okay." She scowled.

I was tempted to break a few traffic laws to get home before Ethan got there but better judgement prevailed. It probably wouldn't have mattered. When I pulled into the driveway, Ethan was already there leaning against his car waiting for me.

"Hi!" I said walking towards him from the garage.

"Hi." He straightened to walk to the house with me. "Where've you been?"

I was glad it was dusk and hoped the shadows would hide my cheeks reddening. "I stopped by the office."

"And what time did you go in today?" He held the door for me as we stepped into the mud room and then the kitchen.

"Uh, when I left your office."

My back was to him as I could imagine the look on his face. He caught my arm gently.

"Kay, please tell me you haven't been working all this time?" The pleading look on his face stabbed me right in the heart.

"Well, I wasn't actually working." I said turning to face him.

He put his other hand on my shoulder. "Kay, you have to take care of yourself. I don't want anything else happening to you, do you understand?" His eyes were warm and gentle, and I wanted to kiss him.

"I was just talking to Sherry and reading some get well cards."

"This whole time?" he said, disbelieving.

"Well it was quite a few cards." I blushed again.

"And that is all?" He gave me a sideways glance.

"Yes."

"Okay." He pulled me to him and rested his chin on top of my head. "I worry about you."

I wrapped my arms around his chest. "I know, and I am glad that you care about me like that."

He squeezed me slightly before releasing me.

I looked up and he looked like he wanted to say something more but didn't.

"Would you like something to drink? Have you had dinner?"

"Yes, and no." He laughed.

"Me, too."

I fixed us a dinner of fried chicken and collards with fresh sweet corn.

"Do you cook like this all the time?" Ethan asked.

"Well, when I have a reason to but not if I'm having dinner alone."

"Well, that was excellent," he said, wiping his mouth with is napkin, and setting it next to his plate.

"Thank you, shall we sit on the porch?" I suggested.

"Sure, after I do the dishes," he offered.

"They can wait," I said definitively.

"Yeah, and if they wait then you'll have to do them alone."

I sighed knowing there was no arguing with him. "Can I at least help with the dishes?"

"Absolutely not." He frowned.

I stood leaning against the counter and he cleared the table and washed up everything.

"So, I think Logan liked the brownies." I said once we were seated on the porch next to each other.

"Yeah, I think so."

"Now, what can I do for you to relieve of this guilt you are carrying around about not being the one to pull me off the barge."

"Who told you that?"

I only smiled.

"Tell me I'm wrong."

"No, I can't tell you that," he admitted.

"So, what can I do?"

"Nothing." He looked away and I realized just how deeply he felt about the situation.

"Ethan." I kept my voice low. "You did find me because if it hadn't been for you the Coast Guard wouldn't have known where to look. You brought them to me and for that I love you."

He looked at me. His eyes were moist. "I love you, Kay."

His voice was low and deep like he was using the tone to convey the meaning of his words.

I blinked. I knew he cared for me. He had certainly told me as much and his actions reflected his concern. He was talking about more than that right now.

I knew how badly the loss of that relationship after his divorce had affected him. I certainly hadn't expected that sort of commitment from him. I was realizing that I might have been wrong, and Ethan had the capacity to love again.

I was speechless not only by his declaration but the way his forefinger was tracing my jawline from my ear to my chin. I knew he was going to kiss me, and I knew this time when he did, I would be lost to him forever. I also knew as he held my hand and led me upstairs it didn't matter if his broken ribs were still sore. We would make sweet, passionate love tonight. My heart and soul would forever belong to Ethan.

The End

About the Author

Lynn Story lives in southeastern Virginia, a region that is known by several names, Tidewater, Hampton Roads, and the 757. Her Gates Point series is based on the Tidewater area and you may recognize some familiar names and places if you've ever lived in or visited the area.

Lynn enjoys writing about people and their relationships and prefers sweet stories with just a dash of heat.

She shares her coastal home with her husband and three cats. They enjoy spending time in the great outdoors, as well as book collecting.

If you enjoyed Rescue My Love, please consider leaving a review to help others find Ethan and Kay.

To learn more about Gates Point and its interesting characters join my newsletter[1] for exclusive previews, pre-orders notices and other fun goodies.

Places to find me:

www.stitchesandstories.com[2]

www.facebook.com/authorlynnstory[3]

www.twitter.com[4] @authorlynnstory

authorlynnstory on Instragram[5]

1.   https://mailchi.mp/e89196102100/lynnstory

2.   http://www.stitchesandstories.com

3.   https://www.facebook.com/authorlynnstory/

4.   http://www.twitter.com/authorlynnstory

5.   http://www.instagram.com/